Praise for *The Inheritance*

"A mesmerizing suspense tale which should keep you guessing, breathless, and fearful. This is a classic Gothic type of tale, written with elegant prose, graceful style, and wonderful characterizations." —*Sullivan County Democrat*

"Gothic romance meets suspense thriller in this taut, diabolically clever story. A gripping read in the style of du Maurier." —*Booklist*

"Writing with fierce energy, Savage gives us an extremely clever and gripping novel, marvelously plotted and thoroughly spellbinding." —*Tulsa World*

"Tom Savage has proved himself the master of the surprise plot twist. It's all crackling good fun." —*The Pilot* (Southern Pines, NC)

"[A] Gothic to end all Gothics, with an unusual twist at the end." —*BookNews*

"Tom Savage continues to demonstrate the wonderfully honed sense of plot pacing which is the hallmark of his writing." —*Mystery Lovers Bookshop*

continued on next page . . .

Valentine

"Suspense with a twist."   —James Patterson

"Genuinely shocking."   —*Booklist*

"Effective . . . a truly surprising twist. . . . A stylish suspense novel."   —*Washington Post Book World*

"A thriller with a heart. Savage writes with fierce energy, piercing holes into the shredding fabric of our society, where no one else is safe, no one is free from harm."   —Lorenzo Carcaterra

"A well-crafted tale of madness . . . spine-chilling."
—*Naples Daily News*

"A pleasurable crafty yarn . . . truly awesome."
—*Publishers Weekly*

"[A] pulse-pounding thriller. . . . It's the kind of psychological tale that burns its way right into the reader's mind."   —*Abilene Reporter-News*

Precipice

"An extremely clever and gripping novel, marvelously plotted, and thoroughly spellbinding . . . as good and surprising as anything I've read in years. Do not peek at the last page."
—Nelson DeMille

"A subtle, well-crafted tale of deceit and madness among the rich."　　　—*Chicago Tribune*

"A story on the edge . . . A twisty, quick plummet, a sunny landscape in which nothing—and no one—is what it seems."　　　—Donald Westlake

"A stylish and accomplished novel with a terrific sense of place and a wonderfully complex plot."
—Jonathan Kellerman

"Unexpected twists. Readers' expectations may be blown to bits by the clifftop denouement."
—*Publishers Weekly*

"A cool, smart, and stylish first thriller . . . that features a major twist in nearly every one of its tightly woven chapters. . . . Surprise piles on surprise . . . a finely wrought, unusually clever literary debut."　　　—*Kirkus Reviews*

Other books by Tom Savage

Precipice
Valentine

Writing as T. J. Phillips

Dance of the Mongoose
Woman in the Dark

THE
INHERITANCE

TOM SAVAGE

A SIGNET BOOK

SIGNET
Published by New American Library, a division of
Penguin Putnam Inc., 375 Hudson Street,
New York, New York 10014, U.S.A.
Penguin Books Ltd, 27 Wrights Lane,
London W8 5TZ, England
Penguin Books Australia Ltd,
Ringwood, Victoria, Australia
Penguin Books Canada Ltd, 10 Alcorn Avenue,
Toronto, Ontario, Canada M4V 3B2
Penguin Books (N.Z.) Ltd, 182–190 Wairau Road,
Auckland 10, New Zealand

Penguin Books Ltd, Registered Offices:
Harmondsworth, Middlesex, England

Published by Signet, an imprint of New American Library,
a division of Penguin Putnam Inc. Previously published
in a Dutton edition

First Signet Printing, October 1999
10 9 8 7 6 5 4 3 2 1

 REGISTERED TRADEMARK—MARCA REGISTRADA

Printed in the United States of America

PUBLISHER'S NOTE
This is a work of fiction. Names, characters, places, and incidents either
are the product of the author's imagination or are used fictitiously, and any
resemblance to actual persons, living or dead, events, or locales is entirely
coincidental.

BOOKS ARE AVAILABLE AT QUANTITY DISCOUNTS WHEN USED TO PROMOTE
PRODUCTS OR SERVICES. FOR INFORMATION PLEASE WRITE TO PREMIUM
MARKETING DIVISION, PENGUIN PUTNAM INC., 375 HUDSON STREET, NEW
YORK, NY 10014

for Uris

I would like to thank my family, my friends, and my colleagues at Murder Ink for their encouragement and support. I particularly thank my mother, Lesley Savage, and the Friday Night Club: John Douglas, Jennifer Jaffee, Tina Meyerhoff, Larry Pontillo, Ann Romeo, and S. J. (Shira) Rozan.

Abby Adams graciously allowed me to use her marvelous observation as my epigraph. The quote is often attributed to her husband, Donald E. Westlake, but it was Abby who actually said it.

My editor, Danielle Perez, and her associates at Dutton have worked long and hard on my behalf, for which I am very grateful.

My agent, Stuart Krichevsky, has done more for me than I can possibly acknowledge.

Here is a roughly chronological list of several favorite authors who unwittingly contributed to this novel, and to my lifelong love of Gothic stories: Nathaniel Hawthorne, Edgar Allan Poe, Charles Dickens, Washington Irving, Charlotte Brontë, Emily Brontë, Henry James, Mary Roberts Rinehart, D. H. Lawrence, Shirley Jackson, Phyllis A. Whitney, Mary Stewart, John Fowles, Ruth Rendell, Stephen King, and Mary Higgins Clark.

And, now and forever, Dame Daphne du Maurier.

A Gothic is a story about a girl who gets a house.
Abby Adams Westlake

PROLOGUE

Washing Away the Dream

From a distance Randall House looks perfectly innocent, but you should never be deceived by appearances. There's nothing innocent about it.

I suppose I've been studying the mansion on the Connecticut coast all my life, and I've always suspected that it held secrets. Oh, it may have started out innocent enough, when old John Randall built it a hundred years ago. But then the old man died and his son, the first James Randall, took over things, and it hasn't been the same since. The first James brought the first scandal into the house, but not the last.

From a distance is an excellent way to view it. If you stand at the main road looking through the big wrought iron gates, you can see, beyond the gatehouse and the stables, the graceful curve of the drive as it stretches off to the right among the trees that accentuate the vast lawns, then around in a wide arc and up to the gravel circle in front of the main entrance. The big house stands against the skyline at the top of the rise on the headland, surrounded by the lawns that end in thick forest at the back and sides. From your vantage place outside the gates, the gatehouse blocks your view of the sheer cliff that is off to your right, and the rocky cove some seventy feet directly below it. The facade of Randall House faces the cliff and the Sound, and Long Island on the other side of it. It is a beautiful view. If you happen to catch a glimpse of one or more of the people who live there through the iron bars, you might assume that we are gracious, gentle people, and that our bounty is well-deserved.

As I've said, you should never be deceived by appearances. But I suppose you know that. Everybody knows what happened at Randall House. You know all about our most recent scandal, or you think you do.

I'm back here now after several long periods away, and being here again reminds me of the promise I once made to myself. I've been planning to write it all down for quite some time. I know the whole story now, I suppose, or as much of it as will ever be known. I was here then, and I was part of it. I saw and heard—and did—many things, and my presence often went unnoticed. I guess you could say I was the perfect witness, because I had no real ties to these people, and no stake in what became of them. Or so it was believed at the time.

This is my story. It may not mean much to you,

but to me it is everything. It plays over and over in my mind, like a song.

Here is how it always begins for me, in a bedroom in Randall House on a morning in August, near the end of summer, several years ago:

"Good morning, Mrs. Wainwright."

It was the first sound she always heard, and the first image she inevitably saw when she opened her eyes was the smiling face of the upstairs maid hovering above her. The pretty face would change from time to time, but the office was as old as the house itself. Her grandmother had been awakened thus. The current pretty face was named Martha, so she summoned a weak smile and bade Martha good morning.

The bedroom windows faced east, and she always closed her eyes again as the girl went over to pull open the drapes at the casement and the pure sunlight came streaming in. Then she performed the not unpleasant little ritual of blinking several times to clear her vision as she sat up in the bed. When she could see again, she looked over at the bedside table. Yes, the big, plain, heavy stoneware mug of strong Earl Grey was waiting there, as ever. No delicate, translucent Royal Doulton cups and saucers for her, thank you very much. Alicia Randall Wainwright's day began with a good, solid, sensible mug of tea.

She took a sip of the hot, sweet drink and put the mug down. Then she maneuvered her legs over the side of the bed and reached for her cane. She only needed it first thing in the morning. Once she was up and about, her circulation flowing, she discarded the loathsome implement. It was a symbol of weakness for her, a state to which she would never succumb however the advancing years assailed her. She stood up from the bed, thinking, *There won't be any more advancing years.*

She was going to die soon. Roger Bell, the family doctor and nearly as old as she, had already informed her of the fact, and she had no reason not to believe him. She knew it herself, really. Her heart was giving out. There had been the attack last February, followed by weeks in bed that she hated more than the pain itself. Her first act on rising from that almost fatal episode was a brisk ride through the estate on Lightning, her champion stallion. But now it was August, nearly the end of summer, and she would take advantage of the perfect morning weather with her other favorite activity.

"I shall swim before breakfast, Martha," she told the girl who waited in the doorway for instructions. "Please tell Mrs. Jessel to hold off on the toast until I return."

"Of course, ma'am," Martha said. With a wide smile and a little bob of a curtsy, she disappeared.

Alicia threw aside the cane, removed her nightgown, and donned her black bathing suit. The terry robe went over it, and she stepped into her well-worn rubber sandals. *A swim*, she thought as she picked up the mug again, *to wake me up and invigorate me, and to wash away the dream.*

She finished the tea and made her way over to the

door. She paused there, leaning forward to press her ear against the wood. No, nothing. No sounds from the other side. If her nephew, John, and his wife were up and about, they weren't presently in the hallway here in the family wing. Good. She had never been fond of her brother's younger son, and Catherine, his wife, was what Alicia's mother would have called a simp. Her mother had been gone these many years, resting in presumed peace beside her husband in the little graveyard next to the chapel on the grounds of the estate. Nearly all of the Randalls were there now. . . .

But not all, she mused, boldly pulling the door open and stepping out into the cool, shadowy hallway. The velvet curtains of the big window here at the end of the hall were closed. She glanced around at the doors to the three other bedrooms, the two across the hall and the one next door to hers. Nothing. Her nephew and his wife had the two bedrooms across from each other closest to the center of the house, which had once belonged to Alicia's brothers. John and Catherine were either still asleep or downstairs in the dining room. With any luck, she would avoid them entirely.

The other door at this end of the hall, across from hers, was the master bedroom. She glanced at that door again. Then, with a swift look down the hall to be certain she was not observed, she crossed over to it, opened the door, and peered inside.

It was cool and dark in the big bedroom, and the first thing she noticed was the gleam on the deep brown mahogany baseboard and columns of the enormous four-poster bed. The creamy white canopy and the matching quilt had been recently cleaned, as had the closed, heavy white curtains on the windows that faced the front drive and the east lawn. The silver combs and brushes that had been her mother's were neatly aligned on the vanity table between the two front windows. She drew in a long breath. Yes, the lavender sachets in drawers and closets, the lovely scent she always associated with her mother, had been replaced with new ones. Martha and the other maids had been busy here, and now the room was ready, waiting for its new occupant.

Its new occupant. A slow, wicked smile came to her lips. She couldn't wait to see her worthless nephew's reaction when that new occupant arrived at last and took rightful ownership of the master bedroom. Oh, how she had waited for that!

With this thought, she closed the door on the room and hurried down the hallway. It opened at the end onto the second-floor gallery that ringed the Great Hall, the massive rotunda at the center of the house. She paused again at the marble gallery balustrade, looking down at the ocean of black and white marble squares, the checkerboard-patterned floor of the Great Hall that had been her grandfather's pride and joy. She and her two brothers had once knelt here long after their bedtime, peering through the balusters at the glittering room below, watching their parents and thirty or forty guests dancing after dinner. This house had once been the site of frequent parties, and long weekends when all four bedrooms in the guest wing and the two in the pool house had been occupied by boisterous, laughing men and women. There had been no such gatherings here in many years.

No one was moving about down there now. Alicia raised her gaze to the balcony above her. Nothing: the third story would be empty by now, with the servants already performing morning chores in the kitchen and elsewhere on the grounds. The big chandeliers suspended from the domed ceiling at the top of the house above the Great Hall sparkled in the morning light.

Quickening her pace, she moved around the gallery to the grand staircase and descended, her hand sliding down the smooth, cold marble banister, her rubber-sandaled feet making no sound on the red carpeting. She arrived at the bottom of the wide staircase in the center of the Great Hall. Looking quickly around to be sure the big double doors to the various downstairs rooms were all closed, she walked to the entry hall.

The table against the wall next to the door to the library held a large vase of fresh summer flowers, but the silver tray beside it was empty. Either Mrs. Jessel had not brought the mail from the box beside the gatehouse, or there was no mail for her. Perhaps it hadn't been delivered yet . . . ? No. It was well after ten o'clock now. Mr. Braeden always came at ten.

She looked up into the big, brass-framed mirror on the wall behind the table. The clear, intelligent blue eyes in the handsome, lined face below her close-cropped white hair stared back at her, filled with anxiety.

No mail, she thought. No letter today. Oh, well, perhaps tomorrow. . . .

With a sigh and a little shake of her head, Alicia went out through the big front door into the bright sunlight, and down the steps to the circular gravel drive. The sky and Long Island Sound were clear today, deep shades of blue shimmering in the distance beyond the bright green of the sloping front lawn and the forest at the edges of the estate. Long Island was plainly visible beyond the sailboats, a dark green line far away at the horizon. The salty sea breeze flowed past her, carrying with it the scent of the recently mown grass. She headed across the east lawn, past the summer house in the direction of the trees.

It would be the lake, as always. She'd never had much use for the big swimming pool behind the main house, and the little cove among the rocks at the edge of the point would involve a hundred stone steps from the cliff to the beach. From childhood, she had loved swimming in the little lake in the tiny clearing among the trees beyond the east lawn, at the easternmost perimeter of the property. Her parents had always admonished her and her two brothers, warning that the lake was really just a pond, filled with goldfish and frogs and turtles that did not welcome visitors. But Alicia and Jimmy and Billy had preferred it to the pool and the Sound. The three children had spent many happy hours there, laughing and splashing and playing tag with the big orange fish. What they had loved most about the spot was that it couldn't be seen from the house: it had been their own private domain. And now, with Jimmy and Billy gone, it belonged to her alone.

She made her way through the trees to the little clearing. She dropped her terry bathrobe on the big rock beside the pond and sat down on it, drinking in the rich green smell of the place and feeling the warmth of the dappled sunlight through the leaves above her.

Jimmy and Billy. She found herself thinking about her brothers more and more lately. Billy, the reckless, grinning youngest, who had never had a chance at adulthood. He'd been shot down over the Philippines more than fifty years ago, at the age of twenty one. She's lost him and her young husband, Charles Wainwright, in the war, within a year of each other. And her older brother, James—well, he had been gone for fifteen years now, and his wife had died seven years before that. Early graves, all of them. But a life lost in wartime was reasonably understandable. James and his wife, lovely Emily, had simply ceased to live, not long after the murder of their older son. Their younger son, now comfortably ensconced here in the family home with his new wife, had never been a source of pleasure for his parents.

Leaning forward to dip her toe in the water before her, Alicia grimaced. She thought about her nephew back at the house, and about the promise she'd made to her brother at his deathbed fifteen

9

years ago. About the letter she had recently sent, and about the reply she now so eagerly awaited. She spent most of her waking hours thinking about it. It was probably the reason she had cheated death herself a few months ago, when she'd had the heart attack. She had to stay alive now, no matter what happened. She had to be sure that Jimmy's dying wish was honored. She had to deliver Randall House and the Randall fortune into the hands of its rightful owner. Then she could rest, then she could die. Until then, she would continue to have the dream.

It had come again last night, as it had come nearly every night for the past few weeks, ever since she'd mailed the letter. She would toss and turn, her arms and legs entangled in the sheets. Then, always at the same point in the terrifying, disjointed scenario, she would suddenly awaken to find herself sitting upright in the bed.

The dream was always the same. In it, she was a little girl again, and she and her two brothers were playing here, at the pond. They chased each other around the rim of their private lake, laughing and screaming. It was summer in the dream, she knew, because it was warm, and her parents were not off at the house in Palm Beach for the winter season. They stood nearby, in front of the closest trees, smiling as they watched their children playing. They were formally dressed for some reason, Father in his black dinner jacket and Mother in her pretty sky blue crinoline evening gown. When she became aware of their presence, Alicia leaped from the water and ran to embrace her smiling mother. The familiar scent of lavender greeted her as she ran, followed by her laughing brothers, toward their parents. But she never reached her mother, who stood, arms outstretched, waiting. Just as she came up to her, the scene would suddenly change.

Now it was many years later, and Billy and her parents were long gone. She was sitting near the fire in the big, formal living room at Randall House. Her brother James and his wife, Emily, sat silently on the couch facing her, holding hands, staring down at the coffee table before them. Mrs. Jessel stood behind them, near the doorway, her eyes filled with tears. Everyone was in black, having just come from the little graveyard beside the chapel. The guests had all gone home, and now the family was alone. Alicia watched them all, feeling the lighthearted happiness from the earlier scene diminish into sorrow and despair. James III, her beloved nephew, was dead, and the police had arrested his young wife, Constance, for his murder. She had not been allowed to appear at the funeral, of course. She was in a cell in New York, waiting for her arraignment, and for the bail that would never be offered. For the eventual trial and the verdict, and the life sentence she deserved.

The big clock in the corner ticked softly in the background as Alicia sat there, wondering how her grandfather, the original John Randall, would react to the scandal and shame that had tainted his otherwise pristine family reputation. She wondered how

11

they would all survive this, knowing that they would not. As she watched the man and woman on the couch across from her, her sister-in-law slowly disappeared, her image fading, fading, until James was alone on the couch. The ticking of the clock became louder, louder, and then the scene dissolved, replaced by another one.

Her brother James—Jimmy—was in bed, and Dr. Bell and Mrs. Jessel hovered nearby. Alicia was kneeling beside her brother, holding his hand. He looked most old now, much older than his seventy years. He had buried his son eight years before, and his wife a year later. His other son, feckless John, was off somewhere, living out his worthless life, waiting for his father to die. For seven years James had remained here alone with his sister; silent, stricken, a shell of the warm, jovial man he had once been. In these, his last moments, he whispered to his sister, his faint voice filled with final urgency.

"The child," he said with massive effort. "You must find the child. Don't let John come back and claim it all. Find the child, Alicia. Promise me. . . ."

"I promise," she whispered to her brother.

"Find . . . Holly . . ." he rasped. Then, in a sudden, ferocious move, he sat bolt upright on his deathbed, his weak arms suddenly powerful as he clutched her throat and pulled her face against his own. His eyes were filled with terror as he shouted the final word, his hot breath exploding against Alicia's startled face.

"Holly!"

The word would echo in her fevered mind as she

came awake, filled with anxious urgency. Even as she realized that it was a dream, that she was alone in her bedroom fifteen years later, it continued.

Holly. Holly. Holly. . . .

Now, on her favorite rock beside the little lake, she shook her head to clear it, silencing the reverberation of her brother's final word. His last will and testament had been succinct: everything— Randall House and the other houses, the stock portfolios, the family's shares in National Food Corporation; *everything*—had been left in trust, to be watched over by Alicia and ultimately given to the child. If the child was dead, or could not be located—well, there were other instructions regarding the settlement of the estate. But James Randall had counted on his sister, Alicia, to find his granddaughter.

And now, at last, Alicia had found her.

It hadn't been easy, and the price had been exorbitant. But it was done, and Alicia was presently waiting for a reply to the letter she had written to the child, now a grown woman, explaining everything.

With a final, decisive shrug of her shoulders, Alicia put all of these thoughts behind her and stood up. The little clearing was so quiet, so green, and the water in the pond looked cool and refreshing. Not for nothing was she a Randall: when the time came, she would see to everything. She would manage, as she had always managed. But now it was time for a swim.

Smiling to herself, she stepped into the water and

slowly knelt down, allowing the cold, bracing water to rise to her neck. She splashed her face and hair and closed her eyes, savoring the wonderful feeling. The cool pond; the fresh scent of grass and leaves; the briefly glimpsed flashes of gold beneath the surface as the local residents made way for her, welcomed her. And the silence: not a sound in the whole world except the soft rustling in the branches, the occasional chirrup of a frog, the—

Her eyes opened, and she made herself be very still in the water, holding her breath as she strained to listen. She had heard something else, some tiny sound from not far away, a muffled thud and a snapping sound, as of a human footfall breaking a dry twig in its path. Instinctively, she moved out farther into the water, away from the mossy bank. She stood up, looking slowly around the clearing.

The trees, the grass, the dappled sunlight. The rustle of leaves, the soft droning of nearby bees, the tinkling of displaced water against the edge of the pond. Nothing else. Silence. Absolute silence.

Oh, please! she admonished herself. I will not go mad. I will not become senile! Now I'm actually hearing things, and imagining eyes peering out from the shrubbery, watching me. Nonsense!

With that, she laughed aloud in the quiet clearing and settled back down into the water. She glided forward, stroking once with her arms, moving through the lily pads. She dipped her head briefly under the surface, which is why she didn't hear the tiny splash at the bank behind her. When she brought her head up, she reached out with her arms to stroke again.

She froze. She slowly lowered her feet until she was once more standing—or, rather, squatting—in the water. She drew in a deep, harsh breath, staring down at the shadow in the water before her. It was the shadow of a person, a human being who now loomed silently above and behind her. A thrill of shock and fear coursed through her. When it passed, she made an effort to find her voice.

"Hello?" she whispered tentatively, unable to will herself to turn around.

The shadow grew larger, darker. She noticed, irrelevantly, that the bees and frogs were silent. Then, at the last possible moment, she pivoted on her feet and turned to face whoever was in the water with her.

She had only the briefest glimpse of the face mere inches in front of her own, and of the arms that were reaching out to grasp her shoulders. Then she was pushed roughly, unceremoniously under the water.

Panic overtook her. She struggled to free herself from the powerful grip on her arms, to break loose and rise to the surface. But she was old and frail, and there were weeds and lily stems all around her, entangling her, helping her assailant to hold her down. Her lungs began to ache, and dark spots appeared before her eyes in the murky water. With a sudden strength born of terror, she reared back with her right leg and thrust it forward. It made solid contact, and the pressure on her shoulders was suddenly gone. She shot up out of the water, filling her lungs with merciful oxygen, moving away from her attacker on unsteady legs. If she could just make it to the edge of the pond. . . .

Worse than her fear was her confusion. Her mind was suddenly filled with images from the dream, even as she strove to free herself. Her brother and her sister-in-law sitting silently on the couch in the living room, gazing at nothing. Mrs. Jessel, weeping silently in the background. Her brother's firm grip on her throat, choking her, as he summoned the strength to shout his final word.

There was splashing behind her, and she knew that her would-be killer was after her once more. She made it to the bank, reaching out to grasp handfuls of long grass even as the hands reached out from behind and whirled her around. She stared into the face before her and opened her mouth, filling her lungs to scream.

The first, electrifying jolt ran down her left arm, forcing the air from her lungs. Her attacker froze, watching warily. The second spasm overtook her, and she sank slowly down to her knees in the water, moaning. Just before the third and final assault within her own system, she drew a last painful breath. The word she managed to croak was the same one her brother had shouted at her before falling back, dead, on the bed. It surged up from the depths of her soul and out into the still morning.

"Holly!"

The last image Alicia Wainwright saw was the sunlight glinting through the leaves above the pond, and the last sound she heard, or imagined she heard, was the laughter of children. Her own laughter, and that of her brothers, long ago. Then the image and the laughter slowly faded, and she sank quietly down into the water.

After a moment the shadow above her moved away, vanishing among the other shadows in the forest one hundred yards from Randall House.

It always begins this way for me, on that sunny August morning, with the "natural" death of Alicia Randall Wainwright. Then, in my mind, the weather changes, and it is autumn.

Holly came to Randall House on a cold, gray day in November, three months after the death of her great-aunt Alicia. The branches of the trees around the estate were bare of leaves but heavy with snow. Everyone was there, in the driveway, waiting for her. As she stepped out of the car to be greeted by her new family and servants, they saw that she was tall and slender, and that she had the Randall eyes: big, clear, pale blue, and remarkably intelligent. She was wearing a thick, hooded white wool coat and boots, and long strands of gold hair spilled down from the fleece lining around her face. She was smiling in what appeared to be innocent anticipation as John Randall and his wife welcomed her. She was the most beautiful woman I had ever seen, and I think I fell in love with her instantly.

Because I know so much more about it all now, I will go back three days earlier than that, to New York City. I will enter the mind of that beautiful

young woman three days before she arrived at
Randall House, to be met by open smiles and secret
hostilities, grudges, hatred, and madness.

And death. . . .

PART ONE

HOLLY SMITH

CHAPTER ONE

"You're Holly Randall Now."

She really had no use for these people.

That thought had first occurred to her as the Delta 747 shuddered down out of the rainy gray sky onto the rainy gray runway at Kennedy International Airport and taxied to a stop at the gray-carpeted mobile hallway into the terminal. Even before that, actually. There was something about the forced heartiness and slightly obsequious behavior of the flight attendants that rather set her teeth on edge. Of course, that isn't really their fault, she supposed. All flight personnel are like that; it's part of the job description. But, for some reason, these particular personnel were particularly annoying.

Oh, and speaking of that, the famous New York smog was everywhere in evidence. God, she thought, how do these people breathe? They might as well be smoking entire packs of cigarettes at a time. And now they had rules against smoking in public places, even restaurants. As if it mattered. Well, she was here now, and she intended to make the best of it.

The best of it. That thought made her smile as she followed the crowd behind the perky flight attendant who led them through the Delta terminal toward the baggage claim area. The best of it, indeed! She had nothing to complain about, and everything to celebrate. So why was she trembling?

Oh, stop it! she commanded herself. Don't be such a ninny. Just get your suitcase and look for the man Mr. Henderson mentioned, the driver with—

"Ms. Randall?"

—the sign that would read—

"Ms. Randall?"

—something or other. . . .

"Holly!"

She stopped so quickly that the middle-aged tourist couple behind her practically walked up her back. She smiled an apology to them as she turned around. There, off to the side of the concourse just behind her, stood a tall, dark-haired man in a chauffeur's gray uniform and cap, holding up a handwritten placard. She stared. The placard read: HOLLY RANDALL.

She looked at the placard, then slowly up at the face above it. An extremely handsome man, she noted, and he was staring rather intently at her. He seemed to be making a study of her, from her scuffed boots and faded jeans to her frayed plaid coat and stocking cap. Nothing in the set of his features told her what he thought of what he saw. She walked over to him.

He continued to stare. "It *is* you, isn't it?"

Holly looked back down at the placard, then up at him.

"Why, yes," she said slowly, smiling. "I suppose it is."

The intense stare dissolved into a delighted grin. "I thought so! You look just like your great-aunt, Mrs. Wainwright—I mean, the painting of her in the—oh, never mind. Welcome to New York, Ms. Randall. I'll get your luggage for you."

He'd actually blushed bright red as he'd stammered all this, so she didn't prolong his apparent discomfort by correcting him. She merely smiled and nodded and led the way to the baggage area. When she pointed at the single, rather battered plastic American Tourister suitcase, he grasped the handle and swung it up from the carousel as if it had no weight at all.

Well, it isn't very heavy, at that, she mused as she followed him out of the terminal to the short-term parking lot. Very few of her earthly possessions had seemed appropriate for this journey. But no matter, she'd been assured. Mr. Henderson, the Park Avenue lawyer who had provided the plane ticket and arranged for all this, would have further instructions for her when she met him at his office tomorrow morning. Those further instructions, he'd said, involved clothing. He hadn't elaborated, so she'd merely agreed to follow his orders. She'd find out soon enough, she supposed.

When she saw the car, she stopped dead in her tracks again. She stood on the curb, staring, as the young man carried her suitcase to the biggest automobile in sight: a long, sleek black Cadillac limousine. He opened the trunk, and her suitcase disappeared inside it.

Oh, she thought, blinking. Of course. This man is a professional driver, and this obscenely luxurious conveyance has been hired for the afternoon, hired by Mr. Henderson. That was very nice of him, but totally unnecessary. She thought all of this, but all she managed to say was "Oh."

He opened the rear door and stood at attention, watching her. She looked from him to the car, then down at her clothes. Then, with a small, determined shrug—the first of many in the next few days and weeks—she stepped forward into the car. He shut the door and fairly ran around to the other side. Holly watched through the thick plate glass that separated the front of the car from the backseat as he slid soundlessly in behind the wheel and started the engine. The enormous car glided silently forward, and she sank back into the soft leather seat.

She had never been inside a limousine before, though she had often dreamed of it. The interior was big, of course, every bit as big as it seemed to be from the outside. Even bigger, somehow, if that was possible: a vast area of soft black leather and thick gray carpeting. A sleek, black cellular phone was built into the wall of the car beside her, and below it were the controls for a radio, a compact disc player, and a tiny television mounted on the armrest in the middle of the seat facing her. That seat was identical to the one on which she now sat, and above it, just below the glass partition, was a gleaming silver handle. It was apparently the entry to some sort of cabinet.

With a swift glance at the back of the driver's head, she gave in to her curiosity. She moved forward across the gray carpet to the other seat and pulled on the handle. A section of the dividing wall came down in her hand, forming a makeshift counter. Inside the space was a fully stocked miniature bar. She grinned with delight as she stared at the array of tiny bottles and cans, tumblers and wineglasses. At the back of the bar was a little compartment containing ice cubes and two small bottles of white wine.

A delicious thrill coursed slowly through her, a voluptuous feeling of luxury and decadence. She closed her eyes, holding on to the experience, savoring it. Then she opened her eyes and gave herself over to temptation. She took one of the chilled bottles from the cooler, uncorked it with a silver corkscrew, and poured into a stemmed crystal glass. She returned the bottle to its compartment, closed the bar, and sat down in her original seat, facing forward. She took a long sip of the dry white wine and smiled.

She could definitely get used to this.

The man was watching her in the rearview mirror. Holly became aware of his gaze, and she peered through the dividing glass at the deep green eyes reflected above the windshield. There was in them an unmistakable hint of humor. She stared, holding her gaze to his somewhat longer than absolutely necessary. Then she grinned, winked, raised her glass toward him in a silent toast, and turned to look through the tinted glass beside her at the rainy Long Island landscape. This held no appeal, she soon realized. She looked through the small selection of compact discs: classical music and jazz, neither of which interested her. She glanced briefly at the telephone, wondering which of her few friends or relations would be most impressed by her calling them from a limousine. Mom and Dad? Rhonda and Mrs. Newman at the travel agency?

Oh, please! she admonished herself. She was just being silly. Smiling at her gaucherie, she took another sip of the delicious wine, settled back in the seat, and reflected on the amazing series of events that had brought her here today, all the way from warm, sunny southern California to rainy, gray New York.

He drove through the rain along the Long Island Expressway toward the Fifty-ninth Street Bridge, glancing up occasionally to observe his passenger in the mirror. She was the most beautiful woman he'd ever seen.

She was aware of his gaze, he noted. At one point she actually raised her wineglass in a silent toast and winked at him before looking away again. It was that wink, accompanied by the irresistible, insouciant grin, that sealed his fate. Here was a woman unlike any he had ever known. Tall, graceful, obviously intelligent—and very, very rich. Oh, he'd been with rich women—several, in fact—but nothing on *her* scale.

Off limits, he could hear the voice of reason saying as he flipped the control for the windshield wipers from low to high and switched on the headlights in the gathering twilight. Do not touch. Don't even *think* about it. She is your employer now, your entire family's employer. . . .

But, of course, he was already thinking about it. He was doing more than thinking. He was *here*.

His father, who would be this young woman's usual chauffeur, was in bed with the flu, under Dr. Bell's strict instructions not to get out until the fever subsided. That's why he was here now, in the first place. Under ordinary circumstances, he would not have had his first glimpse of her until Thursday, when she arrived at the house in Connecticut. Until then she was staying at the apartment in the city.

He glanced again in the rearview mirror and wondered if, perhaps, he could talk Da into letting him come for her on Thursday. Da's uniform fit him well enough. And it wasn't as if he had other things to do. Between jobs again, as he'd informed his mother and Da when he'd arrived on the family doorstep last week. *Fired* again, his mother had corrected him, frowning briefly before taking the prodigal into her arms and ushering him into the gatehouse where his parents lived with his sister, Dora. The gatehouse in which he and Dora had grown up. Hell, he'd been *born* in the gatehouse at Randall one winter night twenty-eight years ago.

He'd never expected to be back there now. He'd expected to leave Randall House behind him a long time ago.

But now all that had changed. Now *she* had arrived.

So now, of course, he had come back.

He glanced at her reflection again, forcing himself to smile, just in case she noticed. No sense in giving away the game now, before it had officially begun. Pressing his lips together in grim determination, he eased the big car expertly over to the left, into the fast lane.

The fast lane. . . .

He nodded to himself as the car increased in speed through the early evening traffic into New York City. He couldn't wait to get there. He couldn't wait for the game to begin.

It was the letter that had begun it, in June, five months ago. Holly remembered the day clearly: hot, dry, the air visibly shimmering above the highway and stretches of parched desert that surrounded the Coachella Valley, where she had lived her entire life.

She'd grown up in Indio, the largest town in that remote section of the country, known primarily for the raceway that was the site of a rather famous annual event. Three miles west of the town of Coachella, "America's Date Capital," and twenty miles east of Palm Springs. Her mom, Mary, owned an interior decorating shop in downtown Indio, and her dad, Ben, was an executive at the California Date Company in Coachella.

Holly had gone to Palm View Elementary and Valley View High before leaving home for four years to attend the University of California in San Diego. She'd come home to Indio after graduation, but she didn't stay with her parents for long. She found a job at Explorers Travel Agency in Palm Springs, and she'd taken an apartment there with Rhonda Metz, one of her fellow agents. She'd been there for three years now; working a little, playing a lot, dating a rather dull succession of men—and wondering what she wanted to do with the rest of her life. She'd majored in English at the university, but she didn't particularly want to write or work in publishing. If she were honest with herself, she knew, she would admit that she was lazy. She didn't like work, period, including Explorers Travel Agency.

Ironically, her biggest desire in life was to be rich enough to become one of her own clients. She wanted to travel, to see the world. London, Paris, Rome, Tokyo, Sydney: she sent others to those places all the time, but she had never seen them. There was a big poster, a gorgeous photo of a beach resort in Crete, on the wall beside her desk at the agency. She constantly found herself staring at it, dreaming of the beautiful Mediterranean so far from southern California, wanting to be there as she had never wanted anything else. . . .

Then, as if by magic, the letter had arrived.

She had just returned home from the travel agency

that afternoon five months ago. Rhonda was having dinner with her new boyfriend, so the little, two-bedroom "bachelorette pad," as they called it, was empty and quiet. She'd collected the mail from the box in the lobby before going inside.

She'd noticed the letter immediately. Shuffling through the usual assortment of bills and brochures, she stopped when she came to the white, business-sized envelope with her name and her Indio address neatly typed on the front. Her mom had crossed out the typed address, written Holly's present one, and sent it on. The words "personal and confidential" were typed in a lower corner, and there was no return address of any kind. The postmark was from New York City.

Inside it was another envelope; small, pale blue, with only her name, Holly Smith, written in a small, elegant hand across the front. The engraved return address was on the back flap:

Alicia Randall Wainwright
Randall House
Randall, Connecticut 06429

She'd held the envelope up to her face and sniffed: lavender. Alicia Randall Wainwright. She'd never heard the name before, and she wondered who the woman might be. Obviously rich, she decided. How else could you explain the woman, the house, and the town itself all bearing the same name?

It was a rather long letter, several pages in the same beautiful hand that had written her name on the blue envelope. As she began to read, she experienced a series of small shocks that added up, as she continued, to the biggest shock of her life.

Randall House
June 22

Dear Ms. Smith,

My name is Alicia Wainwright. We don't know each other, but I am writing to you with certain information of a very personal nature. It will definitely come as a surprise to you, and I cannot think of any delicate way to go about it. But I assure you that, as they said many years ago when I was a young woman, the information is "to your advantage."

Let me begin with the biggest surprise. Your name is not Holly Smith. It is Holly Randall. There, I've stated it, plain and simple. There really was no other way. Allow me to explain:

Your parents, Mr. and Mrs. Smith, adopted you when you were an infant. Before you were born, actually. I will not go into the particulars of it now, nor will I explain the circumstances surrounding your adoption. I will only say that your parents—I mean Mr. and Mrs. Smith—are unaware of those circumstances. Part of the deal your real mother made with the person who arranged the adoption was that you and your new parents would never be bothered, would never be approached by our family. Now I must break that promise—a promise I, personally, never gave— and I trust that you will soon understand why I do so.

I am your great-aunt. My brother—your grandfather,

James Randall—died fifteen years ago, leaving the Randall family fortune to me. But he made certain stipulations in his will regarding the settlement of the estate in the event of my death, and I wish to honor them. Those stipulations involve you.

It has now become necessary for me to approach you. I am not in good health: I don't know how long I have, but last February it became imperative that I find you. For reasons I don't wish to explain at this time, I could not approach your natural mother to learn your present whereabouts. It took two private detectives in my employ the better part of four months to find the person who had arranged for your adoption. That person has agreed to forward this letter to you, wherever you are. I have been told only that your name is now Holly Smith.

Well, Holly Smith, allow me to tell you that you are the principal heir to a great fortune. I know nothing of your life, or of your present circumstances, but I can only assume that this will be good news. I can't imagine it being anything else!

I must make a request of you now, and, as we have never met, you may regard it as an imposition. But I must request it, anyway. Please do not reveal any of what I'm telling you to anyone, even Mr. and Mrs. Smith (I am assuming that's their name), until you and I have spoken further. I promise to tell you everything: who your real parents were, the necessity of your adoption, and the particulars of your inheritance. But I must do that in person. I cannot tell you these things in a letter.

My address is on the envelope. You may write if you

*wish, or you may call me at 203-555-4300. I will
arrange to have you brought to me, or, if you prefer, I
shall come to you. If, for any reason, you do not wish
to contact me or hear more of this, please call my attorney, Gilbert Henderson, in New York City, as other
arrangements will have to be made concerning the
Randall estate. Mr. Henderson's telephone number is
212-555-1000.*

*Holly, it was your grandfather's dying wish that
you inherit the Randall fortune, and now it is my
wish, as well. Please, please get in touch with me, and
soon. I live for the day when I will hear from you. Until then I remain*

*Yours sincerely,
Alicia Randall Wainwright*

Holly sat back against the cool leather backseat in
the limousine, shaking her head at the irony as she
remembered the phone call she'd finally made, last
August. She'd waited until then, but she hadn't
called Mrs. Wainwright.

She'd ultimately called the lawyer, Mr. Henderson. He had been surprised to receive the call, of
course, but he had quickly recovered, and he had
given Holly the inevitable news in a low, clear voice
that conveyed his professional and personal sadness. He had just that morning attended her great-
aunt Alicia's funeral at Randall House. She had
died of a heart attack, while swimming, three days
before.

Then he had told her the rest.

And now, three months and several phone calls later, here she was in a limousine, on her way to New York City and, from there, to Randall, Connecticut. Holly Randall, new owner of fabulous Randall House; a twenty-room house in Palm Beach, Florida; apartments in New York City, Los Angeles, and London; stocks, bonds, real estate, and substantial shares in the National Food Corporation; several "important pieces" of art and jewelry; several cars, three horses, an eighty-five-foot yacht, a sailboat, and round-the-clock access to a National Food Corporation private jet. And—oh, yes, the lawyer had quickly added—a custom-built Steinway grand piano in the music room at Randall House that had originally belonged to, and been composed on by, Rachmaninoff. Total value: well, Mr. Henderson wasn't sure, exactly, but it was somewhere in the vicinity of six hundred million.

She sipped the last of the wine as the car made its silent, smooth way across the bridge into the city. Hell, she thought, the piano alone would be worth more than most human beings will ever see. . . .

No. She wouldn't think about all that. Not now. Now, she would just get through the next step, meeting the lawyer at his office tomorrow morning. There was going to be some sort of test, he'd told her, to assure everyone that she was really Holly Randall. But he hadn't told her the nature of the test.

She hadn't brought up the subject with her parents in Indio, in accordance with Mrs. Wainwright's wish. In fact, they had no idea where she was now,

or what she was doing. A vacation, she'd told them.
A trip to New York City, transportation courtesy of
the travel agency. They had accepted that. They always accepted whatever she told them. Ben and
Mary Smith were good and trusting people.

But they were not her parents.

She'd known that, at least, for quite a long time,
ever since Ben's accident in the date fields six years
ago, when she was eighteen. He'd been cut on the
wrist by a date thorn, a sharp, clawlike edge of the
palm bark that surrounds and protects the fruit at
the top of the tree, and it had severed a vein. He'd
been rushed to the emergency room, where Mary
and Holly had soon joined him. He'd lost a lot of
blood, and he needed an immediate transfusion.
Both women had offered to donate blood. A quick
check of the family's medical records showed that
neither Mary nor Holly was eligible to do so, and
the blood was taken from the hospital's stored
supply.

That's when she'd found out. Her blood type was
O positive, which didn't come close to matching
that of either parent. While the doctors stitched up
her father in the emergency room, Mary sat her
down on a hard, cold chair in the cold waiting room
and told her. They didn't know who her real parents were. They'd gotten her through an adoption
agency in Los Angeles, which had represented an
anonymous party in New York. That was all Mary
knew. Ben was sterile, she explained, had been all
his life, and they'd always wanted a child.

She'd assured her mother that it was all right,

that it really didn't make any difference to her. And that had been the truth.

Until now. . . .

The car came to a sudden stop. Holly blinked and looked around. The rain had ceased, and the limousine had pulled up in front of a big building on Central Park South. A liveried doorman was opening the door for her. She put the empty wineglass in the bar compartment and got out of the car.

The doorman grinned at her. "Welcome to New York, Ms. Randall."

She stared at him, then at the handsome chauffeur who was now removing her suitcase from the trunk, then back.

Ms. Randall.

She produced a warm, dazzling smile, hoping it concealed her surprise. "Why, thank you."

Then the chauffeur was leading her inside, across a beautiful lobby to an elevator. Before any of the opulence could fully register in her mind, they were rising swiftly, silently up to what had to be the top floor, or close to it.

Holly smiled at the chauffeur as they ascended. "Thank you, Mr.—umm. . . ." She trailed off feebly, feeling the color burning her cheeks.

His grin transformed the rugged handsomeness of his features, and his bright green eyes flashed. "It's Kevin. Kevin Jessel, at your service." He doffed his chauffeur's cap and executed a small, formal bow. "My father is your chauffeur and resident mechanic at Randall House, but he's in bed with the flu, so he sent me. My mother is the housekeeper there. My parents and grandparents have done for the Randalls since before you and I were born."

Holly continued to stare. "Then that car, that limousine, isn't—rented?"

"No, ma'am, it's yours. And it'll be back for you on Thursday, to take you to Randall."

She was beginning to feel numb inside. "I see. And—will you be driving it?"

He grinned some more, fingering the gray cap in his hands. "It would be a pleasure."

She smiled back at him. He was watching her, she noticed, and she wondered if any of her racing thoughts had shown on her face.

They emerged from the elevator into a little foyer where the single door stood open. An attractive, middle-aged African-American woman in a black uniform and white apron stood there, smiling at her.

"Ms. Randall, this is Mrs. Wells, your New York housekeeper," Kevin said as he stepped into the apartment and set the suitcase down.

"Welcome, Ms. Randall," the woman said.

Ms. Randall. Again.

"Thank you." Holly smiled as Mrs. Wells helped her remove her coat. Then the housekeeper bustled off, murmuring something about dinner being ready soon, and Holly stepped forward into the huge penthouse apartment with a terrace overlooking Central Park. She tried mightily not to stare around at everything, acutely aware that Kevin Jessel was still hovering in the doorway, watching her. She

37

turned to face him again, smiling to mask her sense of wonderment.

"Anything else, Ms. Randall?" he asked.

"Yes, one more thing—Kevin. I want you to call me Holly."

He looked confused. "You mean, now?"

"I mean *always*. It's my name. Holly Smith."

He grinned once more as he twirled the cap in his hands. "Okay, I'll call you Holly if you insist—"

"I insist."

"But you're not Holly Smith. Not anymore. You're Holly Randall now. I'll be back for you at two o'clock Thursday afternoon. Good night—Holly."

With that, he was gone. After a moment, Holly took a deep breath, walked slowly into the beautiful living room, and sank down onto a couch.

It's all too much, she thought as she stared around at the apartment and the terrace and Central Park in the background. I'll never be able to get used to this. I won't be able to sleep in this place. I won't even be able to *eat*!

It was just going on nine o'clock that evening at Randall House as the lovely, dark-haired woman in the beaded red evening dress made her way slowly down the main staircase to the Great Hall. Dinner had been over for half an hour, and she could hear the faint sounds from the dining room as the servants cleared the table. She'd been up in her room, changing into more comfortable shoes and freshening her makeup, and she was smiling at the prospect of a drink and a quiet game of cards with her husband in the library. As she came down the stairs, she saw the housekeeper, Mrs. Jessel, approaching from the direction of the kitchen. She produced an outward smile and inwardly braced herself.

"Mrs. Randall?" the woman said as they met at the bottom.

"Yes, Mrs. Jessel?"

"We're finishing up in the kitchen now, and Mr. Randall is in the library. Will there be anything else this evening?"

"No, thank you," she replied, still smiling automatically— and rather artificially—at the grim-faced woman who always seemed to be fingering the folds of her severe black uniform. "I'm sure we can manage now."

"Very good, ma'am." The housekeeper started to leave, then turned briefly back to her. "Oh, please tell Mr. Randall that my son is back from New York, and he'll be up from the gatehouse to speak with him as soon as he's finished his supper."

"To—speak with him?"

"Yes, ma'am, just as Mr. Randall requested. Good night, Mrs. Randall."

"Good night."

She watched the woman go, then continued on her way across the Great Hall to the library. She didn't care for Mrs. Jessel, and that was a fact. Always so formal, and so completely humorless. She imagined that the two of them were close to the same age, yet the housekeeper could practically pass for her mother. Mildred Jessel was one of many things she'd had to get used to in the eight

39

months she'd lived here, ever since Alicia Wainwright's heart attack last February, when John had insisted they leave Europe and come to Randall House to be near his ailing aunt. Well, Alicia was gone now, but Mrs. Jessel . . . no, she didn't like her. Mrs. Jessel reminded her of a nun, or a prison matron, with her sour frowns and her constant air of disapproval.

She glanced at her reflection in the mirror above the hall table next to the library door. She paused for a moment, smiling in satisfaction at the attractive, elegant-looking woman with the brown eyes and the short, glossy black curls who smiled back at her. Yes, she should wear this red dress more often. She'd just celebrated her forty-eighth birthday, and she could definitely pass for the daughter of Mildred Jessel, who was probably about fifty-five. Well, to be fair, Mrs. Jessel had never had the benefit of that clever cosmetic surgeon in Zurich, but, even so. . . .

Her husband looked up from his book as she came into the cozy, green baize and dark mahogany room. He was seated in his favorite armchair in the corner, as usual, the blue smoke from his Havana floating in the light from the green glass–shaded floor lamp beside him. She smiled, as she always did when she saw him, feeling the flood of warmth that invariably coursed through her. Two years they'd been man and wife now, and she still couldn't get over it. John Randall was fifty-two, trim and handsome, and the years had been kind to him. That masculine face, that thick blond hair, those amazing, pale blue eyes, the signature of the Randalls.

"Hello, Cathy," he said.

She went over to his chair, leaned down, and kissed him lightly on the forehead. "Hello, yourself." She turned and went over to the bar between the bookcases near the door. As she poured her red wine, she said, "How's your drink?"

"Fine," came the reply. She heard the tinkling of ice in his scotch and soda.

She walked back over to him. "Mrs. Jessel says Kevin will be here presently—as you requested." She hadn't meant to make it sound like a question, but she was aware that it did. She heard his quiet laugh.

"Yes, I thought we'd get a—preliminary report." He laughed again. "You really don't like Mrs. Jessel, do you?"

Now she, too, was laughing. "Oh, she's fine, if you like people who wear black all the time and skulk around the corridors like the wrath of God."

"Yeah," he agreed, still chuckling. "I've never much cared for her, either. Her mother-in-law, the original Mrs. Jessel, was much nicer. She practically raised us, James and myself. She was a very cheerful woman. But Mildred—well, I don't think she likes me, and the feeling is mutual." Still smiling, he returned his attention to the book in his hands.

She watched him a moment, then glanced over at the card table by the windows. "I thought we might have a game of cards."

"What, gin?" he breathed, not looking up. "You always beat me."

"Poker, then. Five-card draw. . . ."

"You always beat me at that, too," he reminded her. He held up his leather-bound volume. "You should try reading."

She shook her head. "I've done enough reading to last me my whole life." She glanced at the cover of his book: *Wuthering Heights.* "I've read *that*, God knows. Many times. You know, I got my name—"

"Yes, Cathy," he said with a sigh, cutting her off, "I know. You got your name from here." He waved his free arm, indicating the walls of books around them. "There must be something you haven't read, something that would interest you." Then, with an impish grin and a twinkle in his blue eyes, he added, "I think I saw a copy of *Lady Chatterley's Lover* over there somewhere. . . ."

Her eyes widened in mock surprise, and she reached over and playfully slapped his cheek.

"Watch it," she warned, giggling.

They were still laughing quietly together when there was a knock on the door, which immediately opened. Kevin Jessel came into the room, still in his gray uniform.

"Good evening," he said. "My mother said you wanted to see me."

She turned around, and her husband rose from his chair.

"Good evening, Kevin," John said.

"Hello, Kevin," she said, smiling at the tall, handsome young man, who smiled and nodded to her.

My God, she thought. How on earth did that dreary Mildred Jessel ever produce such beautiful children? And Kevin and his sister, Dora, were definitely beautiful.

"Yes, I wanted to speak to you," John said, moving over to the bar. "Join me in a drink?"

"No, thank you, sir."

"Oh, put a lid on that 'sir' stuff! You and I don't have to stand on ceremony. Boola boola, and all that."

She watched as her husband refilled his glass and turned to face the younger man, thinking, Yale. John was always doing that, reminding the younger man of their common link. Of course, he never mentioned that he'd been asked to leave their alma mater under a cloud, something about a girl, whereas this man, the son of his servants, had graduated with honors. Kevin, as far as she could see, always responded to her husband with polite but rather chilly formality.

"So," John was saying now, "you picked up Ms. Randall at the airport?"

"Yes, sir—uh, Mr. Randall."

"And you took her into the city?"

"Yes. She's at the apartment. Mrs. Wells is taking care of her, and I'm bringing her here Thursday."

"Good, good," John mumbled, nodding. "And she's seeing the lawyer, Mr. Henderson, tomorrow?"

"I believe so."

She rolled her eyes in exasperation and went over to join them. At the rate her husband was going, they'd never get anywhere.

"What does Holly look like?" she asked abruptly.

Kevin blinked. Then, for the first time since he'd entered the room, the expression on his face softened.

"Oh, she's—she's lovely," he said. "Tall, blond, with blue eyes, just like. . . ." He trailed off, vaguely waving a hand to indicate her husband.

So, she thought. The girl is beautiful.

"I see," she said. "And how would you say she's feeling about—all this?"

"Feeling? I—I don't know, exactly. She seemed very happy, I guess. Excited. A little"—he searched for a word—"overwhelmed."

He shrugged his impressive shoulders and glanced over at the door.

"Well, thank you, Kevin," she said, smiling. "We won't keep you any longer. We were just anxious to hear about our—our new niece." She looked at her husband. "Weren't we, darling?"

"Oh, yes, absolutely," John stammered. He raised his glass and quickly drained it.

Kevin Jessel looked from one to the other of them. "Well, good night, then."

"Good night, Kevin," she said.

"Yes, good night," her husband added.

Kevin went over to the door, turned for a last, polite nod to them, and left.

They stood there for several moments, husband and wife, regarding each other in silence.

"Well," John said at last.

"Well," she echoed thoughtfully. "She must be

44

something. That young man is already in love with her. Yes, she must be quite—quite *something*."

He was studying her face. "Will that be a problem, Cathy?"

She shook her head decisively. "No, of course not. It doesn't change anything. Have you—have you found anyone suitable?"

"Maybe," he said, smiling. She thought he was probably smiling because they were both whispering, despite the fact that they were quite alone in the room. "I'm meeting someone in a couple of days, as a matter of fact. But I won't bore you with those details. The less you know about it, the better."

She nodded. "Okay. Just be sure they understand the importance of making it look like an accident."

"Of course."

"It has to be done right."

"Of course."

"And it mustn't be traced to us."

"Of course."

"All right, then." She went over to the card table and sat. Producing a deck of cards from the drawer under the table, she began expertly shuffling them. John refilled his glass at the bar and brought her wine bottle with him as he came over to sit across from her, his book apparently forgotten.

She smiled as he filled her glass. She'd known all along that they would eventually play cards. She was in charge of this, as she'd just been in charge of the interview with Kevin Jessel, and they both knew it.

"Five-card draw," he said. "One game. Then bed."

She handed him the deck.

"Deal," she said. She meant the cards, of course, but she meant something else as well. They both knew that, too.

"But first," he said, "a toast." His blue eyes twinkled as he raised his glass.

She reached for her wineglass. "What shall we drink to?"

He grinned. "To Holly."

They laughed quietly as they clinked glasses, sealing their bargain and Holly Randall's fate, their gazes locked together.

"Yes," she said. "To Holly."

As it turned out, Holly was wrong about not getting used to her new situation in the apartment on Central Park South. She ate the dinner Mrs. Wells had prepared for her as if she'd never seen food before in her life. After that, the housekeeper unpacked for her and ran her a hot bath. Holly bathed, dried herself with soft towels, and crawled into the big bed in the bedroom that was nearly twice the size of her bedroom at home. As her head hit the pillows, she thought once more of Kevin Jessel, the astonishingly handsome man who was apparently her servant, and of his astonishing words.

"You're Holly Randall now."

Then, almost immediately, she was asleep.

* * *

The rain began again just at the stroke of midnight, but the woman in the black cloak paid no attention to it. She pulled the hood of the cloak closer to her pale throat with her one free hand and continued on her way. Through the trees beside the curving front drive, around the big main house, and down the sloping back lawn she floated, quiet as a whisper.

As the downpour strengthened in its intensity and the cold wind whipped across the headland from the Sound, she held her precious little package closer to her breast, shielding it from the onslaught as best she could. It was very dark here on the back lawn, as the lights of Randall House were far behind her now. But no matter: she knew every step of this journey by heart. She had made it many times before.

A blinding flash of autumn lightning glinted on the wrought iron fence that enclosed the little cemetery beside the chapel, and by the time she reached the gate the answering thunder was resounding through the dark landscape. The woman slipped past the gate and glided over to her usual corner, a shadow among shadows, careful not to disturb the monuments as she passed them. When she arrived at her destination, she sank to her knees on the muddy ground, gently laid down her package, and reached behind the nearest headstone for the little spade she always kept concealed there.

Before she began, she extended a pale white arm, pulled the crude little wooden cross from the earth where it stood, and laid it aside. Then, using the spade with quick, efficient strokes, she began to dig.

The earth, soaked as it was, came away remarkably easily tonight, and her task was soon completed. Even so, she turned her head to glance up at the lights of the distant house several times as she worked, just to assure herself that she was not being observed. It was an evil house, she knew *that* well enough, and evil people lived there. No, she told herself again each time she looked, they are not watching me. They are not pursuing me. Not now, at any rate.

She put down the spade and reached for the little bundle. She cradled it in her arms, raising her eyes to the stormy sky. The rain pelted her upturned face, mingling with her tears. She silently mouthed the words she'd learned long ago in the chapel behind her, the lovely words about the Shepherd. *He maketh me to lie down in green pastures. He restoreth my soul. . . .*

She had never believed the words, or even fully understood them, but they seemed appropriate for this, so she used them. She was not good at memorizing, and she knew few things by heart. And the psalm was more suitable than the poem she'd had to recite in school when she was little, the one about the ringing and the singing of the bells, bells, bells, or whatever it was. She couldn't remember all of it, anyway.

When she came to the end of the psalm, the part about dwelling in the house of the Lord forever, she rearranged the little blue blanket she had knitted with her own hands and gently laid her tiny burden down in the hole, which was rapidly filling with water. Using the spade and her hands, she quickly filled the hole with muddy earth and patted it down. At last, she picked up the little wooden cross and replaced it, to mark the site. She leaned forward to kiss the cross, stood up, and moved swiftly back through the burial ground to the gate.

Another bolt of lightning lit the sky as she came out of the cemetery, and she shrank against the big oak beside the gate as the thunder crashed around her, ignorant of the fact that it was the worst place to be if lightning struck. She was drenched, her garments clinging heavily to her thin, shivering body. No matter, she decided: I feel better now.

A sense of elation coursed through her as she broke away from the shadow of the tree and ran lightly up the sloping lawn toward the side of the house. Be careful now, she cautioned herself. Don't let them see you. Don't let the Devil see you.

She passed the building and continued on her way down the drive toward the massive front gates, toward home. She smiled as she ran through the pouring rain, the deafening thunder, the whole wild night, blithely unaware of the single pair of eyes that watched her progress, as they had watched her ritual in the cemetery.

She always felt better after she buried the baby.

CHAPTER TWO

The Legacy

Gilbert Henderson, Esquire, was exactly as Holly had imagined him to be. His handsome face and tall, slender form; his charcoal gray Brooks Brothers suit; even his oak-paneled offices on Park Avenue went perfectly with the deep, mellifluous, upper-class New England voice she'd been hearing on the telephone for the last three months. In his mid-fifties, or thereabouts. He sounded like a television network anchorman, and he looked like one, too. Another Yalie, she decided, by way of Choate. Some of the framed sheepskin certificates that lined his walls would probably bear this out.

"Good morning, Ms. Randall," he intoned when he came out of his inner sanctum into the large reception area where she'd been waiting. "I'm pleased to meet you, at last."

She smiled and murmured the usual amenities as

she followed him back into his office, acutely aware of her clothes. She was wearing the faded jeans and scuffed boots from yesterday: she really didn't have anything else for the bitter-cold weather outside, and snow had been predicted for later in the day. Even so, she was uncomfortable. The lawyers and clerks and secretaries were all so beautifully dressed, and she looked like—well, she didn't fit in here, certainly.

He offered her a seat in a big leather chair and went around to sit behind his massive desk. He folded his hands on a file folder on the blotter before him and leaned forward, smiling. She knew he was inspecting her, so she looked elsewhere, at Park Avenue through the big windows behind him. He asked her if she would like coffee, and she smiled and nodded. He pushed a button and spoke into an intercom, and moments later a pretty young Asian woman in a wheat-colored suit and matching shoes came in with a silver tray. Holly looked at the woman, at her glistening black hair and subtle makeup and tasteful jewelry, then down at her own well-worn sweater. She felt a sense of relief when the woman left the room.

"Now," Mr. Henderson said at last, smiling. "Richard Lawrence of the Tri-State Trust Bank will be joining us shortly, but first I want to explain a few things to you. In this folder are all the necessary papers, as well as the report from your doctor in California. I thank you for cooperating in all this: it may seem silly, even old-fashioned, to need all this proof of your identity, but I'm sure you understand. The circumstances are definitely unusual."

She leaned forward in her chair, glancing down at the folder on the desk. "I assume Dr. Kelman's report was—um—satisfactory?"

"Oh, yes," the lawyer quickly assured her. "Age, blood type, et cetera. Your Dr. Kelman's report matches this." He opened the folder, pulled the top sheet of paper from it, and held it forward. She took it from him.

It was a photocopy of a birth certificate. Holly Alicia Randall, born Christmas Eve, twenty-four years ago. She glanced at the names of the parents, and then up at the logotype at the top of the document. A chill of apprehension, or perhaps merely of wonder, coursed slowly through her as she stared, aware that the lawyer was once more watching her intently.

"You were born there, in the infirmary," Mr. Henderson whispered. "It's—it's a women's detention center here in New York. Your mother was awaiting her trial at the time. You see, Ms. Randall—"

"Yes," she said, raising her gaze to meet his. "I know. My mother killed my father. She shot him twice in the chest, on April first—April Fools' Day—in their apartment in Greenwich Village. The media called it the April Fools' Murder. He was thirty-one, she was twenty-four. My age now. . . ."

Holly recited the story she'd recently learned. Her mother was an actress her father had met when he saw her in an off-Broadway play. They were only married about a year and a half when the murder occurred. She didn't even know she was pregnant until after her arrest. She had Holly in the infirmary and gave the baby to someone to put up for adoption, because her own family and the Randalls refused to help her. She claimed self-defense, but no one believed her. She was tried and convicted of second-degree murder, and sentenced to life. Five years ago, after serving nineteen years, she was released. She went to live in a cottage in a beach community on Long Island, near where she'd grown up. She lived in complete seclusion, because nobody would have anything to do with her. She lived there for nearly one year. Then, on April first, exactly twenty years to the day after the murder, she doused the cottage with kerosene, set it on fire, and shot herself. She was identified from the prison dental records. The media had another field day, thanks to the second "April Fools' " tie-in. She was buried in a public cemetery on Long Island, at the expense of the state.

". . . Her name was Constance Hall Randall," Holly finished, "but everyone called her Connie. I don't look like her, judging from the photos I've seen, but I'm definitely my father's daughter." She smiled at the attorney, picked up her cup and saucer, and took a sip. "This coffee is delicious."

They sat in silence for a moment, regarding each other across the desk. Then the lawyer nodded.

"Well," he said, "you've certainly made my part in this interview a great deal easier."

Holly laughed. "Yes. I spent the better part of

three days at the library in Palm Springs, after I received the letter from Mrs. Wainwright. She'd been so cryptic about the circumstances of my adoption, and I was curious. I wasn't prepared for what I found. I was just looking up the name Randall in *Who's Who*. I figured, with that kind of money, there must be something written about them. What I found was the Randall Fish Company, which had eventually merged with National Food Corporation. My great-grandfather was chairman of the board. I also found out about the scandal. It was mentioned in the biography. So I went to the microfiche section, where all the newspapers are stored. I read everything available from the New York papers at the time. Quite a story. Quite a legacy." She shrugged. "I mean, one minute my mother was a very nice interior designer named Mary Smith, and the next minute my mother was the April Fools' Killer."

Mr. Henderson was watching her again. "Is that why you didn't immediately respond to Alicia's letter?"

She nodded. Then she leaned forward again. "Tell me, Mr. Henderson, how did she find me?"

Gilbert Henderson leaned back in his chair, smiling. "No mystery there. She hired private detectives. They started at the detention center, which somehow got them onto the adoption agency in L.A. I think she must have bribed someone there, because they finally relented and opened a confidential file, which led her to the anonymous party who had arranged everything." He continued to smile as he looked at her.

Holly nodded again. "The family lawyer. You."

"I wasn't the family lawyer at the time," he corrected her. "In fact, I've only been working for her—for *you*, actually—since she tracked me down some four months ago, just before her death."

She shook her head absently. "Then, why did you . . . ?"

There were two silver-framed photographs next to the telephone at the side of his desk. He reached over, picked one up, and held it out to her.

Despite the warmth of the room, the silver frame was cold in her hands. She stared. Two young men against a snowy landscape, wearing identical Yale sweaters and stocking caps, their arms across each other's broad shoulders, laughing into the camera. The dark-haired hunk on the left was obviously this man, Gilbert Henderson, some thirty years ago. The blond, blue-eyed beauty on the right was James Randall III.

Her father.

Oh, she thought, of course. They were classmates and best friends, and arranging for my welfare was the least this man could do for my father after his death. She thought all of this as she replaced the picture on the desk, but all she managed to say was "Oh."

Mr. Henderson stood up and came around the desk to stand before her. "Ironic, isn't it? The man responsible for spiriting you away is now the man responsible for bringing you back." His smile faded, and he leaned down to take her hand in his. "If it *is* you, and I hope it is. But I must ask you to please indulge me." He sat on the edge of the desk, his two warm hands still holding her single cold one. "I was there, at the detention center infirmary, when you were born. I was the first person, aside from your mother, to hold you." He suddenly blushed bright red. She thought it was at the memory, but she was wrong. "I—I noticed something then, something I've never forgotten."

He let go of her hand, turned to the desk, and pressed a button. After a moment, the pretty Asian woman in the wheat-colored suit came back into the room.

"This is Ms. Choi," the attorney said. "Paula, this is—uh, well, I *think* this is Holly Randall. Ms. Randall, I want you to do one last thing. I want you to submit to a test. You don't have to, of course, but I would be grateful."

The test he'd mentioned on the phone: she'd forgotten all about it. She smiled at Paula Choi, who was looking down at the floor, and shrugged.

"What do I have to do?" she asked.

"Paula will explain," he said, heading for the door. He was still blushing. "I'll be right outside."

When the lawyer had gone, closing the door firmly behind him, Holly turned to the other woman. Ms. Choi, too, was blushing, and still apparently inspecting the carpet. For one odd, suspended moment, Holly felt a sudden, unaccountable stab of fear.

Paula Choi took a deep breath and at last raised her gaze to Holly's face, and the pink glow on her cheeks subsided.

"I'm sorry about this," she said. "He—he wants you to take off your clothes."

Holly stared. "My *clothes*?"

"Well, the top, anyway . . ."

Holly stared some more. "The top . . ."

Then, all at once, she got it. So, this was the test. She actually laughed as she reached up and pulled her sweater over her head. She'd cursed the thing every day of her life, but now she silently thanked Heaven for it. It had always been a scar to her, a blot, a blemish. Now, as it turned out, it was something else entirely.

She unbuttoned the flannel shirt and removed it. She wasn't wearing a bra. She stood before Ms. Choi, naked to the waist. Then she reached up with her left hand and cupped her left breast, pushing it gently upward. With her right index finger, she pointed at the now-smooth skin just under the fold below her breast.

Paula Choi stared at the small, wine-colored stain, the slight imperfection in the otherwise perfect skin. Then she smiled, clearly relieved, and raised her gaze to the face of the woman who stood grinning before her.

"Welcome home, Ms. Randall," she said.

"Thank you," said Holly Alicia Randall. "Thank you very much."

* * *

The old man was standing at the window, staring out, when the butler came into the room and silently placed the lunch tray on the table near the bed.

"Thank you, Raymond," he said.

"Of course," came the reply.

He could hear the butler behind him moving toward the door, but there was something he had to know first. "Raymond, is it—is it confirmed? Is the young woman from California really arriving?"

"She is, so far as I know," Raymond said. "Mrs. Jessel and the girls are getting everything ready. Mrs. Randall told us to expect Miss Holly at four o'clock Thursday afternoon."

The old man processed this information, nodding slowly to himself. "Thank you."

"I'll be back for the tray in a while," Raymond said. "Call down to the kitchen if you want anything else." There was a slight pause, followed by the sound of the door being quietly shut.

When the butler was gone, he turned from the window to face the room behind him. So, he thought, it's true. This woman who is apparently Holly Randall is coming here.

I must be ready for her.

He thought about that. After a moment, he moved rather unsteadily over to the bookshelves and selected a big scrapbook from the upper shelf. Slowly, with careful effort, he carried it over to the table near the bed and lowered his withered body into a chair. He pushed the lunch tray aside and placed the book on the table. He opened it and began to pore over its yellowing pages, pausing from time to time to read a faded newspaper clipping or to study a face in one of the many old photographs.

The familiar images seemed oddly new to him today, because he was imagining that he was seeing them through Holly Randall's eyes. He wondered what she would make of them, how she would feel about everything that had come before. The family history. Well, it was her history, too, and she was now a part of it.

Then his vision cleared. He was no longer that unknown young woman looking at the albums, but himself again. These people in the photographs were not strangers, but people he had known and loved. As he stared down at them, he felt the rush of old pain suffuse him. And he felt the newer, more alien emotion that had recently entered his catalogue of sensations: suspicion.

He had a horrible suspicion, and he was afraid.

Yes, he thought again. I must be ready for her. . . .

Holly was fully dressed and seated again, sipping coffee, when Mr. Henderson came back into the room. She clutched the cup and saucer tightly in her hands to keep them from rattling together, because she did not want the lawyer to see how nervous she was, or the full extent of her great relief. She smiled warmly up at him as he briefly squeezed her arm, and the smile remained as she watched him go around the desk and sit. And all the while the phrase blared and jangled in her mind, over and over: *I'm Holly Randall. I'm Holly Randall. I'm*—

"So," Mr. Henderson said. "You're Holly Randall."

"Yes," she replied, still smiling. "I am."

His little sigh was accompanied by a single, decisive nod. "Well, then, we can proceed now. First, Mr. Lawrence and I will arrange for you to have access to your money. We've opened a checking account for you, and he'll have your new credit cards with him. You may want to merge your old accounts, your Holly Smith accounts, with the new ones. Mr. Lawrence can do that for you."

She stared at him, trying mightily to take it all in. She smiled blankly, idiotically. *I'm Holly Randall.*

"You're going to be signing a lot of papers," he continued. "I hope your wrist is up to it." He laughed at that, and she joined him. Then he leaned back in his chair, regarding her. "So, do you have any questions, Ms. Randall?"

She nodded. "Mr. Henderson—"

"Gil. Please. May I call you Holly?"

"Of course. In fact, I insist. Gil, what can I expect when I get there? Randall House, I mean."

"Ah, yes," he said. "Your new family. Well, there was your great-aunt Alicia, of course, but I'm afraid you won't have that pleasure. . . ."

"I guess not. What, um, pleasures *will* I have?"

They laughed together again. She had the distinct impression that Mr. Henderson—Gil—was stalling, playing for time. He was arranging information carefully in his mind: she could read it on his face. At last he continued.

"Your uncle John is currently living there with his wife, Catherine. I only met her once, at Alicia's funeral, but I know him. Jim—your father, James—

and I were seniors at Yale when he arrived as a freshman. I can't say I ever liked John. Jim didn't like him, either. They were never close, the Randall brothers. Anyway, John's been in residence at Randall House since last February, when Alicia had her first heart attack. I understand he'd been living on the Continent for several years before that, where he met Catherine. They were married two years ago. If I were you, I'd watch out for him."

Holly stared, confused. "What do you mean?"

Gilbert Henderson sighed. "Well, it's no secret that John is the reason you're here now. His brother wasn't the only one who didn't get along with him. Alicia loathed John, and so did his own father. James Randall, your grandfather, changed his will shortly before he died. After Jim was dead and your mother. . . ." He trailed off, glancing down at the framed picture on his desk before clearing his throat and continuing. "Anyway, your grandfather passed over John in favor of you."

"Do you have any idea why he did that?" she asked. She leaned forward in her chair, studying his face.

He grimaced. "My dear, all you have to do is meet John Randall. I can't speak for your family, but I wouldn't give him cab fare, much less a fortune. He was expelled from Yale in his sophomore year. He's spent his entire adult life wandering around the world on his trust fund, being a sort of international playboy and doing absolutely nothing constructive. He's a leech, a freeloader, and he always was. Now, he'll only get a fortune—I mean a *big* fortune—under certain circumstances."

"And what are those circumstances?"

The lawyer shrugged. "Well, there's a contingency plan for the estate. Your grandfather designed it, and your great-aunt continued it in her will. Since you've been located, and you've proved your identity, all you have to do is get through a grace period. This was put in as a stopgap, for your sake as well as the family's. A period in which you may decide whether or not you really want the fortune, and in which I and Mr. Lawrence may observe you, to be certain that you are—please forgive me, it was your grandfather's request—that you are suitable. That you deserve the name Randall."

Holly nodded. "I understand. How—how long is this grace period?"

"One year. One year in which you must stay at Randall House. You'll have access to the fortune, or a reasonable percentage of it. If at the end of the year you want to run the estate, and if Mr. Lawrence and I give our approval, you inherit the bulk of the fortune. Certain amounts go to charities, of course, and your uncle John will receive five million dollars, in addition to his lifetime annual allowance of two hundred thousand."

"I see," Holly said. "And what is the contingency?"

Mr. Henderson folded his hands together on the desk in front of him. "If you hadn't been found, which you *were*, or weren't deemed 'suitable,' which I'm sure you *will* be, or if you refuse the inheritance, or in the event of your death before the year is up, the Randall estate is settled quite differently. Barring another heir, three-fourths of it will be divided as your grandfather instructed, a lot of it in scholarships to Yale, and a lot more, including Randall House and its property, to the State of Connecticut. The Heart Association, Amnesty International, UNICEF—oh, various things. Alicia added a few, notably the Humane Society and the ASPCA."

Holly could see where this was going. "And the other one-fourth?"

He nodded again, knowing that she'd figured it out. "Your uncle John."

She stared at the man across the desk. "I see. If I inherit, he gets five million and an annual allowance. If I don't inherit, he gets, let's see, about a hundred fifty million."

"Exactly. Barring another heir."

"What does that mean, 'barring another heir'?"

The lawyer shrugged. "A technicality. Your grandfather and great-aunt left everything specifically to the issue of your grandfather's children. So far as anyone knows, that means you, period. Jim had no other children, and John and his wife don't have any, either."

"What if they adopt?" Holly asked.

He shook his head. "Alicia's will is specific: only children extant at the time of her death. She named you as principal beneficiary, despite the fact that you were adopted out of the family, and therefore not necessarily entitled to the fortune. The passage now reads"—he shuffled through some papers until he found what he was looking for—" '. . . to be *divided equally among the issue of my brother's children, regardless of new adoptive status.'* That was obviously for your benefit. Alicia then mentioned you by name: *'the child born Holly Alicia Randall, later adopted by others.'* "

She nodded. "I see. So, Uncle John may not exactly be overjoyed by my arrival."

Gil Henderson grimaced. "As I said, I'd watch out for him if I were you. John Randall is—" He broke off, waving a hand dismissively. "Well, judge for yourself. You'll meet him soon enough." He smiled then, and rose to come around the desk. "Speaking of which, I'm sure you'll be very busy tomorrow. You'll want to be ready for Randall House. I doubt whether a girl from southern California has the right wardrobe for a New England winter. And with Thanksgiving and Christmas coming up, you may be attending a few parties. . . ."

"Oh, gosh!" Holly said. "Clothes!"

He chuckled. "Are you familiar with New York?"

"No, not really. I've only been here twice before, briefly. I guess I can find Macy's and Saks again, but . . ." She shook her head at the overwhelming prospect of shopping in this city.

"I think we may be able to help you," Mr. Henderson said. "I've taken the liberty of recruiting someone, a sort of guide for you. One of your new neighbors, actually. Melissa MacGraw. She's about your age, and her family and the Randalls go back quite a way. She's at her apartment in town now, and I called her and explained the situation. She was delighted. She said it would combine her two favorite pastimes: meeting new people and shopping. If anyone knows everything about buying clothes in New York, it's Melissa. She'll call you tonight."

Holly stared, smiling involuntarily at the man's finesse. It was so smooth, what he'd done, and so kind. Not knowing her until an hour ago, he had no way of knowing whether she was up to this, the adventure she now faced. He hadn't known if she was the sort of person who would be able to buy the proper clothes and accessories. For all he knew, she'd be completely stymied and make a fool of herself. So he'd provided a guardian, a young woman of unquestioned stock and presumably impeccable taste, to help her. Melissa MacGraw, whoever she was, was obviously to the manner born. Holly vaguely imagined a dull, rather homely rich girl who spoke through clenched teeth, all blushes and giggles and Bryn Mawr. But she'd know where to get the right clothes, and for that Holly was grateful.

"I don't know how to thank you," she said to the lawyer.

He smiled. "It isn't necessary. I work for you now, remember?"

She shook her head. "What you've done—*everything* you've done—goes way beyond the employer-employee relationship."

He looked over at the picture on his desk again. "I'm just glad I can do this for Jim." Then he turned his attention back to her. "So, tomorrow you can get whatever you need, and Thursday you'll go to Randall. It's quite a beautiful house, you'll find. I hope you'll be happy in your new life, Holly. Jim would have wanted you to be happy."

She was watching him closely again. "And—my mother? Would she have wanted me to be happy?"

Gilbert Henderson blinked. He looked away a moment, then back at her.

"I have no idea," he said at last. "I only met her the one time, at the detention center, when you were born."

"Oh." She looked from him to the photograph of him with her father. It stood on the desk beside the other framed picture. That one, she saw now, was recent: Gil Henderson as he looked today, his arm across the shoulders of a dark-haired younger man. His son, she supposed. This man had gone on from Yale to have a life as a father and a lawyer, but it had obviously been separate from his old friend, her father. Why didn't he know Constance? she wondered. Why wasn't he at least at their wedding? What had happened to the college friends? She was actually opening her mouth, forming a question, when the intercom buzzed on his desk.

"Yes, Ms. Choi?"

"Mr. Lawrence of the Tri-State Trust Bank is here."

He grinned and winked at Holly. Then he turned back to the intercom. "Show him in, please."

The woman in the black cape was standing at the fence on the edge of the cliff, staring out over the water, when the confusion came upon her.

It happened to her frequently, more frequently than she would have admitted, had anyone ever asked. She had inured herself to the world's disinterest, even its occasional derision. It was her lot, she supposed, and she did not question it. She had learned long ago not to assert herself in any way. Had the dark spell not clouded her mind this afternoon, she would never have dreamed of doing what she did next.

This was her favorite place, this cliff, and she had been standing here for a long time, watching as the ominous clouds gathered above the Sound. She was thinking about the conversation she'd overheard this morning, the one that had struck fear in her and sent her running, gasping from the shock, out across the lawns. She'd been trying to control her terror, trying to sort it out in her mind, trying to decide what she must do. And she must do something, she knew. She must prevent this catastrophe from occurring. But, how?

The conversation had been very clear. There was a woman in New York, a young woman named Holly Randall. And she was coming here two days from now, on Thursday. She was coming to Randall House to stay.

She was the new owner of Randall House.

Just before the veil fell over her eyes, the terrified woman in the cloak was thinking, No! She can't come here. She *mustn't* come here! If she does, she might be . . .

The thought, disjointed as it was, was never completed. At that moment her vision faded, and she stared out over the Sound, not seeing it. Then, as in a trance, she slowly turned around and focused her unseeing eyes on the mansion in the distance.

And she began walking toward it.

Her pace quickened steadily as she approached the house, and the hood of her cloak fell back, unleashing long tresses of jet black hair that floated out behind her. Her breath was coming in little gasps, and her pale hands were clenched together at her bosom. By the time she reached the front steps, she was running. Up the steps she flew, heading for the front door. She did not stop when she arrived at it, did not so much as hesitate. She threw open the big oak door and glided silently into Randall House. Had she been conscious of her actions, she would not have been here, not in a million years. It was the one place in the world she avoided.

What happened next was never very clear to her, even after she had regained consciousness, after she had been told what she had done. She did not remember it.

Mr. Wheatley, the butler, was the first person in the house to get to her. He was in the library across the entry hall from the living room, restocking the bar with Mrs. Randall's favorite red wine, when he heard the shrieking and the first crash, which was followed almost immediately by a second one.

He later reported his actions: he ran to the open doorway of the living room and froze, startled, staring at the cloaked figure standing beside the open breakfront, her pale arms and black hair flying, watching in incomprehension as she pulled display plates and figurines from their shelves and hurled them at the far wall. Another crash, and another. One pretty Dresden shepherdess, Miss Alicia's favorite, actually struck a portrait and shattered. It was this that galvanized him.

He threw himself at the shrieking young woman, knocking her to the floor. As he shouted for help, he grasped her flailing arms and pinned them down. The woman struggled mightily for several moments, but he somehow managed to keep her where she was. He was an old man, and she was amazingly, inhumanly powerful, and he wondered how he was able to do it. Only then did he realize that he was actually sitting on her, and that several other people were crowding into the room behind him. And he at last became aware of what the young woman on the floor was shouting. Her voice was high-pitched, frantic, echoing from the walls all around him, filling the room with her madness.

"She can't come here! She can't come here! Please, God, don't let her come here! She has to be stopped! Don't let her come here!"

Then Mildred Jessel, the housekeeper, was helping him to his feet. He rose slowly, painfully, and moved aside to allow Mrs. Jessel to kneel beside her daughter.

"Dora! *Dora!* Stop this at once, do you hear me? *Stop it!*"

Still lying flat on her back, Dora Jessel blinked, coughed, and stared up at her mother.

"Wha—?" she murmured, blinking around at the strange room and the stricken, concerned faces of

Mr. Wheatley and the cook, Mrs. Ramirez, and the maid, Frieda. "Mother? What happened? Where— where am I?"

She was lying on something sharp, a sliver of broken glass, but what on earth was she doing here? And where was she? There was more broken glass on the floor all around her, and she was apparently in a large room with pale blue walls, perhaps a living room. Yes, it was a living room, the living room of—

She sat bolt upright on the floor.

—Randall House!

Her mother was reaching out for her, attempting to take her in her arms and comfort her, when Dora Jessel, still disoriented, looked past her at the face of the person who had just that moment arrived in the living room doorway. She froze, staring into those eyes. The eyes of the Devil.

Slowly, deliberately, she opened her mouth, filled her lungs, and screamed.

CHAPTER THREE

Arriving

"Well, it's a start," Missy said. "You can get everything else you'll need later."

Holly smiled at her new friend, wondering what else she could possibly need, and reached for another shopping bag. This one was from Ralph Lauren on Madison and Seventy-second, one of three bags from that place alone. She glanced around the pale blue carpeted floor of the bedroom. Fifteen bags in all, crammed with boxes of dresses, sweaters, blouses, skirts, slacks, shoes, boots, and lingerie.

This was the haul from yesterday, not counting the belted Florentine leather coat, the two evening dresses, and the suit that were being altered to fit her. These last items would be delivered to Randall House in the next few days. She looked over at the white wool coat with the fleece-lined hood that lay so casually across the bed, thinking about the strapless, low-cut royal blue satin evening dress and matching pumps that would soon be sent along. She shook her head in wonder: for the coat and that gown alone, she had paid what one would normally pay for a modestly priced car.

Now, in the bedroom, Holly and Missy had finished packing the treasure trove into five new Louis Vuitton suitcases and a brass-studded steamer trunk, which were now shut and standing ready near the bedroom door beside the shabby American Tourister she'd brought from California. This contained faded jeans, sneakers, a pantsuit, the plaid coat, and her one good evening dress. Holly stared at the contrast of the old luggage and the new, smiling, realizing yet again that her life would never be the same.

Melissa MacGraw—Missy, as she insisted on being called—was a pleasant surprise in a day chockfull of pleasant surprises. Far from being the plain, bucktoothed, simpering cliché Holly had envisioned, she was a strikingly pretty Scotswoman with lovely russet-colored hair. She was considerably smaller than Holly, but she laughingly insisted that Matthew, her fraternal twin, had claimed all the height and weight their parents could muster. There was a generous smattering of freckles on her fair skin, and her hazel eyes were definitely her most arresting feature.

Holly had been amazed by her energy. She'd arrived here for breakfast at eight-thirty yesterday morning, and then she'd immediately whisked

Holly off to Fifth Avenue. The light snow that had followed the rain the night before did not slow her down. The next twelve hours were a blur to Holly: Saks, Bergdorf Goodman, Donna Karan, Aquascutum, Ralph Lauren, Bally of Switzerland, and two or three shops on Madison bearing the names of designers Holly didn't know. But Missy knew them, and now Holly owned at least two items from each of them. The brand-new credit cards were presented at each place, and Holly noticed the reactions of everyone in the shops, even the department stores, when they saw the name Randall. Her selections were boxed and bagged and silently, smilingly taken away for delivery to the apartment.

Perhaps the most interesting event yesterday, Holly now reflected, was lunch. In the middle of the whirlwind invasion of shops and stores, Missy had taken her to the Polo Bar and treated her to a delicious meal. Payback, she'd laughed, for Holly's having allowed her to live vicariously through someone else's shopping. It had been over grilled chicken salad and white wine that the other woman had enumerated a few salient points about her new destination.

"Two things you have to remember about Randall," Missy had announced. "One: practically everybody is rich. Two: most of them are rich thanks to your great-great-grandfather, old John Randall. He came to America from England not long after the Civil War. He was a fisherman in Dover, where the industry was awfully crowded, and he decided he'd have a better chance over here. He started out up in Mystic, with a small fleet of boats. Later, he got the idea of drying and smoking and packaging, and he bought up several hundred acres near Greenwich to build a plant. He also built the house on the point for himself and his wife. By the time he died, the business had grown a lot. His son, the original James, took over the running of things.

"The town of Randall sprang up around the Randall Fish plant. Workers, mostly, but the managers and executives built big houses nearby, too, including my great-grandfather. When the National Food Corporation made an offer to buy the Randall Fish Company, old James managed to turn it into a merger. He died shortly after World War Two. His son—your grandfather, James Junior—got the corporation in on the ground floor of the frozen food industry, specifically frozen fish. Later, when NaF-Corp went public . . . well, everybody got rich, including my family, but nobody more than *your* family. So, that's how a lot of frozen cod and herring got us both where we are today!"

Holly laughed politely, holding back the question she was burning to ask, presenting Missy with another one instead.

"What is it like in Randall now?" she asked.

Missy shrugged. "Well, the plant was torn down years ago, so the town changed. Now we have three distinct groups there: the old upper-middle-class group of onetime Randall executives, which includes my family; the former plant workers, who now have other jobs, I guess; and the new people. The rich New Yorkers who did the suburb thing in the fifties and sixties. The richer they were, the farther out of the city they got. Larchmont, Greenwich, Darien; all those places. Randall was particularly attractive, a picturesque little waterfront village just across the border from New York, with lots of rolling hills nearby that would be perfect for big houses. So now we have fresh blood, a brand-new upper-class enclave. And a lot of their kids are our age. I went to school with them. You'll be meeting as many of them as I can talk into coming to Randall House—with your permission, of course."

"What do you mean?" Holly asked. "Why would you have to talk them into it?"

Missy blushed and looked away. "Sorry, that slipped out."

Holly reached for her wineglass, staring at the other woman. "You're referring to my parents, aren't you?"

After a moment, Missy nodded.

So, Holly thought. This is it, the subject I wanted to bring up in the first place. She leaned forward.

"Tell me," she said.

Melissa MacGraw summoned the waiter and asked for more wine. When the glasses were refilled, she took a deep breath and looked directly at Holly.

"Okay," she said.

And she had told her.

Now, as they packed the last of the bags, Holly looked over at her new friend, grateful for her honesty. Thanks to Missy, she was better prepared for what she would find in her new home. She was now, as a result of her grandfather's will, the principal heir of a once highly regarded family whose reputation had been sullied by scandal. The local gentry had stopped coming around, and her great-aunt Alicia had lived out the final years of her life in relative seclusion. There had been no parties at Randall House in a long time, and the family was not included on many guest lists. It was difficult to believe; it seemed so old-fashioned, somehow. But there it was.

As she led her friend out of the bedroom for lunch in the dining room, she made a silent vow to herself. She, Holly Alicia Randall, was going to change all that. If she was to join this family, share in its great fortune, she was going to bring something into it. She would meet the local families, get to know them, and improve their opinion of the Randalls.

It was, she decided, the least she could do.

Almost exactly at the time that Holly was making this decision on Central Park South, one of her new relatives at Randall House was making a similar one. She sat in the rarely used office on the ground floor of the house, at the big oak desk from which her husband's grandfather had once run the family business. Occasionally she would pause to sip her coffee and gaze out the window at the snow that fell softly on the lawn. Then she would pick up her pen and continue writing, carefully copying the words from the etiquette book that lay open beside her notepad.

John and Catherine Randall request the pleasure of your company at a birthday party for their niece, Holly Randall, on Christmas Eve, December 24. . . .

There was a little smile on her face as she wrote. This would be her first act as a hostess at Randall House, and she was certain that most of the one hundred fifty people she planned to invite would attend. The scandal was twenty-five years old now, a quarter of a century. Besides, even the die-hard snobs would not be able to resist the chance to meet the new member of the Randall family. Oh, no: she was counting on their curiosity to overcome their reserve.

She would hire an orchestra, and extra help, and she had already placed a call to Madge Alden, the most sought-after caterer in Greenwich. There would be a great tree, twelve feet high, near the bottom of the staircase in the Great Hall, as in the old days when the Randall Christmas party had been the social highlight of the year in this part of Connecticut. Of course, Emily and Alicia had entertained three or four hundred guests at a time, or so she'd been told, but that was long ago. This party would be smaller, perhaps, but it would be memorable.

On Christmas Eve, she and John were going to show the world how happy they were, how proud they were of Holly, their new relation.

After Christmas—well . . .

She smiled again as she finished writing out the invitation, and glanced at her watch. There would be plenty of time to drive into town now, to the stationery shop on Main Street. Gilt-edged cream card stock, she decided. Then back here, to get ready for Holly's arrival. At four o'clock, she and her husband would be standing at the top of the front steps before the house, waving as the car came up the drive. The servants would be there, too, organized by Mrs. Jessel. Everyone would be smiling, welcoming the young woman into their midst. And no one would be smiling more than John and herself. They would appear to be the two happiest people in the world.

It was all going to be absolutely perfect.

Holly replaced the receiver on the phone in the living room and waited several minutes, undecided. She had just told Mrs. Newman that she would not be back to work at Explorers Travel Agency, that "unforeseen circumstances" were keeping her in New York indefinitely. Mrs. Newman had been very nice about it, assuring her that her job was always there if she wanted it again. Then she'd put Holly's fellow agent and roommate, Rhonda, on the line, and Holly had said good-bye to her, adding that she'd send her half of the rent every month. She hadn't told either woman about the Randalls.

Her hand still rested on the receiver, but she didn't pick it up. The next call would be to Mary Smith, and she wasn't sure what she was going to tell her adoptive mother. It was odd, really. She'd been in New York for fewer than seventy-two hours, and she had yet to arrive at the house she would have to reside in for at least one year. But she was already beginning to think of Indio and the Smiths as her former life.

She looked at her watch: one o'clock. Missy had left a few minutes ago, right after lunch. Kevin Jessel would be here in one hour to take her to Randall.

It was ten o'clock in California. Mrs. Newman and Rhonda had just opened for the day when Holly called them. Mary Smith would just now be opening Smith/Pierce Interiors, her shop in downtown Indio. Bracing herself, Holly picked up the receiver and dialed, trying to form coherent phrases in her mind.

Mary answered on the first ring. "Smith/Pierce Interiors. May I help you?"

It was the clear, cheerful voice of the woman Holly had always thought of as her mother. The familiar, soothing voice she'd heard every day of her life. *Good morning, dear. Good night, darling. I love you, Holly . . .*

"Hello, Smith/Pierce Interiors," the voice, now tentative, questioning, repeated into the silence.

Holly opened her mouth to reply, but no sound would come. In a sudden, overwhelming instant, she realized that she was unable to speak.

"Hello? Hello?"

Tears arrived in her eyes, burning them, blurring her vision as she pressed the receiver to her ear, drinking in the sound of the voice on the other end of the line.

"Hello . . . ?"

Before she was aware of what she was doing, Holly slammed down the receiver. She sat there in the living room on Central Park South, twenty-seven hundred miles from Mary Smith. She swiped at her eyes with the back of her hand as she wept, waiting for her vision to clear, filled with an acute sense of sadness, of loss. She had not expected to feel homesick for Indio, yet here it unaccountably was.

She imagined Mary shaking her head in mild annoyance as she hung up, assuming that someone had dialed the wrong number. Then she would return her attention to her work. Later today, in some quiet moment, she would think about Holly, her daughter who was on vacation in New York, and wonder whether or not she would be home in time for Thanksgiving.

Holly drew in a deep breath and stood up from the couch. She would go into the kitchen and ask Mrs. Wells to have someone come up for the luggage. She would go to Connecticut, meet these people, see how she felt about it all. And sometime in the next few days, when she was settled in at Randall House, she would decide on the best way to tell her nice, loving, respectable, middle-class parents that their daughter was the daughter of a murderer, and that she was now one of the richest women in America.

The meeting took place at a roadside diner outside a town several miles north of Randall. The time, three o'clock, had been carefully chosen, an hour when the place would be fairly empty. He was wearing faded jeans, an old sweater, a black pea coat from his college days, and a blue stocking cap. He even wore dark sunglasses, which he did not remove during the interview. A casual observer would assume he was a truck driver or a local fisherman. John Randall didn't want to be recognized, and he didn't like taking chances.

He laughed at that thought as he parked the Honda Accord, the Randall staff car he'd chosen over his own Mercedes, next to a red Infiniti in the diner's lot and went inside. If I didn't take chances, he mused, I wouldn't be here. But here he was.

And there the man was. John had never seen him before, did not even know his name, but he decided immediately that the man in the leather jacket must be the one. For one thing, he was the only person sitting alone in the room. There were two big, burly men at the counter, probably from the eighteen-wheeler outside, flirting with one of the two pink-uniformed waitresses. Four teenage girls, just out of class for the day, whispered and giggled together at a table in the center of the room. None of these people so much as glanced over at John as he made his way to the booth in the farthest corner where the man was waiting. As he arrived there, the man looked up from his coffee.

"You John?" A hoarse, gravelly voice, the accent straight from the meanest streets of Brooklyn.

John nodded silently and slid onto the banquette across from him.

"Ed," the man said. He made no move to shake hands.

John nodded again, studying him as discreetly as possible while the waitress took his order for coffee. A medium-sized man with curly brown hair and dark, heavy-lidded eyes. A solid build under an angular face, the slightly crooked nose its only remarkable feature. Well, that and the dark eyes: they looked directly at you, frank, appraising. There was no warmth in them. The nose had been broken, probably more than once, and the oversized knuckles on his thick fingers had been put to frequent use. A plain gold wedding band and an expensive-looking watch were his only accessories. He was somewhere around forty, as nearly as John could guess. An ordinary-looking man who was anything but ordinary: strong, cold, capable, and obviously dangerous.

In his travels, John had become friendly with a lot of interesting people, not all of them on the right side of the law. One such acquaintance was J. T. Benson, a dedicated gambler he'd first met several years ago at a table in Vegas. J.T. was an importer/exporter, the extent of whose inventory had never been made very clear. He and his wife were amusing, adventurous types, and John had liked them immediately. He'd taken them on gambling junkets to Nassau and Jamaica and Puerto Rico on the *Emily,* the Randall yacht, and he'd been their houseguest on several occasions, in several houses. They'd even flown to Paris for his wedding two years ago.

Recently, when it was confirmed that Holly Smith had been located and was definitely going to arrive at Randall House, John had called J.T. Without going into any details, he'd told his friend that he was looking for a certain type of person for a certain type of job. He'd figured J.T. might know someone who knew someone, and he'd figured correctly. J.T. had asked no questions, but he'd arranged today's meeting.

The waitress placed coffee before him and refilled the other man's cup. As soon as she was gone, Ed leaned forward.

"So," he said, "what can I do for you?"

Money, John thought as he looked into the cold eyes of the man before him. This is going to cost a lot of money. Then again, if all goes well, money will not be a problem. I don't know this man, and J.T. has probably never met him, either. He's a friend of a friend of a friend. He can't be traced to me, whatever happens. He's perfect.

John looked at his watch—three-ten. He had to get back to Randall House and change clothes, to be ready to greet Holly on the doorstep at four o'clock. With a quick glance around the diner, he also leaned forward. The two men's faces were now mere inches apart.

"I have a problem, Ed," John said, "and you may be able to help me with it."

The man, whose name was probably not Ed, didn't even blink. This was obviously what he did for a living.

"I'm listening," he said.

Keeping his voice low, barely more than a whisper, John began to talk.

* * *

Holly didn't help herself to wine from the little bar this time. She sat very still on the plush backseat, her gloved hands folded primly in her lap, and braced herself for whatever she would find at her journey's end.

At least she was now suitably dressed for the occasion. She was wearing a blue, green, and gray diamond-patterned sweater, a gray midi-length wool skirt, and boots. The beautiful white wool coat was over all this. She was grateful for the new wardrobe, for the confidence it instilled in her. Most of the luggage had gone into the car's big trunk, and the rest was on the front seat beside Kevin Jessel. She would need every bit of what she'd bought, and more.

One year. She would have to spend one year at Randall House. Mr. Henderson—Gil—had told her as much on the phone in one of their conversations in the last three months, but it hadn't really registered, become real to her, until he had repeated it in his office the other day. A whole year in this strange new place with—with . . .

With whom? she wondered. With Uncle John, apparently the black sheep of the Randall family, who could hardly be blamed for resenting her. And with Catherine Randall, his wife, the unknown quantity; the mystery woman Missy MacGraw had seen only a couple of times and Gil Henderson had met only once. What would she be like?

There would be others there, too, at Randall

House. Friends and allies, like Missy and this handsome man driving the car, Kevin Jessel.

Kevin Jessel. He would be there for a while, at least, or so he'd said when she'd asked him. His parents were the housekeeper and the chauffeur, and Holly was certain that they would be nice, too, just as nice as their son seemed to be. Mrs. Wells had told her about the butler, Mr. Wheatley, and a cook and two gardeners and several maids. She would make a project of learning everyone's names.

Hell, she thought, I'll have to get used to all these people being around all the time. Waiting on me, cleaning and cooking for me, tending to and anticipating my every need. *That's* what I'll have to get used to.

She was determined to do just that.

Kevin steered the car off of the turnpike and onto a smaller road that wound through a snowy, wooded landscape. We're nearing our destination, Holly reasoned. The car had crossed the border into Connecticut ten minutes ago, and she knew that Randall was close to it.

Even as she thought this, she saw the little carved wood sign looming up on the right side of the car: WELCOME TO RANDALL, CONNECTICUT. The sign glided by, and now there were buildings on both sides of the road.

She stared out through the windows, delighted. It was as if the car had gone through a rift in the time-space continuum and been deposited in a turn-of-the-century New England village. First there were houses with picket fences and immaculate little yards and pretty, latticework-edged porches. Then came the shops and stores of Main Street. A little redbrick public library beside a big white clapboard building with three blue and white police sedans parked in a neat row before it. Two pretty little churches across the street from each other, one Catholic and one Methodist. A tiny movie theater with an old-fashioned, plastic-letter marquee. Rows of lovely storefront display windows: stationer, drugstore, barbershop, beauty parlor, antique shop, dress shop. An ice cream parlor beside—could it be?—Stahl's Grain and Feed. A diner and an Italian restaurant. There was even a town square surrounding a charming little park with a bandstand. A columned, gleaming white Town Hall and courthouse with an American flag flying before it. Down the side streets on the right she glimpsed clusters of small boats in the gray water of a little bay that she imagined would be blue and sparkling in the summer.

"This is beautiful!" Holly cried.

Kevin glanced over his shoulder and grinned. The glass partition between them slowly lowered.

"You ain't seen nothin' yet," he promised.

And he was right. They passed through the picture-postcard village and went on through snowy forest for another half mile. Suddenly, through the trees ahead, she saw more water and cloudy gray sky in the distance. Huge wrought iron gates rose up on their left, flanked by high stone walls. The limousine slowed and turned in through the open gates. There was a big metal plaque set into the wall to the right of the gates, announcing that this was RANDALL HOUSE.

Kevin pointed to the little, two-story stone building with leaded glass windows just inside the gates. "My house."

She smiled. "Very pretty."

As she looked out at Kevin's home she noticed something, a slight movement at one of the small upper windows. A white lace curtain was pushed aside, and a face nearly as pale as the lace peered down at them. Holly had a brief impression of two big dark eyes in the face, a woman's face, watching the car as it went by. Then the pale face disappeared, and the curtain fell back in place.

There were two long buildings on her immediate left beside the drive. As they passed the second building, she looked in through an open door and saw a beautiful white horse. A burly, bearded man was brushing the animal, watched by a blond teenage boy and a German shepherd. Everyone turned to stare at the limousine as it passed, including the horse and the dog. The burly man grinned and waved. Holly waved back.

"Stable and garage," Kevin said.

Then the drive ascended slightly and curved through a grove of trees toward the Sound. The trees ended abruptly, giving way to wide lawns on either hand. And there it was.

Randall House.

It was on her left across a vast expanse of lawn,

framed by trees and the hazy blue hills in the distance. A massive, graceful three-story mansion with ivy-covered white walls, tall columns, chimneys, and at the top, like a crown, a wrought iron–railed widow's walk. Two identical wings sprawled out at its sides from the slightly higher, forward-thrusting center section. It stood on the promontory facing the water, which was now on her right, its rows of windows reflecting the winter sky. The car glided around the wide curve of the hill, and they were directly approaching the building.

As they drew nearer, Holly could see the people standing by the steps in front of the columns that flanked the big front door. A handsome blond man and a lovely dark-haired woman stood together just in front of the door, waving as the car approached them. At the base of the steps stood another dark-haired woman, this one clad all in black. An elderly African-American man in a formal black suit stood at attention next to her, and beside him was a heavyset Hispanic woman in a cook's white dress and apron. Three women and two men stood in a row beyond the cook, the women in black dresses with white aprons and the men in work clothes. Ten people in all, watching as the car came around the drive toward them.

"Looks like everybody's here," Kevin said as he slowed to a stop. "Except Da, of course. He's still not up and about. He sends his regrets."

When Holly looked back on the scene later, she remembered that the snow had begun to fall again just as Kevin ran around the car and opened the door for her. She remembered reaching up and pulling the fleece-lined hood of her coat over her head, aware of the fact that her gloved hands were trembling uncontrollably, though not from the cold. And she remembered the warm smile on Kevin Jessel's ruggedly handsome face as he reached in to help her out of the car. It was that smile that got her through the following moments.

The beautiful dark-haired woman remained by the front door, but the tall, handsome blond man bounded down the steps to the drive. He was grinning, and his eyes—the same pale, clear blue as her own—twinkled as he held out his hands.

"You could only be Holly," he said as he clasped her gloved hands in his own. "I'm your uncle, John. Welcome to Randall House." He leaned forward and brushed her cheek lightly with his lips.

"How—how do you do?" Holly whispered, trying with all her might to smile. But the smile never arrived: she stared blankly at him, and around at the others. She struggled with her sudden, overwhelming nervousness as the man took her gently by the arm and led her to the end of the row of servants.

Then came the introductions. As Uncle John presented each person, he or she stepped forward from the line. The cook and the maids curtsied, and the two workmen bobbed their heads and grinned. Mrs. Ramirez, Martha, Frieda, Grace, Zeke, Dave. The butler, Mr. Wheatley, actually shook her hand and bade her welcome in a thick, mellifluous West Indian accent. Last came the imposingly serious, dark-haired woman in the long, rather old-fashioned black dress. As Holly arrived before her, Kevin stepped forward.

"Ms. Randall, Mrs. Jessel," he said, grinning. "Mother, this is Holly."

Kevin's mother glanced over at him, and Holly could see from her expression that she did not approve of his using their employer's Christian name. Then the woman turned her attention back to her new mistress, and Holly was pleasantly surprised when she actually smiled.

"Welcome to Randall House," Mrs. Jessel said. "I hope you will be very happy here."

At last Holly was able to summon a smile to her own lips. "Thank you, Mrs. Jessel, I'm sure I will. Your son has done a wonderful job filling in for his father. Please tell Mr. Jessel I hope he's feeling better soon."

The woman's dark eyes widened in astonishment. Then she melted. She smiled again, and reached out to take Holly's offered hand. "Thank you, Ms. Randall. I will."

Holly knew without looking that Kevin was grinning his approval at her, just as she knew that she had passed some sort of test and made a friend of his mother. The woman was positively beaming. Holly relaxed a little as she smiled around at everyone.

Then Uncle John took Holly's arm again and led her up the steps to the woman who stood smiling in the doorway.

"Catherine, may I present Holly Randall?" he said.

Holly smiled at the woman, forming a polite greeting in her mind, but whatever she was about to say went forever unspoken. With a little moan of joy, the woman stepped forward and took Holly into her arms.

"Oh, my darling!" she whispered into Holly's ear. "Welcome! I'm so glad to meet you, at last." She kissed Holly's cheek, as her husband had done, and when she pulled back, Holly was surprised to see that there were tears in her eyes.

"Hello, Aunt Catherine" was all Holly could think to say.

"You must call me Cathy," the woman said, "and I shall call you Holly. Now, let us show you your new home." She reached out to take Holly's hand.

At that moment, the distant bark of a dog made Holly turn around. The servants were still at the base of the steps, smiling up at her. Kevin, standing beside the limousine in his gray uniform, caught her eye and winked. Beyond him, the front lawn rolled away in all directions, and she could see the sky and Long Island Sound through the light flurry of snow that continued to fall. Down the drive, near the edge of the forest, the blond boy and the German shepherd from the stable stood, watching the scene. As she looked at them, the dog wagged its tail and barked again. She smiled and waved. The boy did not wave back, nor did he smile. He merely nodded once. He continued to stand quite still in the falling snow, watching her.

Holly turned back to face the open door that loomed before her. Ignoring the other woman's extended hand, she took a deep breath, bracing herself, preparing herself for whatever awaited her on the other side of the door. Then, summoning another smile to her lips, she stepped across the threshold into Randall House.

We all stood there that cold, snowy afternoon, watching Holly go into the house. She walked forward into the front hall, her white coat visible for only a moment before it was engulfed by the shadows, and she was gone. The image was unsettling, prophetic: it almost seemed as though the big house on the headland had devoured her, swallowed her alive.

There was a moment, just before she moved, when everything might have been changed. She might have felt something, become aware of the warmth that cut through the frigid air, a subtle but unmistakable undercurrent of malice. It was certainly there that day: I could feel it myself. But Holly apparently did not feel it, or she would never have entered. She would never have come here at all.

That was my perception then, but time has altered it, as time has altered so many things. There were such goings-on at Randall House, so many plots and counterplots, and the ever-present, ever-growing threat of violence. It has taken me a long while to sort out everything that happened later, between that second week of November and the end of the year. That fateful New Year's Eve, with the police and the paramedics swarming all over the house, the flashing red and blue lights of their vehicles glinting on the snow in the driveway. The still figure on the carpet in the library, and the other sprawled on the black and white tiles of the Great Hall. And upstairs, the splash of blood on one bedroom wall, darkening as it dried. But on that day in November, I didn't know how it would affect us all. I didn't realize that people were going to die.

I was to realize it, though, soon enough.

I see it all clearly from this distance in time. I know as well as you that it had really begun earlier, quite a while earlier, and you may think you know the rest. Well, if all you know are the rumors and the newspaper accounts, you don't know the rest of the story. Trust me.

Holly's arrival was the catalyst, the factor that set all the plots in motion. That was the official beginning, and everything else was destined to follow. There was no escaping it, I suppose. We can never escape destiny. If anything, we are drawn inexorably toward it, as Holly was drawn to Randall House.

And then she went inside.

PART TWO

HOLLY AND THE IVY

CHAPTER FOUR

First Impressions

"Good morning, Ms. Randall."

It was the first sound she heard, and the first image she saw when she opened her eyes was the smiling face of the upstairs maid hovering above her. Her great-aunt Alicia had been awakened thus, she supposed, by she had to think a moment—Martha. This woman's name was Martha. She summoned a weak smile and bade Martha good morning.

When the maid was gone, she sat up in the big four-poster bed and gazed slowly around the room. She'd barely noticed it last night when she'd first been brought here. She'd been given a quick tour of the downstairs rooms by Aunt Catherine before being led into the huge dining room for a sumptuous dinner she'd barely touched. The house, the new relatives, the servants: everything was a blur. She'd been overwhelmed, exhausted by the glut of sensations that coursed through her as each new thing arrived before her eyes. Now, rested, in the bright light of morning, she studied her new bedroom. It was beautiful, the most beautiful bedroom she'd ever seen.

She was going to like it here.

Someone had unpacked for her. She got out of bed and made a tour of the room, stopping first at the little table in the corner where Martha had placed a silver tray bearing a pot of coffee, a cup, milk, sugar, and a single red rose in a crystal bud vase. Her new dresses and coats were in the walk-in closet, and her blouses and sweaters and underwear were neatly arranged in the drawers of the mahogany bureau. Her makeup case was on the vanity table between the big front windows, resting beside a beautiful collection of silver-plated brushes and combs. She picked up a brush and inspected the engraved initials on the back: ELR. She wondered whose initials they were, whose combs and brushes were so carefully, lovingly laid out for her. She would ask Catherine at breakfast. . . .

This thought propelled her into the bathroom, where she took a quick shower and dried her hair with the brand-new blow-dryer she found there. She brushed her teeth, noting that the toothpaste, soap, and shampoo that had been provided were not her usual brands. She decided to take a trip into town after breakfast.

She smiled at her reflection in the bathroom mirror as she thought this, realizing that all she had to do was give one of the servants a list of everything she wanted, and it would silently, magically appear. This was the way things were done here at Randall House, here in her new life. But no; she wanted to explore the little waterfront village she'd only glimpsed from the car yesterday.

She donned new clothes—jeans and boots and a beautiful blue sweater Missy had insisted she buy. This first full day would be one of exploring, the town in the morning and the grounds of the estate in the afternoon. When she was ready, she left the room and made her way down the long hallway, past the other bedroom doors to the gallery above the Great Hall.

She paused at the marble balcony, staring down at the immense room with its black and white marble tiles, rising up, up, the entire three-story height of the building to the domed ceiling high above her. Her gaze rose slowly to the glittering chandeliers. Then, shaking her head in sheer wonder, she came around the gallery to the top of the stairs.

As she descended the red-carpeted staircase, she was reminded of one of her favorite movies. In *Anastasia*, Ingrid Bergman had come down a staircase exactly like this one to greet the waiting reporters. It was the press conference where it was announced that the suicidal, amnesiac former mental patient had been verified and accepted as the true Grand Duchess, the youngest daughter of the czar, the heir to the Russian throne. When Holly reached the bottom of the stairs, she shrugged, amused, remembering more recent news reports.

The bodies of the royal family had been found in the forest near Ekaterinburg. Now, with the advent of DNA testing, it had been proved beyond all doubt that the woman was *not* Anastasia, that she had been an impostor all along. Oh, well, she thought as she turned in the direction of the dining room, no matter. She preferred the film's romantic ending to prosaic, pathetic reality.

She smiled at this thought, and then she went in to join her new family for breakfast.

The old man watched the young woman descend the front steps below him and walk forward to the waiting car.

Yesterday he had watched from this window as she got out of the limousine, but it had been snowing and she had been surrounded by people, so he'd had only a brief glimpse of her face. But he had seen the face, and the lovely, warm smile. She was the most beautiful woman he'd ever seen.

It wasn't the limousine today, he noted. She had apparently instructed Kevin Jessel to bring round the blue BMW sedan, and to lose the formal gray uniform as well. Kevin stood now with his hand on the open passenger door, waiting, clad in his usual black leather bomber jacket, jeans, and boots.

This told the old man something else about the new mistress of Randall House, something that might turn out to be crucial. She was not brought up as the Randalls had been, so she did not stand on formal ceremony. She obviously preferred to treat everyone as an equal, even her new servants. She apparently had the more practical, more democratic personality of someone who was from what had once been referred to as the middle class. Well, it *was* the middle class, he reminded himself, and not a bad thing: she would not be afraid of a challenge, or of a potential mess. For his purposes, that might prove to be a very *good* thing. . . .

He held aside the curtain, watching the pantomime below from the upstairs window. Kevin grinned and said something as the girl arrived beside him, and she replied. Then, just before she allowed the young man to hand her into the front passenger seat, she turned around and glanced briefly up at the house behind her. He ducked swiftly behind the curtain, but not before he had another look at her face.

Oh, dear, he thought. Oh, dear me, that girl is most definitely a Randall. Yes, it is she.

He peered through the curtains again. The young man ran around to the driver's side and got in, and the BMW glided away around the curve and down the snowy drive toward the front gates. In moments, it had disappeared beyond the trees.

So, he reasoned, she is on her way to see the town that bears her family's name.

Her family . . .

He thought about his sister again. He stood there for several moments, head bowed, and presently the tears of impotent frustration arrived at the corners of his eyes and made their way down his desiccated, disfigured cheeks. But then he collected himself. He drew himself up and swiftly, roughly wiped the useless tears away. He was an old man, and uncertain, but he would not, *must* not give in to despair.

And now, at last, he began to form his plan of action, knowing as he did that it would not be easy. This new character, this Holly Randall, might be the answer he needed, and he would have to ascertain that as soon as possible. In order to do that, he would have to do something he had not done in years, something he had long ago forbidden himself to do. But now, he realized, it was necessary.

He would have to let the young woman see him. He would have to let her see his face.

It would not be easy, but it would have to be endured. He had to meet Holly Randall. Talk to her. Get to know her.

Warn her. . . .

"So," Kevin said, apparently to break the silence in the car, "how was your first night in your new home?"

Holly smiled, gazing out at the snowy trees that lined the road into town. "All right, I guess. It's a beautiful house, and my bedroom is gorgeous."

"Yes," he said, "but, I mean, how *was* it? You know, being there with—with—"

"With my new family, you mean," she finished for him. "Ah, well, it was a little . . . strange. But I'm sure I'll get used to it quickly. Everybody is being very nice. Your mother is lovely, and Uncle John and Aunt Catherine—Cathy—are bending over backward to make me feel welcome."

Kevin nodded and glanced over at her. "Well, that's good. Now, where would you like to go first?"

She thought a moment. "How about the town square, or whatever they call it?"

"The Green."

"The Green," she repeated, savoring it. "That's wonderful. Yes, the Green. You can just drop me off there, if you would, and then I think I can manage on my own."

He glanced over at her again. "I thought I could show you around the village, if you—well, if you don't mind some company."

Holly smiled. It was what she'd been hoping he'd say.

"I'd like that," she said. "If you're sure you want to. I mean. . . ."

Now Kevin smiled too. "At your service, ma'am."

They laughed together, and it was settled. He drove into the center of the town and parked in a little lot on the edge of the square. As she got out of the car, Holly noticed that the sun was shining brightly down on the trees and the bandstand in the park across Main Street. Even so, she immediately pulled the hood of her white wool coat up over her head and put on her gloves. Sun or no sun, she decided, this place is a hell of a lot colder than California.

Their first stop was the drugstore. She remembered it from the drive through town yesterday, and she immediately turned in that direction. Kevin held the old-fashioned oak and glass door for her as she paused outside, staring past the arched gilt letters on the picture window—MILLER'S PHARMACY, EST. 1927—at the quaint display inside. Dusting powder and bath salts. Holly smiled and stepped past Kevin into the delightfully Old World, wood-paneled, dimly lit chemist's shop.

There were five people in the big, well-stocked room. A middle-aged man and woman in identical white smocks were behind two large oak counters, and each was waiting on a customer. The woman was helping a heavyset, elderly woman at the perfume counter, while the man stood at the back counter facing a pretty young woman with a well-bundled baby in a pink plastic stroller. A bell tinkled above the door as Holly and Kevin came in, and the woman behind the counter looked over from her customer and smiled warmly.

"Good morning, Kevin," she called. "How's your father feeling today?"

"Much better, thank you, Mrs. Miller. Hello, Mr. Miller. I have a new customer for you." Kevin smiled over at Holly. "This is Holly Randall."

Holly stepped forward, smiling. "How do you—do?" She stopped, the words dying on her lips, as she regarded the people before her.

Everyone, with the exception of the sleeping baby in the stroller, had turned at the same moment, and all conversation in the room stopped. Holly stood there, her smile fading, as the four adults regarded her. There was a moment of awkward silence. Then Mrs. Miller blinked and said, "How do you do?"

Holly forced her smile to reappear. "What a lovely shop you have!" she said, coming forward. "We don't have places like this where I come from. Just, you know, chain stores with plastic counters and industrial lighting. This is beautiful."

"Thank you," Mrs. Miller said, and then she turned back to her customer, who resumed her inspection of the various scents displayed on the counter. The woman with the stroller handed a slip of paper to Mr. Miller, who went off into a back room to fill the prescription.

Holly glanced over at Kevin, who shrugged. Then she pulled the list she'd made from her purse and went quickly around the room. Soap, toothpaste, shampoo, makeup, tampons, vitamins, aspirin. For an old-fashioned shop, the pharmacy was well-stocked with a wide variety of brands. By the time she and Kevin came over to place her purchases before Mrs. Miller, the other two customers had gone. Holly smiled again at the woman and produced her new MasterCard.

"That won't be necessary, Ms. Randall," Mrs. Miller mumbled as she quickly placed everything in a paper shopping bag with the shop's logo on the side. "I'll just put it on your account." She held out the bag, which Kevin took from her, but she did not smile. "Good day."

"Thank you," Holly murmured before turning and fairly running toward the door.

She had to get out of there.

She heard Kevin and Mrs. Miller laughing and exchanging good-byes behind her as she pulled open the door and went out into the cold air of Main Street. She stood before the pharmacy, her back to it, breathing slowly in and out, calming herself. From the moment Kevin had announced her identity to the people in the shop, not one of them had smiled. The proprietress's greeting had been perfunctory, distant, cold. Never before had Holly been made to feel so politely, formally unwelcome.

Well, that isn't exactly true, she mused, remembering a young man in college in San Diego, and his rich parents. She had been invited to his family home in Palm Springs to meet them, and she'd sat through a horrible, unendurable dinner party during which she'd felt the eyes of everyone at the table scrutinizing her, assessing her, dismissing her. That had been the beginning of the end of her brief liaison with that particular college sweetheart.

By the time Kevin joined her on the sidewalk, Holly had forgotten all about Gregory Sanford III and his condescending clan. She glanced at Kevin, wondering briefly whether she should mention how she felt about what had just happened. She even considered asking him if there was another drugstore in the area where she could do her shopping from now on. But then she thought better of it and looked away from him, in the direction of the water.

"I want to see the harbor," she said, and she walked away, leaving him to follow with the shopping bag.

The waterfront, down the little paved walk beside the sloping side street, was beautiful. She emerged from the walk onto a tiny, cobbled seaside road that ran along an esplanade. Across from her was a miniature marina, with three parallel wooden docks jutting out from the rocky shore. There were perhaps twenty small craft here, tied to the docks or moored nearby. Sailing vessels, most of them, with tall masts rising into the gray sky above the Sound. A few men were about, busy on the boats or chatting idly in front of the wooden structures that faced the water on this side of the road: Bob's Bait & Tackle and a seafood shop/restaurant called, by someone with a sense of humor, Herringbone. The chill wind from the water whipped past her as she gazed off to her right, toward the far end of the cove. There was a larger configuration of docks, wider and more solid-looking, in the water at that end, and behind them, at the base of the hills that ringed the town, was a big, square, three-story clapboard structure with a wraparound wooden porch and many green-shuttered windows.

"Randall Inn," Kevin said as he arrived beside her and followed her gaze with his own.

She nodded, pointing. "Why are those big docks down at that end deserted? All the boats seem to be over here, at the smaller place."

He shrugged. "Those docks were built for bigger boats—you know, freighters and fishing scows. And they're not safe anymore. They haven't been used since long before I was born, since the fish company went public and relocated upstate. The inn was built on the site where the old packing

107

plant used to be. Your great-grandfather tore it down years ago."

"Oh." She continued to stare off at the empty docks in the distance, weather-worn and crumbling, a ghostly reminder of the bustling industry that had once been this town's lifeblood. And the pretty inn, once the packing plant, now undoubtedly filled for approximately six months of the year with adventurous and invariably obnoxious New Yorkers who would roam the quaint village streets for photo opportunities and hire local men to take them out for day sails. She could imagine them catching the occasional fish, shrieking with amusement through their beer and martinis, while the silent former fishermen, now reduced to tourist guides, looked on. Another summer adventure, another wonderful story to tell friends back in New York, over dinner at Le Cirque. Any locals fortunate enough to have kept their fishing or packing or carting jobs when the Randall Fish Company had been swallowed by NaFCorp must have long ago moved away to the new upstate location, wherever that was. Those who remained probably took the tourists sailing, or worked in that inn over there, or manned the cutesy gift shops she'd passed on Main Street. Cunning driftwood centerpieces and charming bouquets of dried sedge and sea grass, twenty bucks a bunch.

Her great-grandfather had done this. She remembered the expressions in the eyes of the local natives in the drugstore a few minutes ago, thinking, No wonder. . . .

"Good morning, folks."

They both turned around, in the direction of the big, hearty voice. There stood a tall, lanky blond man in a dark blue uniform with brass buttons on the front. A badge over his left jacket pocket identified him as CHIEF. He was about forty, Holly decided, with brown eyes and a thick mustache the same dark blond shade as the hair above, which went well with his ruddy, wind-chiseled face. A seafaring face, the face of a fisherman.

"Hi, Pete," Kevin said. "Pete Helmer, Holly Randall. Holly, this is the head of the Randall Police."

"Such as it is," Pete Helmer said, laughing and reaching out a big hand.

Holly took it. "How do you do?"

"Welcome to Randall, Holly Randall."

"Thank you," she said, and they all laughed at the irony. "What do you mean, 'such as it is,' Chief Helmer?"

"Pete," he corrected.

"Holly," she replied.

"Well, Holly, there's just the three of us, don't you know, myself and two overpaid, good-for-nothing deputies. Four, if you count old Mrs. Proctor, our secretary. Not that we're called on to do much, mind you. It's a quiet town."

She nodded, avoiding his eyes. He had a frank, penetrating gaze, a way of looking straight at her that was vaguely unsettling. She looked down at his left hand, noticing that he wasn't wearing a wedding ring, then wondering why she'd noticed that. Disconcerted, still staring at his hand, she nonetheless produced a weak smile, grateful for the warm welcome from at least one of the townspeople.

"It's a very pretty town," she finally offered, looking away from his hand toward the little harbor.

Pete nodded. "That it is. I hope you'll be happy at Randall House. If there's anything the local constabulary can do for you, just give us a buzz."

"Thank you."

The chief glanced over her shoulder, raising a hand and waving to someone behind her. "Well, if you'll excuse me, I think old Tod Farley has another complaint. That'll be, let's see, the third one this week. He says one of the Delany boys has been filching his catch. Oh, well, it's always something. See you around, Kev. Nice meeting you, Holly."

"Good-bye," she said as he walked off toward the pier. Then she turned to Kevin. "What's that about filching someone's catch? Do the people around here still fish?"

Kevin shrugged. "Some of them, like Tod Farley and the Delanys. They sell some to the Herringbone and keep the rest for themselves. Well, where would you like to go now?"

She was staring off at the docks, watching the police chief trying to placate a wildly gesticulating elderly man. She smiled, thinking, I'm glad some of them still go fishing. . . .

"Hello," Kevin said.

She blinked and returned her attention to him.

"What? Oh—I guess back to the car. Let's go through the Green first, though. It looks beautiful."

He nodded, and the two of them walked back the way they'd come.

Old Tod Farley was in high dudgeon again. Pete Helmer grimaced inwardly as he nodded at the shouting man, thinking that nobody's dudgeon was higher than Tod's. Especially when he'd drunk his breakfast, which, judging from the fumes, was apparently the case. Pete took a step back from him, nodded some more, and sighed, thinking of Holly Randall.

She was the most beautiful woman he'd ever seen. More beautiful than Carol, the former Mrs. Helmer, who'd been Miss Randall High some twenty years ago and was considered the catch of the town.

Well, Pete had caught her, and a fat lot of good it had done him. Carol was off in New Haven now, where she'd lived for the last six years with their two boys, whom Pete rarely got to see, and her new husband, the bank manager. Another police widow, refusing to have anything to do with her former husband but taking a third of his weekly paycheck just the same, thank you very much. Oh, well . . .

Holly Randall, he thought. Holly. Nice name. It made him think of Christmas. Not the lonely, gray holidays of the last few years, but the ones before, the Christmases of his childhood and the early years with Carol and the boys. Holly.

He nodded again at the vociferous Tod and

turned his head to watch Holly Randall walking away up the side street with Kevin Jessel. Yes, he thought with another sigh. Beautiful.

He decided to keep an eye on her.

It happened a few minutes later, shortly after they arrived on the Green. Looking back on it in the next few days and weeks, Holly would wonder at it, replay it in her mind. She even began to have dreams about it.

She walked back down Main Street, Kevin at her side, looking in the various shop windows and asking him about the library and the churches and the restaurants they passed. Kevin was apparently only too happy to be her tour guide. He kept up a cheerful narration of everything they saw: the library was small, but Mrs. White knew how to find any book for you; the diner was okay, and the Italian restaurant was actually very good; the churches kept up a friendly rivalry, with Father O'Brien and Reverend Ellsworth constantly struggling to secure the larger congregation. Of course, if you were Jewish, or anything else that wasn't Catholic or Methodist, you had to drive a fair piece to find places of worship. Typical small town.

Holly smiled at his observations. Yes, she thought, it really is a typical small town, and very New England. Or, at least, what she had always imagined when she'd thought of New England. Thornton Wilder and Norman Rockwell. Now it was her town, too, as different from southern California as it was possible to be.

She was thinking just this as they came back into the square and strolled through the corner entrance into the Green. The sidewalks here were in an X-configuration, merging at the wide space in the center where the bandstand stood. This was an elevated, round structure of wood and wrought iron, with several rows of park benches on all four sides, facing in. There were other benches here and there, off among the trees and well-tended shrubbery on the grass. The trees were bare now, but Holly imagined how they would be in spring and summer, forming large patches of shade on a sunny afternoon.

As they arrived at the bandstand, Holly noticed something else about the park, something she hadn't seen from the street. Off to the side of the big, open air building was a life-sized statue made of some heavy, dark metal on a granite pedestal. It was the figure of a man, his left arm at his side, the right extended out in front of him as if he were pointing, indicating something off in the distance. She glanced over at the figure without much interest, then away, then quickly back again, feeling the breath catch in her throat.

She stared, and she would later remember that the small, growing sense of surprise she experienced very nearly prepared her for what was to happen next. Slowly, as if in a trance, she turned from Kevin and walked over to the statue. She regarded the strong, stern face of the man, felt the power in his torso as he pointed off toward whatever it was that he saw. Then she lowered her gaze to the brass plaque below him, set into the base. She was suddenly aware of the cold, aware of the slight sound as Kevin came softly over to stand beside her.

The plaque read:

JOHN WILLIAM RANDALL
1858–1932
Looking Ever Forward

Her gaze rose to the powerful face again. She stared some more, feeling something of the force of him, thinking, This man was my great-great-grandfather. He started the Randall Fish Company and founded this town. He'd built Randall House for his wife. . . .

She blinked and turned to Kevin. "What was her name?"

"Whose name?"

"This man's wife," she said, pointing.

Kevin smiled. "Alicia."

She nodded and turned back to the statue. Of course, she thought. Alicia. Years later, her granddaughter, my great-aunt, would bear her name. . . .

But first she and old John, this man, would have a son, James. It was he who built the fish company into an industry, and he who merged it with the National Food Corporation, making the Randall family one of the richest in the country. But, in making himself rich, he had turned this lovely place into a ghost town, a marginal tourist trap, a shadow of its proud, industrious former self. . . .

As she later remembered it, she was mulling over

this thought when she turned at last from the graven image of her imposing forebear.

And froze.

They were standing on the sidewalk on the opposite side of Main Street, perhaps fifty yards away. A woman, about thirty, and a little boy no more than ten. Holly looked first at the woman: pretty, slender, blond; then her gaze moved slowly down to the child: pretty, slender, darker than his mother. The two of them stood quite still, so still that she actually had the fleeting impression of a photograph, or of the statue she'd just been contemplating. And they were both staring directly at her, into her eyes.

Then she noticed the others. Two old men were sitting near the woman and the boy, on a bench in front of the barbershop, one with a cigarette and the other with a pipe. They, too, were watching her.

It was very quiet in the square, unnaturally so. Holly was suddenly, acutely aware of this, and of the complete lack of any movement whatsoever. She could hear the sound of her own breathing, feel the blood throbbing in her veins. Slowly, with a vague but growing sense of unease, she looked over to her left. Two women on the walk near the entrance to the dress shop, still, suspended, staring. And, close to them, a teenage boy and girl; lovers, perhaps, holding hands. Staring.

She turned her head to her right. An elderly woman stood on the sidewalk over there with a poodle on a leash, and a young woman about Holly's age stood near them. Even the dog was motionless, regarding her. She turned around to look behind

115

her. There, on the opposite sidewalk beyond the bandstand and the statue, some six or seven others, watching her. She could feel the eyes, the naked intensity of their silent gaze boring into her, violating her. And, most of all, she was aware of the awful stillness of this oppressive, claustrophobic, four-sided, freeze-frame tableau.

When the hand suddenly clamped down on her shoulder she actually jumped, emitting a startled little sound somewhere between a squeak and a sigh. She turned toward Kevin, into the big, solid, reassuring bulk of him, and sagged against his chest. His other arm came up to steady her.

"Let's go," he whispered.

She nodded, mute, dazed, aware of the welcoming warmth as he placed one arm across her trembling shoulders. Then he picked up the drugstore shopping bag and moved her gently forward. One step, then another. Three. Four. They were walking now, gaining momentum, toward Main Street and the parking lot. And by their movement the spell was broken.

The tableau dissolved. The woman with the little boy reached out to take his hand, and they moved away down the sidewalk. The two old men resumed their smoky conversation. The two women turned and entered the dress shop. The young lovers laughed and embraced. The poodle ran off, dragging his mistress behind him. Several cars materialized, moving in various directions about the square. In that long, long walk across the Green, Holly began to hear the sounds: voices and barking and a steeple bell as it began to toll the hour, followed immediately by the identical clangor of its rival across the street. There was even soft music coming from somewhere, from the direction of the diner. A popular rock ballad, probably from a jukebox.

By the time they crossed the street to the car, her breathing and her pulse rate had returned to normal. He handed her in, closed the door, and went around to the driver side. She sat there, staring forward through the windshield, acutely aware of the numbness in her arms and legs. She was grateful for his polite silence as he steered the car out of the lot onto Main Street, in the direction of home.

Home, she thought. Randall House.

Then, as the car swiftly and silently put distance between them and the town, she thought of her mother, not Mary Smith but Constance Randall. She thought of Constance, and she thought of old James, the statue's son. They, the two of them, were the reasons for what had just occurred in the square. They were responsible. Constance and old James: the one had murdered her husband, and the other had murdered the entire town. And she, Holly, their progeny, was a living reminder of their shame. Constance and old James.

She thought about them for a long time. As the car approached the massive gates of Randall House, she finally broke the silence. She actually managed to produce a smile for the handsome man beside her, the strong, kind man who had firmly moved her away from the scene of her ordeal. When she

117

spoke, he did not reply, but merely smiled and nodded in what appeared to be understanding.

"Thank you," she said.

She could see from the way he smiled and nodded that he did not really understand why she was thanking him. She wasn't certain she fully understood it herself.

He stood in the drive near his front door, gazing up through the trees at the lights of Randall House. It was early evening, and he had just finished dinner with Dora and his father. Now Da was comfortably seated in his favorite chair near the fireplace in the living room, a blanket over his knees, and Dora sat near him, knitting. His mother was up at the main house, seeing to Holly's meal.

Holly. He'd thought of little else all afternoon, ever since he'd dropped her off at her front door and she'd leaned over toward him and brushed his cheek lightly with her lips. Then she'd smiled, gotten out of the car, and run lightly up the steps and into the house.

During the drive home, she'd broken their silence only once, to say, "*Thank you.*"

Those two words, and the sudden, tingling thrill of her lips on his cheek moments later had stayed with him for the rest of the day. All through the trip to the supermarket with his mother and Mrs. Ramirez, and the workout at the health club in Randall, and dinner. Everything else about the afternoon was a blur, essentially meaningless. He remembered only those lips, that smile, that *thank you*. . . .

Now the long night seemed to stretch before him, and he wondered what he should do with it. There was a bar at Randall Inn, and another one on Main Street that had a pool table. He knew most of the guys who hung out there—hell, he'd grown up with most of them. He could shoot some pool with his pals. Or there was always Greenwich, not too far away. There were clubs there, with women. Rich Greenwich girls . . .

No, he decided. Not tonight. Not after those lips, that smile, that *thank you* . . .

She would be in the dining room now, still smiling and making light conversation with the strangers who were now her family. Chicken Kiev, he'd heard Mrs. Ramirez tell his mother, with rice and broccoli. White wine in crystal goblets, shimmering in the candlelight. Then coffee and Mrs. Ramirez's famous Key lime pie. Later, perhaps, she would join Mr. and Mrs. Randall in the library for their nightly card game. Then she would go upstairs, to the big four-poster in the master bedroom.

He imagined her there, and he tried to imagine himself there with her. . . .

He blinked, and the distant lights of the house snapped back into focus. From somewhere off among the trees he heard a sharp bark, followed by a faint whistle. He smiled. That kid from the village, Toby, he thought. Toby and his dog love the forest, not to mention the horses in the stable. They always seem to be hanging around. Oh, well . . .

The night was cold: it was time to go inside. With a last, longing glance up at the main house, Kevin went back into his own home, to the warmth of the fire and the quiet company of his family. And as he went he thought, Holly. . . .

Holly was not thinking about Kevin Jessel; not at the moment, anyway. She had other things on her mind.

They were in the library, she and John and Catherine, but they were not playing cards. She and Catherine sat beside each other on the couch facing John's chair. The rich aroma of John's cigar permeated the room, not at all unpleasantly, as she'd have expected, but, rather, the opposite. She figured, correctly, that this was the most expensive cigar to which she'd ever been exposed. Catherine smoked cigarettes, and Holly found herself staring at the rather peculiar way she held them, cupped in her right hand, almost invisible from view. She'd never seen anyone do that.

For the past hour, John had been filling her in on family history. Well, mostly his own history, with a smattering of references to other family members, her father among them. But it was clear that most of John's adult life had been lived away from Randall. Europe, the Caribbean, even South America. He'd knocked around the world, he'd said, several times. When Holly observed that it seemed as though he'd been searching for something, he laughed and shook his head. Not searching, he said. Waiting.

Now he realized that he'd spent his entire life waiting for Catherine.

To give them their due, John and Catherine tried several times to change the subject, to get Holly to talk about her own life. But she merely smiled and shrugged, murmuring something noncommittal about the difference between the Coachella Valley and the real world, and directed the conversation back to them. Where had they met? How long had they known each other before getting married? Where was the wedding in Paris? She wasn't really interested, but at least it kept the focus on them rather than her, which was what she wanted. She didn't want to talk about herself to these people. Not yet. Maybe not ever.

They'd met in Monte Carlo, John told her. They'd fallen in love immediately, and they'd knocked around Europe (that phrase again) for several months ("He *chased* me around Europe!" Catherine interjected) before she agreed to marry him. At fifty-plus, as he put it, John had given up on the idea of ever marrying—until he met Cathy. They were wed at the George V Hotel in Paris, by a local judge. Catherine had been married before, they explained, which put a damper on their original plan, to be wed at Sainte Chapelle.

Holly smiled and said that it all sounded terribly romantic. Of course, she'd done little else but smile at them from the moment they'd arrived here from dinner. She'd smiled all through dinner, as well.

She studied them as they spoke, these attractive, intelligent people who were her uncle and aunt, and she wondered what she thought of them. She wasn't sure, really. They seemed perfectly nice, perfectly pleasant. And yet, she couldn't lose sight of the fact that, but for her, they would be much better off than they were. That was ridiculous, she supposed. Her uncle and aunt were *already* better off than most of the world. But there was such a thing as avarice: Holly knew that only too well. She knew what it could do to people. So, naturally, she wondered what *they* thought of *her*. . . .

Catherine—Cathy—poured her another cup of coffee from the silver service on the table before them. Holly thanked her, sat back on the couch, and smiled some more.

He'd seen the man in the drive a while ago, but now the man was back in the gatehouse. He'd been very careful that the man did not see him. The man's name was Kevin, and he was apparently the chauffeur. Kevin had been with the mark all morning in town, and then he'd brought her back here.

It was nearly ten-thirty. The man John Randall knew only as Ed was stationed in a grove of trees about halfway between Randall House and the front gates. He'd been on the grounds for two hours now, slowly circling the house and the outbuildings. He was very careful to remain out of sight among the trees as he moved around, getting the lay of the land. It was freezing, and he couldn't wait to get back to his car.

His name was not Ed, but Alec. Alec Buono. Alessandro Buonaventura, truth be told, but who the hell wanted to be saddled with a name like that? This was America, not the old country, and Alec Buono was about as much as anyone here could handle.

As a low-ranking member of a prominent crime family, Alec had a lot of time on his hands, which was why he occasionally took freelance work. Off the books, he thought, grinning as he glanced down at the wedding ring he still wore: money his ex-wife would never know about. Not that he was *on* the books with the Family, but she and her lawyer could estimate his income there with unnerving exactness. His permanent employers were aware of his extracurricular activities, but they politely looked the other way. He performed an invaluable function, and what he did when he was not serving them was all right with them, as long as they were never involved in it.

Alec liked women, and he always had a lot of them. Hell, that's what had broken up his marriage in the first place. He still wore his wedding ring so none of the women would get any ideas. But lots of women meant lots of expenses, which was why he was here now, freezing his ass off.

He raised his binoculars and peered through them at the two lighted windows to the left of the main entrance to the house. The curtains of one window were open, and he could see the heads of the two women on the couch. They were facing into the room, and Alec knew his employer, John Randall, was there, though he couldn't see him. But no matter: it was the young woman with blond hair

123

who commanded his attention. He gazed at her profile through the binoculars, sighing.

This one wasn't going to be easy. He'd never done a job on a woman before. And she was such a lovely young woman. He'd almost turned John Randall down cold in the diner yesterday—until he heard how much the man was offering. Hell, for that kind of money, he figured he could ignore his love of women just this once.

But this woman, Holly Randall, certainly was beautiful. He'd stayed the night in a motel by the highway, and he'd discreetly followed her today. He'd watched her and the man, Kevin, in the drugstore, and on the waterfront with the police chief, and later in the park, when she had suddenly become upset. She had every right to be upset, he supposed: all the townspeople were staring at her. Staring and whispering.

Now it was just a matter of learning her habits. He would give her time to settle into a new routine in her new home. He would come back next week to observe her again, and several times after that. John Randall wanted it done sometime after the new year. By then, Alec would know all he needed to know about Holly Randall.

He would get the job done.

The front door of Randall House opened and a woman stepped outside, closing the door behind her. As he watched, she switched on a flashlight, came down the steps, and began to walk directly toward him across the lawn.

He felt a brief prickling of panic as he stepped

back into the darkness behind a tree. Had he been seen from the house? Should he go now, get away from here and back to his car by the main road before she arrived to confront him? His right hand began to move instinctively toward the holster inside his jacket. . . .

No. She wasn't coming toward him, after all. He relaxed, expelling his breath in a long, silent sigh as the woman with the flashlight continued down the sloping lawn toward the drive. She passed by him several yards to his right, and he got a glimpse of her face. It was the housekeeper, Kevin's mother, on her way back to the gatehouse. Because the drive curved in a wide arc before it reached the house, she was taking a shortcut across the lawn. Of course.

He watched the beam of the flashlight move away down the road toward the lights of the gatehouse. The woman opened the front door, switched off the flashlight, and went inside. The door closed.

He returned his attention to the main house. The lights in the library windows went off, and a few minutes later lights came on in a couple of the upstairs bedrooms in the wing to the right of the main entrance. So, everyone was going to bed for the night. Good: it was time he did the same. He'd stay at the motel tonight and drive back to the city in the morning—

A sharp barking from somewhere very close to him made him jump. He immediately crouched down at the base of the tree, reaching again for his gun, listening. He heard a low whistle, also very near, and the barking stopped. That damn kid with the dog, he thought, the one he'd almost hit with the car earlier this evening, when he'd come here from the motel.

He'd taken the road from town, and as he'd neared the estate he'd switched off his headlights. There was a little lane, John Randall had told him, leading to an old, abandoned farm, just before the turnoff to Randall House. He could leave his car there for reconnaissance missions on the grounds. He'd slowed, peering through the darkness in search of the lane, when two figures had suddenly loomed up almost directly in front of the car. A boy, about fifteen, walking along the road with a German shepherd. He'd slammed on the brakes. The boy and the dog had turned around, startled, and the dog had begun to bark. Then, taking the dog by the collar, the boy had moved to the side of the road to let him pass. He'd driven quickly past them, found the lane, and parked.

Now, it seemed, the kid and the dog were roaming around these woods somewhere nearby. Kids, Alec thought with disgust. He'd have to be very careful around here. A gatehouse with a family living in it, a stable with three horses, and a kid and a dog skulking around the place. The grounds of Randall House were alive.

He looked back up at the facade of the enormous house. The only lights that were on now were in the corner bedroom on the right. The master bedroom, her room. John Randall had described the house for him in some detail. There were alarms on all the windows and doors, but Alec knew his way around those. There wasn't a door he couldn't pass, an alarm system he couldn't circumvent, once he'd put his mind to it. It was one of his special talents.

But his biggest talent was accidents. He could make any death look like an accident. And that was precisely what he was planning for Holly Randall.

She sat at the vanity table in her new silk bathrobe, brushing her hair with the silver-plated brush that had belonged to her great-grandmother. Uncle John had told her at dinner that the initials engraved in the silver, ELR, stood for Ellen Louise Randall. After dinner, before going into the library, Uncle John had led her into the big living room on the other side of the foyer. There, above the massive fireplace, was a life-sized portrait of an elegant blond beauty in a blue gown. Holly had stared at the painting of Ellen Randall, noting that the woman's coloring and features were not unlike her own. She regarded her own image in the glass as she once again raised the silver brush to her hair.

And now, at last, she thought about Kevin Jessel. She smiled at the thought of him, coloring slightly as she remembered the moment in the car when she had leaned over to kiss him. It had been an impulse, a gesture of gratitude, but now, in retrospect, she did not regret doing it. He was certainly handsome. . . .

And she was grateful to him. A shiver ran through her as she remembered that awful moment in the park, when she had stared around at all those silent figures, confronted those frosty, oddly accusing eyes. Her sudden panic, an overwhelming sense of claustrophobia. And then that arm around her shoulders, that reassuring voice, that gentle touch as he led her across the grass to the car.

With a last little smile at the memory of kissing his cheek, she put down the brush, rose, and went over to the bed. She dropped the bathrobe on a chair, slipped naked between the sheets, and reached over to turn off the lamp on the night table. Then she lay back against the soft pillows, listening to the low, steady hiss of the ancient radiator as it filled the bedroom with warmth.

She must have fallen asleep immediately, she would later decide. Otherwise, she probably would have reacted differently to what followed.

She was definitely dozing, in that borderland between sleep and full alertness, when she began to drift, and then to dream. It was very bright where she was, very warm, and she was holding someone's hand. Slowly, in the way of dreams, the scene around her became clear.

She was standing in the main quadrangle of her college campus in San Diego, surrounded by buildings. On the sidewalks in front of the buildings stood several motionless, staring people. She recognized classmates, and several professors, and Gregory Sandford III and his family. Her roommate from Palm Springs, Rhonda Metz, was there, too. Even her parents, Ben and Mary Smith. They surrounded her, staring silently from the distance. With a gradual, sickening certainty, she realized that she was naked. She looked over with mounting horror to realize that the man holding her hand was Kevin

Jessel, and that he, too, was naked. Clutching his hand, she gazed wildly around at the silent, accusing faces of everyone she knew, everyone she'd ever known, feeling the cold, raw chill surge up through her exposed body as the bright California sunlight faded and the scene dissolved into another.

They were still naked, still holding hands, but now they were on the Green in front of the bandstand. The horrible tableau from earlier today came back to vivid life, only now the townspeople were staring at their nakedness. The little boy beside his mother raised his arm and pointed directly at her, and then he began to laugh. One by one, the others joined in. They moved slowly forward toward the two figures in the center, their demented laughter rising in pitch.

With a cry of anguish, Holly broke free of Kevin's grasp and began to run, pushing through the enclosing mob as she fled across the grass, faster and faster. Then, somehow, her feet no longer touched the ground. She was flying, soaring down the road as the trees rushed past her and the wind whipped her nude body and the iron gates of Randall House loomed up before her. She floated through the gates and up the curving drive, aware all the time of the derisive, high-pitched laughter behind her. Through the open front door, across the Great Hall and up the carpeted marble stairs, around the gallery and down the long hallway to the master bedroom. She melted through the solid door and sailed across the darkened room to land, light as a feather, between the sheets. She pulled the covers up over her head, trying to drown out the sound of the laughter, knowing that the townspeople were even now filling the room, crowding around the bed, reaching out their bony fingers to point accusingly at her.

Then she opened her eyes.

She was sitting up in the bed. She listened for the laughter, but the only sound that reached her ears was the steady hissing of the radiator. As her vision focused, she saw that there was not a crowd of figures standing at the foot of the four-poster bed.

Only one.

It was the figure of a man. He stood at the baseboard gazing down at her, clad in what appeared to be a monk's robe and hood. Light streamed in on him from the hallway beyond the bedroom door, which now stood open. As she peered up at him, he turned quickly away from her, in the direction of the light. She had a fleeting glimpse of his face, or, at least, half of it. A long, wrinkled face beneath a shock of white hair. But she could only see half of it, the left half. Where the right half of his face should have been there was—nothing. Darkness.

Then the robed figure moved, as she had moved moments before, in her dream. He floated across the room, the cassock flowing out behind him, and through the door. He reached out a ghostly, skeletal hand and closed the door behind him.

When she heard the soft, distinct metallic click, Holly came fully awake. She blinked several times, and her heart began to pound. She realized in a sudden rush of wakeful clarity that the last part of her dream had been real. There *had* been a man here, at the foot of her bed, seconds ago. An old man—a *very* old man—with only half a face. And when she'd woken to see him there, he'd silently left the room.

She lunged for the bedside lamp and switched it on, flooding the room with light. The alarm clock next to the lamp indicated that it was one thirty-five. She already had the receiver of the bedroom telephone in her hand before she stopped, confused, staring down at the many buttons. There was a little typewritten list pasted to the side of the phone: dial 1 for the kitchen, 2 for the butler, 3 for—for what? Whom would she call? Everyone was asleep by now, including her aunt in the next room. And what could she possibly tell them that they'd believe? That an old man in a monk's robe who had something terribly wrong with his face was wandering around the house? No, they wouldn't believe her. They'd smile and tell her she'd been dreaming. And perhaps she *had* dreamed him. Perhaps she'd seen a ghost. . . .

No. If he'd been incorporeal, nothing but ectoplasm, he would not have needed the door.

In a flash, she was out of the bed. She grabbed the robe from the chair, pulling it around her as she hurried over to the door. She took a deep breath, bracing herself, and yanked the door open.

There was no one in the hall. The light from the brass wall sconces illuminated every corner of the passage, every shadow. Nothing.

Holly stepped out into the hallway, softly closing

the door behind her. She cocked her head to one side, listening. She thought she could hear a rustling, a whisper of movement, from the darkness beyond the far end of the hallway. She moved swiftly, silently in that direction, glancing nervously over at the doors of John's and Catherine's rooms as she passed them, half expecting one or the other door to fly open to reveal a sleepy relative gaping at her.

She emerged from the hallway onto the gallery that ringed the Great Hall. Here, all was in darkness. She stood at the railing, her hands resting on the cold marble, peering down into the gloom. No sound, no movement. Nothing down there. Slowly, her gaze rose to the gallery itself, and to the dark hallway of the guest wing beyond it, on the far side of the Great Hall. At that moment, from down that dark hallway, she thought she heard a soft click, identical to the sound of her bedroom door closing moments before. She held her breath, straining to hear any further sound from that direction. Nothing. Silence.

With a sigh of relief, she turned from the railing toward the lighted hallway.

A dark figure loomed before her, backlit by the lights of the hall. She gasped and brought a hand up to her breast.

"Is everything all right, miss?"

Holly sank back against the marble balustrade, grasping it for support, and strong hands reached out to steady her.

"Miss?"

It was the butler, Mr.—Mr.—Mr. Something-or-other. She recognized the mellifluous West Indian accent immediately. When she caught her breath, she began to giggle.

"Yes," she managed to say. "I'm all right, Mr.—umm. . . ."

"Wheatley, miss."

"Mr. Wheatley. Yes. I'm sorry. I thought—I thought I heard a—a noise. . . ." She waved a hand limply in the direction of the Great Hall behind her, trying mightily to control the laughter that was welling up inside her.

Mr. Wheatley took her gently by the arm and led her forward into the light of the hallway. Now, in the light, she saw that he was wearing a beautiful red satin smoking jacket over striped pajamas. Definitely not a monk's cassock, she thought, and she began to giggle again. Besides, he was African-American, and the man she'd seen—or thought she'd seen—was definitely Caucasian. . . .

"It's a big house, miss," Mr. Wheatley was saying. "Sometimes, you hear things in the night. It's usually nothing, nothing at all. Of course, I thought I heard a sound, so I came down to look—and it was *you*! Don't you worry, Miss Randall. You'll get used to this big old house soon enough. Can I get you anything? A warm drink from the kitchen?"

"No, thank you. I'll just go back to bed. I'm sorry to have disturbed you."

"Not at all. Good night, Miss Randall."

"Good night."

She watched as he faded back into the shadows

of the gallery, and after a moment she heard the faint sounds of his climbing the stairs to the third floor. Then, with a last, nervous glance toward the darkness above the Great Hall, she went back down the hall to her room.

This time, she locked her door.

As she lay back down and pulled the covers up around her, she began to giggle again. After a while, she drifted off to sleep once more, and this time her sleep was undisturbed.

It was the end of her first full day in residence.

CHAPTER FIVE

The Burial Ground

In the next few days, the mansion on the Connecticut coast became the focus of a great deal of attention.

Nobody was later certain how it began, but the arrival of the new heir to the Randall fortune could hardly have remained a secret for long. The whole town of Randall knew, for one thing, as did everyone in Mr. Henderson's law firm and several banks and boardrooms. Along with the house and other properties on two continents, Holly now owned an impressive share of interest in a major corporation. So, somebody talked.

Ben and Mary Smith learned about it as everyone else in America did: in the news. It first appeared as a local story in the tristate area of New York, New Jersey, and Connecticut, and it billowed out from there. By the end of Holly's first week at Randall

House, her new good fortune was a national item. One can hardly blame the media in this particular case, because there is nothing more irresistible— and certainly nothing that sells more newspapers and fills more airtime—than a Cinderella story. Thus it was with Holly.

She was America's flavor of the week. On her third day in the house the phones began to ring, and they didn't stop, despite her flat refusal to grant anyone an interview, or to make a comment of any kind. News vans began to gather outside the estate, which prompted Brian Jessel, Kevin's father, to leave his sickbed and lock the gates. There were even a few helicopters flying over the point, taking aerial pictures of the house and grounds that were printed and broadcast everywhere. An angry call from John Randall to the governor of Connecticut finally put a stop to that.

No one was able to trace the mysterious heiress to her roots, which caused much speculation as to her life before the day she arrived at Randall House. There were no photographs of her, for one thing, except for a blurred, grainy one of her walking on the grounds, taken from a great distance with a tele-photo lens. Not even Mary and Ben would have recognized her from it. After that picture was taken, Holly did not leave the house for several days, but she finally called her erstwhile parents. She later said that they had been understandably surprised to learn that she, their own Holly Smith, was the golden girl being discussed by everyone in the country.

I did not meet Mary Smith until later, after these events, so at the time I had no idea what she looked like. I assumed she was a pretty, fiftyish woman, dark-haired, with kind eyes and a warm smile. As it turned out, she was very much as I imagined her. Ben Smith, on the other hand, was a surprise. He was not exactly handsome in any classical sense, but he was very tall and powerfully built, and his gray hair and age-lined face only added to his distinguished appearance. For some reason, I don't know why, I hadn't expected him to look like that. But they were both very nice, and I could see why Holly had always spoken so fondly of them. Their primary concern was her well-being, and they had placed her first and foremost in their lives, even after her abrupt departure to Connecticut. Their loyalty to her never wavered.

The worst part of the publicity blitz that greeted Holly's arrival was the obligatory rehashing of the notorious murder case involving her parents. That story was reprinted everywhere, as a sidebar to the new item, complete with all the old photographs and garish headlines. Not only was Holly Randall an overnight success story, but she was also the daughter of the April Fools' Killer. As far as the media were concerned, it was almost too good to be true.

At the end of a week, her first at Randall House, Holly was given a reprieve, of sorts, by the least likely of people. A farmer named Cullen, in a remote part of Montana, assaulted a young hitchhiker, a drifter to whom he'd offered a ride. The young man got away from him and reported him to the police.

In a routine search of Cullen's house and grounds after his arrest, the police unearthed the skeletal and partial remains of seventeen other young men, some of them dating back nearly twenty years. Every journalist in America immediately took off for Montana, and Holly was off the hook.

But not for long.

In her second week there, a few days before Thanksgiving, she began to learn the secrets of Randall House.

The two horses burst out from the woods and cantered across the big field behind the apple orchard, manes and tails flying, their breath steaming out in snorts that formed puffs of smoke in the freezing air. When they arrived at the other end of the field their riders reined them in, slowing their pace to a comfortable walk.

Despite the cold weather, Holly was exhilarated. She hadn't been riding in several years, since high school, and she'd almost forgotten what a wonderful feeling it was to soar through space on a horse's back. And this white stallion, Lightning, was the most magnificent animal she'd ever encountered. She grinned over at Kevin.

"Race you back to the stable!"

He laughed. "Forget it! You'd win by a mile. Miss Alicia had Lightning carefully trained by a professional, and he's won several trophies and blue ribbons in his day. He was her pride and joy, and for very good reason. In fact, he has a date next month with a lady horse in Darien. He's already sired two other prizewinners. This nag"—he pointed down at his own mount—"would probably take off in the wrong direction. Hell, I'd be in Greenwich before I could stop her!"

"Oh, well," Holly said. "In that case, let's take the scenic route." She pointed toward the woods ahead of them.

"You're on."

They entered the forest. Holly gazed around at the bare trees, and presently she heard the sound of running water. Looking over to her left, she saw a stream running down from the hills behind the property. A few minutes later they arrived at a small clearing in the woods. There was a pond here, partially frozen in this weather, its icy crust glistening in the weak sunlight. On the far side of the pond, the water continued on its way down the wooded slope toward the Sound.

"How lovely!" she cried.

She noticed that Kevin had become very quiet. He had a slight frown on his face as he gazed around the clearing. He apparently didn't share her enthusiasm for the spot.

"This is where it happened," he said at last. "I mean, where your great-aunt . . . Miss Alicia . . ." He trailed off into silence, nodding mutely toward the pond.

Oh, she thought. That explains his tension. That's what he's thinking about. She thought all of this, but all she managed to say was "Oh."

They rode on through the trees, and soon they emerged from the wood on the east lawn. The sun had grown in brightness, it seemed to Holly. As if the same thought had occurred to Kevin, he pointed out over the Sound. "Look."

Holly looked. The horizon and the distant coast of Long Island had disappeared from view in a thick mist.

"The sun is out now," Kevin explained. "There's a warm front up against the cold one. The fog will roll in soon."

She nodded. "Let's get the horses inside."

They trotted across the lawn, past the summer house and down the drive to the stable. George, the groom, arrived beside them as they dismounted, then took Lightning's reins from Holly and led the animal into his stall. As Kevin started to follow him into the stable with his own horse, Holly put a hand on his arm to stop him.

"Thank you," she said. "That was fun."

He grinned at her. "Anytime, ma'am."

"Tomorrow?"

"Sure!" he said, unable to conceal his obvious pleasure at the prospect.

They laughed. Before he led the horse away, she kissed him again. She had intended another kiss on the cheek, but just as her lips arrived at what should have been his cheek he turned his face to her, and her kiss landed on his warm lips. They gazed at each other a moment, smiling. She noticed that his green eyes twinkled when he smiled. Irishmen, she thought.

"Well, see you later," he said at last, and he and his Irish charm were gone.

Still smiling, Holly walked away up the drive. As she walked, she began to hum softly to herself. She stopped abruptly, giggling at her own idiocy when she realized that she was humming "When Irish Eyes Are Smiling."

She giggled all the way home.

Dora Jessel watched her brother and Holly Randall through the lace curtains of her upstairs bedroom in the gatehouse. They were returning the horses to the stable across the drive, and they were smiling at each other. Suddenly, Holly Randall leaned forward and kissed Kevin on the lips. Then Kevin went into the stable, and Holly Randall went skipping off up the drive toward the main house.

She smiled briefly, remembering a boy named Leonard Ross. He had taken her to a dance once, years ago. Her senior prom. He'd brought her a corsage of white orchids that she still had, pressed between the pages of one of her journals. She had been dressed all in white, and Mother had helped her with her hair, and none of the other kids had laughed at her. As they danced in the school gymnasium, Leonard had suddenly leaned forward and kissed her, as Holly Randall had just kissed her brother. It had been the loveliest night of her life.

Then her smile faded as she remembered what had happened to her soon after that magical night.

She turned from the window and went back over to the little desk where she had been sitting all morning, working on her current diary. She would

141

record the scene she had just witnessed, she decided. She would describe the way her brother and Holly Randall had laughed together under her window. She would write for another fifteen minutes, and then she would devise a way to get out of the house.

It would not be easy, she knew, with Da sitting in his favorite chair in the living room. Mother had instructed Da to watch her carefully, ever since the terrible day she'd come out of one of her confusing spells to find herself lying on the floor of the living room in the main house, surrounded by broken glass, screaming. That day was now more than a week in the past, but she remembered her confusion and her sudden, sharp fear as if she had experienced them mere moments ago.

Dora had given Da his lunch and his prescription pills an hour ago, and the pills always made him drowsy. With any luck, he would be asleep in the chair now, and she would be able to steal away. She'd managed to do it yesterday, when she went back to the cemetery to dig up the grave. And she would have to do it again today.

She wanted to meet Holly Randall. She wanted to approach the woman and introduce herself, and she wanted to warn her. Tell her to leave Randall House now, today, and never come back. She would tell her calmly but firmly, and she would try not to become confused. Perhaps Holly Randall would listen to her, she thought, before any damage was done. She knew that she would have to try to make the woman understand the danger she was in. But, in order to do that, she would have to get past Da and out of the gatehouse.

Besides, it was time to bury the baby again.

Holly was at lunch in the dining room with her aunt and uncle when the messages arrived. Mr. Wheatley came in with a silver tray and placed two small envelopes, one pink and one white, on the table beside her.

"Excuse me, Miss Randall, these are for you."

"Thank you," she said, putting down her soup spoon and reaching for them. Mr. Wheatley left the room as silently as he had come.

Catherine glanced over at the envelopes with obvious interest. "What's this?"

Holly opened the pink one first and read the matching card inside. "We're invited to a cocktail party. Missy MacGraw. A week from this Saturday at five—oh, gosh!"

"What?" Catherine asked.

"It's in my honor. To introduce me to her friends."

"How nice," Catherine said. "I don't know the MacGraws. In fact, this is the first real invitation we've received from anyone in Randall." She smiled over at her husband. "I told you Holly's coming here would be a good thing!"

"I never doubted it," he said. "It's certainly improved our social life."

Then Holly opened the other envelope and took out a folded piece of stationery. It was formal notepaper, and the writing was obviously done with a fountain pen, sloping and neat. She read a moment, puzzled. She read it again. Then she looked up at the other two. "Do I have a great-uncle Ichabod?"

John's eyes widened in surprise, and Catherine gasped.

"Don't tell me you've actually heard from *him*!" John exclaimed.

"I can't believe it!" Catherine added.

Holly looked from one to the other of them. Then she held the note up and read. " '*My dear Miss Randall, I present my compliments. I would be honored if you would take tea with me tomorrow afternoon, four o'clock, so that I might have the pleasure of making your acquaintance. If that is inconvenient for you, please let me know when you might be available. I look forward to meeting you. Sincerely, (your great-uncle) Ichabod Morris. P.S.: RSVP via Mr. Wheatley.*' " She looked up at John. " 'RSVP via Mr. Wheatley.' What on earth does that mean? There's no return address."

Husband and wife exchanged nervous glances. After a moment, John broke the uncomfortable silence.

"He's here," he said. "At Randall House. He—he lives in one of the guest rooms. He's been there for"—his brows came together in concentration—"about twenty-four years. Ever since . . ." He trailed off, apparently flustered, staring down at the table.

"I see," Holly said. "Since the murder. Morris. My grandmother, Emily, was his—sister? And he came here to be with her after . . .Oh, yes, I see."

"She died a year later," John said, his voice now a

144

whisper. "But Father and Aunt Alicia told Cousin Icky he could stay as long as he liked."

"Cousin—Icky?" Holly wasn't sure she'd heard him properly.

At last John smiled. "Oh, Lord, we've called him that since we were children. He's—well, you'll see for yourself soon enough. He's a recluse, a hermit. Always has been. I've only met him a few times myself. He never leaves his room, and this is the first time I've *ever* heard of him *inviting* someone there. Hell, I'd all but forgotten he was here."

"That's probably why no one's told me about him until now," Holly said dryly. Then she leaned forward. "You say he's a recluse. Why?"

John glanced over at his wife, then back at Holly. He shrugged. "Well, Icky's a little—strange. I can only repeat, you'll see for yourself."

Holly smiled. "In that case, I can hardly refuse such a rare opportunity. Excuse me."

She rose and left the dining room. Across the Great Hall was the office, she remembered. She went into the office and sat in the padded leather chair behind the big desk. There would be writing paper here, she guessed, some sort of official Randall House stationery that would be suitable for her purpose. She pulled open the desk drawer.

Her first thought when she looked down was, I've been here before. There, in the drawer, were several sheets of paper covered with what appeared to be her own handwriting. She picked up the top sheet and held it up to the light, studying it.

145

John and Catherine Randall request the pleasure of your company at a birthday party for their niece, Holly Randall, on Christmas Eve, December 24. . . .

Oh, she thought. So, they're planning a party for me. That's very nice of them, and I must remember to look surprised when they tell me about it. She shoved the paper quickly back where she'd found it, staring briefly at it again, shaking her head at the neat, sloping hand. It was uncanny. This must be Catherine's writing, she reasoned, but it looks almost exactly like mine.

In the top drawer beside the desk drawer she found pens and pencils and plain white linen stationery. She took out two sheets and envelopes. She selected a pen, hurriedly scrawled an affirmative reply to Missy's invitation, found a stamp, and sealed it. On the second note she slowed down, taking great care with her penmanship. She wrote:

Ms. Holly Randall accepts with pleasure your kind invitation to tea. I look forward to meeting you at four o'clock tomorrow afternoon.

She signed it, simply, *Holly*. She folded the note and slipped it in an envelope, on which she wrote *Mr. Ichabod Morris*. Then she picked up the phone on the desk and summoned Mr. Wheatley.

"What do you think?" his wife asked as soon as Holly had left the dining room.

John shook his head, frowning. "I don't know. Maybe he's just curious."

"Curious!" she hissed. "Indeed! *I've* been here nearly a year now, and he's never asked *me* to tea."

Despite his trepidation, he smiled.

"Lucky you," he murmured.

She stared at him. Then they both began to laugh.

"Yes," she conceded. "Lucky me."

An hour later, Holly put on her warm wool coat and left the house again. She had yet to take a good look around the estate by herself, the news vans outside the gates having kept her a virtual prisoner in the house until a few days ago. Now the vans were gone, and she was determined to see just what her new property entailed. She'd seen some of it already, of course, but now she was in a mood to explore.

A fine mist lay on the ground and among the bare branches of the trees, and the water and sky beyond the cliff had nearly disappeared in the approaching swirl of white vapor. She pulled the hood up over her head as she walked across the flattened brown grass toward the summer house.

The pretty iron and glass structure held little allure for her. She went inside and gave the big, well-appointed room a perfunctory inspection, and almost immediately she went out again in search of more interesting prospects. From the sheer cliff she regarded the stone hillside staircase and the rocky beach below, hazy in the gathering mist. Very nice, she thought, and maybe good for swimming in the summer.

The thought of swimming led her off around the main house to the backyard. The swimming pool was here, drained for the winter and covered by a wood platform that made the area a temporary extension of the tiled patio surrounding it. She imagined there would be furniture around the pool in season, chaises and umbrella-covered tables.

The pool house was a handsome stucco building with sliding glass doors. She went up to the glass doors of the house and peered inside. It was a veritable guest cottage, with tables and easy chairs, a little kitchenette at the back, and two big couches that probably opened into beds. Very attractive, she thought as she continued on her way around the side of the building toward the back lawn.

There was a little door here, in the side of the pool house. She tried to look through the frosted glass pane in its center to see what was inside, but the glass was opaque. Curious, she tried the doorknob and found that the room was unlocked. She pushed the door open and went inside.

It was very dark in the little room, but the mingled smells of chlorine and turpentine told her where she was before she found the light switch beside the door. She snapped the light on, revealing a crowded but neat storage room. There were utensils stacked in the corners, scythes and shovels and rakes, and long-handled nets for skimming the pool. Two wheelbarrows, one stacked on top of the other. A big white plastic drum in one corner was labeled CHLORINALL.

The walls of the room were lined from floor to ceiling with wooden shelves crammed with every imaginable maintenance and gardening need: rubber gloves, spades, hedge clippers, and paint trays with a wide assortment of well-used brushes and rollers. Two entire shelves contained only paint cans, each labeled with its specific function: POOL, IRONWORK, GATEHOUSE, etc. Below these was a shelf given over to various chemicals, a long row of cans and jars and bottles, most of them marked with an ominous skull and crossbones—cleaning agents, weed killer, ant and roach sprays, and a big jar of clear liquid felicitously labeled BEE-GONE.

She stared around at everything, taking in not the sight but the significance, what it represented. This little room indicated the vast size of all that was Randall House more acutely than anything else she'd seen so far. Here was the domain of the groundsmen, Zeke and Dave, and their several part-time assistants. The house and grounds were huge.

And now they were hers.

With a last glance around the place and a bemused shake of her head, she turned off the light and went outside, closing the door behind her.

Beyond the pool house was a small lawn that ended at a row of trees. The drive from the front of Randall House curved around the west side of it to become a small road leading past the pool area and through the trees. She went over to the road and walked down it, away from the main house.

Past the row of trees was another lawn, this one containing a little chapel and a small, fenced-in cemetery. Behind them was the apple orchard, and she knew from this morning's ride that there was another lawn behind the orchard before the forest took over completely, stretching outward to the high stone walls that ringed the property.

The road ended in a little parking lot beside the chapel. This was a tall structure of fitted stone with a domed roof and big oak double doors. There were beautiful little stained glass windows on either side of the doors, and substantially larger ones on each sidewall. The big side window before her depicted the Ascension. She knew without having to go around the building that the opposite window would be the Crucifixion.

Never having been religious, she was always leery of such places. As a child, she'd attended regular Sunday services with Ben and Mary Smith, who were Catholic, but she'd later begged off, and neither parent had forced the issue. Odd, she thought now, staring up at the pretty stone edifice: Catholicism. The one thing the Smiths and the Randalls had in common. The *only* thing . . .

Oh, well, she decided. I'm here now, and this is my chapel, and I might as well take a look.

She was about to go up the two steps to the big oak doors when she heard barking behind her. She whirled around, startled, to see the German shepherd bounding across the lawn from the direction of the forest. Behind him, just emerging from the trees, was his master, the blond teenage boy.

The boy stopped when he saw Holly standing there, and he whistled sharply to the dog, but the shepherd paid not the slightest attention to the command. He ran straight up to Holly, all lolling tongue and wagging tail. With a smile, she sank to her knees and removed a glove, extending her bare hand to stroke the glossy black and tan coat.

"Hello, Tonto," she whispered.

The dog, in an apparent paroxysm of ecstasy, rolled over onto his back, presenting his tummy for petting. With a laugh, Holly obliged.

She had not been afraid, because she already knew the dog was friendly. Mr. Wheatley had told her that when he'd told her the dog's name, and the boy's. She'd seen the pair several times from the windows of the house during her forced imprisonment in her first week, and she'd asked the butler who they were.

Now she studied the boy as he slowly, almost reluctantly made his way across the lawn to her. His name was Tobias Carter, he was called Toby, and he was about fifteen. His parents were teachers at Randall High School, which he attended. They lived in town, but Toby was on the grounds of Randall House nearly every day after school. He worked here part-time in winter and full-time in summer, helping Zeke and Dave. Maintaining the swimming pool was his principal summer responsibility, and sometimes he helped George with the horses, which he was occasionally allowed to ride. He also was a favorite of Brian Jessel, because he was as interested in the cars as the horses. In addition to the wages he was saving for eventual college tuition, he was allowed to swim in the pool and the pond and the cove beneath the cliff.

He'd been a fixture on the grounds for two years, ever since Alicia had first met him in the stable and invited him to ride with her. Mr. Wheatley had frequently seen the old woman and the boy riding together, the dog running along behind them. They seemed to have become great friends, the butler told Holly. But, despite Alicia's occasional invitations to lunch or dinner, Toby never entered Randall House.

He also almost never spoke. At least, that's what Mr. Wheatley had told her. In two years, Mr. Wheatley had not heard him utter more than a few words.

As the boy arrived before her, Holly got her first good look at him. He was tall and rather thin, and his golden hair tumbled down into his blue eyes. The eyes were his most arresting asset; large, grave, and full of what she could only describe as a remarkable intelligence. Very handsome, she decided, and then she immediately squelched the thought. Here she was, having impure thoughts about a virtual child. She smiled to cover her vague embarrassment as she rose to face him.

"Hello," she said, extending her hand. "You're Toby, right? I'm Holly. I'm pleased to meet you."

He looked down at her hand. After a moment, he nodded and briefly took her hand in his own. Then his arm dropped to his side. He stared down at the dog, and a troubled look came to his face.

"Oh, it's all right," Holly said quickly, interpreting his look as censure for the dog's overfamiliarity. "I love dogs, and Tonto here is charming." She reached down to pet the dog again, which set off another fit of tail-wagging. She laughed, and the boy actually smiled at the dog's antics. "If he's Tonto, then you must be the Lone Ranger."

He shrugged, looking off toward the house.

Far from unnerving her, his silence was oddly comforting. She immediately felt an affinity for him, and she wondered why this was. She also wondered why he was always here when he wasn't in class, and why he wasn't playing football or basketball at this time in the afternoon. Surely there were plenty of other boys his age in the vicinity, and that's what they were probably doing now. That, or spending quality time with girls. Sports and sex: the twin obsessions of most fifteen-year-old boys. Toby was apparently more interested in earning his college tuition, which was certainly admirable. But she couldn't help feeling curious about him.

She knew instinctively that she would not ask him questions about himself. Not that he'd answer them, anyway. He seemed more a man than a boy, serious and silent as he was. She decided that he could make his own decisions.

"Well, I'm glad to have met you, Toby," she said. "I'm sure we'll be seeing each other around the place. Perhaps you'd like to come riding with me sometime."

Now he was looking at the distant apple orchard. He had not once met her gaze with his own. He nodded again and reached down for Tonto's collar.

The dog immediately rose and stood at attention. With a last brief smile and a little bob of his head, Toby turned and walked away down the road toward the house. The dog began to follow him, then pivoted and ran back to her for one more pat on the head. He licked her outstretched hand, wagged his tail vigorously, gave a little yap of farewell, and took off after his master. When they were a little distance away, the boy suddenly turned around. He looked directly into her eyes, grinned, and raised his hand in a small salute. Then he and Tonto continued on their way.

Holly smiled, watching them go. She put her glove back on, turned around, and went into the chapel.

It was dark here, dark and silent. There was an altar at the end of the red-carpeted center aisle, which was flanked not by pews but by several rows of red velvet–upholstered chairs. Weak light glowed through the stained glass windows. In the nave before the chancel railing was a low table containing the obligatory rows of candles. A single candle was lit, its tiny flame reflected on the gold and brass fixtures of the altar behind it. Above the altar, mounted on the rear wall, was a large gold cross.

She wondered who had lit the candle.

Catherine had told her that this place had last been used for Alicia's funeral three months ago. It had been built when the house was built, a century ago. The original Alicia Randall was devout, and the local priest had performed the Sunday service here every week for the family and their servants.

But successive generations of Randalls were not as pious as their antecedents, and the little church was now used mainly for funerals and the occasional baptism or servant's wedding. Kevin had been christened here, twenty-eight years ago. So, she supposed, had Uncle John and her father.

Her father.

She was struck by a sudden feeling of curiosity. With a last glance around at the beautiful room, she turned and left the chapel.

John walked swiftly out through the front gates of the estate, grateful for the weather. The fog would obscure him from view, which, at the moment, was precisely what he wanted. He didn't want anyone noticing him.

He glanced at his watch—four forty-five. He was late, but he was certain that Ed—or whatever his name was—would be waiting. Hell, for what John would eventually be paying him, Ed could wait for hours. For ridding John of the obstacle that was Holly, Ed could buy a new house, or take several trips around the world. So, let him wait.

He walked along the edge of the road toward town, peering through the mist for the turnoff that led to the abandoned farm. Ed's car would be there, parked far enough along to be out of sight of the main road. He found the lane and proceeded.

Somewhere off to his left he heard the barking of a large dog. That damned brat, Toby Carter, he thought. Always underfoot. Alicia had tolerated him, and now he had the run of the place. John had never understood Alicia's indulgence. He didn't like children, and he didn't like dogs.

The red Infiniti arrived before him in the thickening fog, and he saw the silhouette of a man leaning against the hood, smoking a cigarette. John walked up to him, and the two men nodded in greeting. They did not shake hands: John knew, instinctively, that in Ed's world this was not done. Hands were for holding weapons.

John had arranged this meeting by calling the New York City number Ed had given him from a pay phone in town. He was being very careful not to have any record, anything at all that could possibly connect him to this man. When the time came, he would pay Ed in cash and send him on his way.

They stood on the little dirt road in the forest, regarding each other. At last, John broke the silence.

"You've been here twice now, right?"

Ed shrugged. "Yeah."

"Know your way around, I guess."

"Yeah."

"Good. My wife and I are giving her a party on Christmas Eve. That's her birthday. We'll probably do something with her on New Year's Eve, too. In the second week of January, my wife and I are going to Europe to visit some friends. We plan to be gone two weeks. That's your best time, while we're safely away. Any ideas on how to do it?"

Ed took a last drag on his cigarette, dropped it to the ground, and crushed it out with his heel. "A couple. She rides horses. I saw her and that guy, Jessel, riding this morning. Does she drive?"

"I think so," John said.

"That's another possibility. The best accidents are natural. Two weeks in January . . . hmmm. Yeah, I can arrange something."

John heard a faint noise, a rustling in the trees nearby. He leaned closer to the other man. "Do you plan to continue coming out here every week?"

"Yeah, for a while, anyway. I've found a place to stay, a little motel a couple of miles away. The Kismet."

"I know it," John said. "If I need to get in touch with you from now on, I'll leave a message for you there." A pay phone to a motel, he was thinking: better than a call to Ed's home in Brooklyn, traceable or not.

Ed nodded. "I have other things to do in the next few weeks. Some business in New York. But I'll keep an eye on her, once a week. By January, she'll have my undivided attention."

"Do it," John said. "I want her dead."

Ed smiled, a slow, lazy curling of his lip. "I'll try not to make her suffer."

"I don't give a damn about that," John snapped. "Just do it."

Ed continued to smile at him. Then he nodded.

"Sure thing," he said.

She must have been inside the chapel longer than she'd thought. It was dark now, and the mist had intensified into a dense gray fog that had settled down around everything. Randall House was no longer visible from here, and she could barely see the wrought iron fence of the cemetery mere steps away across the road. Shivering in the cold, damp air, she walked down the steps and over to the gate of the cemetery. She lifted the latch, pushed the gate open, and stepped inside.

It was a small, well-tended place, perhaps thirty feet by thirty. She nearly collided with a headstone, and after that she made her way slowly around, finding her way as much by feel as by sight. The fog obliterated everything that wasn't directly in front of her.

She found the largest, oldest markers in the far corner. The biggest was an elegantly simple mono- lith of polished pink marble, perhaps three feet high and four across. Engraved in the stone was the an- nouncement that here lay John and Alicia Randall, *Beloved of God and of each other*. The two large marble stones nearest this were the final resting places of James and Ellen Randall, her great-grandparents. Then came a William Henry Randall, 1921–1942, *Taken from us in the glorious service of his country*. She passed the next headstone, for Charles Franklin Wainwright, who'd also apparently died in World War II. Beside him was the most recent monument, and Holly paused at this one for a few moments, gazing down. Alicia Rose Randall Wainwright. Next came James II and his wife, Emily, her grandparents.

She found the grave she'd been seeking a little apart from the others in the family grouping, under a small tree near the wrought iron fence. Other, lesser stones dotted the ground on the opposite side of the enclosure, clearly those of servants, including Mrs. Wheatley and at least two Jessels. Next to the Jessel graves a single, crudely made wooden cross rose up from a patch of freshly turned earth: a pet, she supposed, recently deceased. But the simple white stone that stood off by itself under the tree now commanded her attention.

She approached it slowly, almost cautiously, as if she were loath to disturb the spirit within. That's silly, she reasoned: there are no spirits here, only earthly remains. Yet she could not shake the feeling that they were all here, now, watching her. She peered nervously around and behind her, but she could see nothing in the fog.

She sank slowly to her knees before the little white headstone. She reached out a gloved hand and carefully cleared away a small tangle of dead brown ivy vines draped over it.

JAMES WILLIAM RANDALL III

Under the name were the dates, and under these a series of smaller lines, his epitaph. She stared at the words etched into the face of the stone, memorizing them so that she could recall them in the future, whenever she chose.

Beloved son, beloved brother, beloved father,
Struck down by the hand he held most dear.
He is in Heaven now.
Requiescat in Pace

Holly took off her right glove, leaned forward, and pressed her bare hand against the stone. She closed her eyes and tried to feel something, anything. Anything at all.

Beloved father: those words obviously referred to her. This man, not Ben Smith, had quite literally planted the seed that had become her, Holly.

Beloved husband was conspicuously unmentioned. He had been struck down, taken before his time, *by the hand he held most dear.* His wife. The woman who had been her mother; the woman who was not Mary Smith; the woman whose absence from this place, whose unmourned grave in a common field on Long Island, said all that needed to be said about her.

This man, this victim of murder, was her father.

And yet she felt nothing. She was kneeling in a freezing graveyard in the fog, her hand pressed against his monument, and no tears, no remorse, no righteous anger would come. Nothing at all. Had Ben Smith lain here, she would be weeping now. But this man meant nothing to her.

"He isn't here, you know."

The voice, low and clear, emanated from somewhere in the fog behind her, near the gate of the cemetery. Holly jumped to her feet and whirled around, the glove falling from her hand. She held her breath, peering through the swirling mist. A dark shape was all she could make out, a shape standing quite still not ten feet from her. She took an involuntary step backward, nearly tripping over her father's stone as the figure slowly began to move toward her.

"They're gone now," the figure said, gliding closer, closer. "They're in Heaven."

It was a woman, Holly now saw, as tall as she, dressed all in black. She was wearing a long black cape, or cloak, its deep hood framing an unusually pale face. Dark eyes and hair. She might have been about Holly's age, or older, or younger; it was impossible to tell.

As the woman arrived before her, Holly had the distinct impression that she had seen the face before, though she couldn't place it. But at least it wasn't the old monk, or whatever, from her dream. This woman was certainly not a ghost, she reasoned, conjured from this ground by her own anxieties. Besides, she had spoken, and civility demanded a reply. Holly licked her suddenly dry lips, cleared her suddenly dry throat, and spoke.

"Yes, I know they're in Heaven. I was just—"

"You shouldn't be here," the woman said. "You could lose your way in this weather."

"Yes," Holly said again, and now she began to move, edging slowly around the woman, who stood between her and the gate. There was something wrong with her; she made Holly nervous. "I was just going back to the house. . . ."

Now the woman shook her head, reaching out a pale white hand to clutch the sleeve of Holly's coat. "You shouldn't be *there*, either!"

"I live there," Holly said, pulling her coat rather roughly from the woman's grasp and backing toward the gate. "It's my house now. I'm Holly Randall."

The woman followed her, grabbing at her sleeve again.

"I know who you are!" she hissed. "You shouldn't be there! A pretty girl like you—"

"Don't!" Holly cried, yanking her arm away. The sharp iron bars of the fence were behind her now, pressing into her back. "Please don't touch me! Just—"

"*You shouldn't be there!*" The woman's eyes were wild, pleading, her breath coming in a series of panting gasps. She continued to advance, reaching out once more.

Holly stared at the pale white fingers of the woman's right hand as they came toward her. Then her gaze traveled to the left hand, and she saw that the woman was clutching something in it, something limp and grubby that dangled down against her cloak. A surge of pure revulsion coursed through her as she realized what it was: an old, battered, naked baby doll, its glass eyes staring vacantly, its remaining sparse patches of downy hair matted with dead leaves, its plastic head and limbs encrusted with dirt. Graveyard dirt.

Holly ran. A small cry escaped her as she caught her coat on the pointed tip of a rail, and she heard a ripping sound when she tore herself loose and staggered through the open gate just as the woman's fingers were about to snatch her. She ran blindly through the wall of fog in what she hoped was the right direction.

"You shouldn't be there!" she heard once more from the darkness behind her.

A tree loomed up before her, and she tripped over an exposed root and went sprawling on the damp ground. She was up again in a second, up and running through the trees and across the lawn. She had the sensation that she was running underwater, which wasn't far from the truth. The fog, wet and freezing, clung to her face and hair and clothes, drenching her. The patio and the covered swimming pool floated by her in a hazy blur as she fixed her gaze on the light ahead, the beacon that suddenly, mercifully arrived before her, shining through the mist—the brightly lit windows of the kitchen.

She flew across the final stretch of walkway and stumbled up the three stone steps to the kitchen door. She fell heavily against it, panting, and grasped the knob in her shaking hand. Only then did she summon the courage to turn around to look behind her.

There was nobody in sight. She couldn't see very far from here, only as far as the edge of the patio, but the black-cloaked woman was not there. She had vanished in the fog, along with her grisly burden.

Holly pushed open the door and barged into the kitchen. A sudden blast of warmth assaulted her wet, freezing body as she stopped, blinking around through the glare. Three women were here, Mrs. Ramirez and Mrs. Jessel and one of the maids, whose name she could not remember, and they had all turned to stare at her.

"Ms. Randall!" she heard one of them say. "Are you all right?"

"Yes, I—I'm fine," she murmured, sinking into a chair at the big table in the center of the room. "I just got lost in the fog, and I fell down, and. . . ."

"Oh, my dear, you must be careful in this weather," someone said. "Grace, pour Ms. Randall a cup of tea."

It was Mrs. Jessel who had spoken. She sat down beside Holly and reached for her coat.

"You're fairly soaking wet," she said. "Take off that coat and stay here, near the fire."

Holly shrugged the coat from her shoulders, gazing around. The big brick fireplace was roaring, and the stove and oven were in use. Of course, she thought as she relaxed in the warm room, they're making dinner. She smiled up at the maid—Grace; her name was Grace—as a mug of tea was placed on the table before her. "Thank you."

"Are you all right?" Mrs. Jessel asked her again. "You've torn your coat."

Holly followed Mrs. Jessel's gaze down to the right sleeve of her wool coat. There was a small rip there, where she'd caught it on the iron bar of the cemetery fence. "I'm fine." She noticed her bare right hand. "I think I dropped my glove in the—" She stopped herself abruptly. For some reason, she didn't want to tell these women where she'd been, what she had been doing. "Near the chapel."

"Well, we can look for it tomorrow," Mrs. Jessel said, "and Martha can sew this sleeve for you. Grace, close that door. The cold is coming in."

The maid went over to the open kitchen door as Mrs. Jessel picked up the coat. Holly reached for the mug, steadying herself, forcing the obscene image of the pendulous, filthy doll from her mind.

"Oh!" Grace cried from the doorway.

Holly and the other women turned to look as Grace stepped out through the door, leaned down, and picked something up from the top step. She came back inside and shut the door.

"Here you are, miss," Grace said. "You dropped it right here, just outside the door."

Holly stared. The girl was holding up the glove she'd dropped on her father's grave in the cemetery.

The woman in black, she thought. She picked up my glove and brought it here. She was right outside this door, clutching that ghastly thing to her, probably seconds ago. . . .

Holly turned to Mrs. Jessel. "There was the most extraordinary—"

For the second time in as many minutes, Holly stopped herself. She was looking at the housekeeper. Now, in the light, she noticed something about Mrs. Jessel that hadn't registered before. The pale skin, the dark eyes and hair, the severe black dress. Her face . . .

The face that had emerged from the fog in the graveyard. The face at the upstairs window of the gatehouse, Mrs. Jessel's house, on the day Holly had arrived here from New York. A pale face with dark eyes, framed by dark hair, and a pale hand moving aside the lace curtain of the window. A younger, prettier version of the face before her now.

Mrs. Jessel was watching her. "The most extraordinary—what?"

Holly blinked at the woman, shrugged, and forced herself to smile.

"Oh, nothing," she whispered.

Still smiling at Mildred Jessel, she picked up the mug in her trembling hands and drank.

CHAPTER SIX

A Game of Chess

He looked nervously around the room to be sure that everything was ready. He was about to receive his first guest in years, and he wanted to make a good impression. It was vital that she like him, trust him. Especially if his growing suspicion was correct.

Of course, there was every chance that the girl was an idiot, or took after her mother, in which case he would keep his own counsel. He would fill her with tea and Mrs. Ramirez's excellent pastries, chuck her under the chin, and send her on her way. No harm done. But he hoped she wasn't an idiot. And he fervently hoped she didn't take after Constance Hall Randall. . . .

He shook his head, smiling at his trepidation. *Ichabod Crane:* that's what Emily had always called him.

Emily . . .

Oh, well, he told himself. Let's cross that bridge when we come to it.

Raymond Wheatley had helped him with the table. The two men had moved it out into the center of the room, and Raymond had placed a white linen tablecloth over it and set it with good silver. My sister's silver, he thought as he went into the bathroom and checked his appearance for the third time in ten minutes.

He was wearing his white dinner jacket, with the black bow tie and piped trousers and patent leather shoes. He hadn't worn these clothes since Emily's wedding to James Randall nearly sixty years ago. He'd never worn them in his public appearances in the old days, comfortable sweaters being more suitable for long sessions at chess tables with all those lights and cameras aimed at him. He shuddered now, remembering that he had once actually allowed people to photograph him, and to film his matches.

Yes, his tie was straight, not that it really mattered. The little medicine cabinet mirror was the only one in his rooms. He didn't care to look at himself, any more than others cared to look at him. But maybe, with any luck, Holly Randall wouldn't mind.

Mr. Wheatley was turning out to be a treasure. He had taken Holly's note to her great-uncle yesterday, then come back with the confirmation. When Holly asked, he was only too happy to give her some background information on her mysterious host.

Now she knew a few things. As it happened, her preparation was fortunate.

She had dressed with care, deciding after much thought on the blue velvet cocktail dress. It covered more of her than the others she'd bought that would be appropriate for afternoon tea, and she was aware that a gentleman in his late eighties who sent formal notes of invitation would disapprove of anything that could be construed as provocative. She kept her makeup simple and wore no jewelry, and her hair hung down her back in a single braid. She briefly considered but ultimately discarded a pair of white gloves. Almost as an afterthought, she sprayed herself lightly with the distinctly old-fashioned, lavender-scented toilet water she'd found on her bureau with the silver-plated brushes. She felt like Pollyanna, but she was certain the overall effect would be appreciated.

She knew, in the way that one knows these things, that this meeting could be important. She was in a new house with a new family and a new way of life, but she distrusted her aunt and uncle. This ancient relative, this man in the guest room, could not possibly want or need anything from her. Mr. Wheatley had informed her that Ichabod Morris had once been world-famous, and that he was wealthy in his own right. That alone made him valuable to her: he, of all those present, would tell her the truth.

She was planning to ask him about her parents.

He would certainly have been around at the time of the murder, and he could probably give her a personal view of the events of twenty-four years ago. Holly had already accepted his invitation when she visited the cemetery yesterday, but ever since she'd seen what was etched into her father's headstone she'd been consumed with questions, questions she had never thought to ask. Questions she would never ask Uncle John.

At the appointed time, she left her room and went down the hall, around the gallery above the Great Hall, and into the guest wing, to the first door on her left. At precisely four o'clock, she raised her hand and knocked.

A thin, tremulous voice on the other side of the door said, "Come in."

Holly opened the door and went inside. She stood in the doorway, her hand on the knob, gazing around her. The first thing she saw was the little table laid for tea, all crisp white linen and heavy, sparkling silver. There were two red velvet overstuffed chairs pulled up to the table, facing each other. On another table in a corner was a big, beautiful marble chessboard, the rows of ivory and ebony pieces gleaming, ready for a game. She took in the many crowded bookshelves, the heavy damask curtains at the large windows, and the bulky, state-of-the-art computer terminal on the desk near the corner, its screen saver flashing endlessly repeated patterns of stars and asteroids and the U.S.S. *Enterprise*. She smiled at this anachronism in the otherwise old-fashioned room, shut the door softly behind her, and turned her attention to the tall, white-haired gentleman in the white dinner jacket who stood looking out at the front drive from a window, his back to her.

After a moment he said, "Miss Randall." A statement. He did not turn around.

"Holly," she said. "I'm Holly. What shall I call you, sir?"

She heard his low chuckle. "You may call me Ichabod. Or you may call me what your delightful father and your rather loathsome uncle always called me."

Holly laughed. It was an easy, unaffected sound. He'd caught her off guard: she hadn't expected anything like that statement from him. She respected him immediately.

"He *is* rather loathsome," she said, "and it's a loathsome nickname. I'm pleased to meet you, Ichabod."

"Check," the old man said.

"I beg your pardon?"

He reached out with an arm, gesturing toward the chessboard. "A term we use in my profession. You are an intelligent young woman, and you have just completed an excellent move. Forgive me for keeping my back to you all this while, Holly. I'm going to turn around now, but before I do, I feel I must—"

"It's quite all right," she said softly, cutting him off. "Mr. Wheatley has told me. Not that it matters. I have one myself."

There was silence in the room. Then the old man nodded once, took a deep breath, and slowly turned away from the window to face her.

She thought she would be prepared, but she was not. She blinked to keep from staring at him. The deep red stain was there, just as Mr. Wheatley had described it, completely covering the right side of his face and neck. Otherwise, it was a handsome face, or would have been. He was old, most old, older than she'd expected. But neither his age nor his disfiguring birthmark was the reason for her surprise. With a massive, but invisible, effort, she managed to smile and extend her hand. After a moment, he smiled and came over to take her hand in his.

She stood there, smiling, shaking the hand of the specter from her dream, the monk at the foot of her bed.

"Checkmate," he murmured, and then he led her over to the table. They sat facing each other in the plush chairs. He smiled at her again and reached for the telephone on the little table beside him. "Mrs. Ramirez, please tell Mr. Wheatley we're ready for tea. Thank you."

She was prettier up close than she was from a distance, but this did not surprise him. He made a slow, appreciative study of the face and hair, the dress, and the hands now folded in her lap. Yes, he thought. Quite beautiful. She looks like Emily, and a little like Alicia Wainwright. Not like her mother, though; more like her father.

"I compliment you on your perfect manners, Holly," he said at last. "You recognized me immediately, of course, but you didn't let on. Yes, it was I, the menacing figure in your bedroom, for which I apologize. I gave in to an overwhelming urge."

The young woman grinned and raised an eyebrow. "And what overwhelming urge was that?"

They laughed.

"If I were sixty years younger, or even forty, I would be insulted," he said. "As if I would have any other reason for stealing into a woman's bedroom! Alas, that is no longer the case." Then his smile faded, and he leaned forward, gazing into her eyes. "I just had to be sure. That it really was you, and that you really were here."

She stared at him, and now she, too, leaned forward. She opened her mouth to speak.

The door opened, and Raymond Wheatley came in with the tea tray.

"Thank you, Raymond," her great-uncle said.

"Of course, Ichabod," Mr. Wheatley replied. He set down the tray and departed.

She watched her great-uncle as he poured, and as he offered her the plate of pastries. She took one, something warm and flaky with chocolate drizzled over it, and grinned at him again.

"Raymond," she said. "I've never heard anyone use his first name before. And I've certainly never heard him call anyone else here by *their* first name."

He nodded. "We are of a certain age, Raymond and I. He was never my servant, nor am I his. We are on a first-name basis."

They sipped their tea. Then she noticed the trophies covering nearly every surface on one side of the room, and the framed ribbons and citations on the wall above them. "I didn't place your name when I first heard it yesterday, but I certainly know who you are."

He nodded absently. "Oh, yes, I suppose. As you probably know Babe Ruth and Jack Dempsey and Sonja Henie. A legend from the remote past."

"You were America's greatest chess player," Holly said, remembering what Mr. Wheatley had told her.

He laughed again. "It's a good thing Fischer didn't hear you say that. He'd have had a fit!" Then he glanced sharply at her. "Do you play, by any chance?"

Her eyes widened, and she blushed. "Not like you."

"I was thinking, perhaps we could have a game when we finish our tea. . . ."

"Oh, sure!" she said, giggling. "But a quick one, please. I promised to play tennis with Martina later this afternoon."

He reached out and took her hand in his. "Holly, indulge an old man. I have so few visitors, and Raymond does not play. For longer than I care to admit, my only opponent has been *that*." He waved, indicating the computer on the desk.

Holly smiled. "You play chess with a computer?"

"My dear, I was one of the first people in the world to do so. Fischer, Spassky, and me—they tried it out on us. And I must tell you, *we* always won. It's rather boring."

She regarded him a moment. Then she nodded. "I'd be honored—if you promise not to slaughter me."

The old man smiled. "My dear, who on earth would want to slaughter *you*?"

He liked her. At the same time, he was aware of the tension, something unspoken between them. He wondered what it was.

"And now," he said as soon as Raymond had reappeared to take away the tea tray, "a game."

The girl immediately rose and went to get the chessboard. She lifted it slowly, carefully, and brought it over to the table. He noted how gently, almost lovingly, she set it down. He was pleased: she respected beautiful things.

She won in eleven moves.

He let her win in eleven moves.

She didn't flatter herself: he'd carefully set it up so that she couldn't help but win. But he looked surprised and shouted bravo, so she smiled and went along with it. When she offered to play again, he shook his head, pushed the board aside, and sat back in his chair, gazing across the table at her.

"So," he said at last. "You're from California. You must find the weather here dramatically different."

"Yes. That fog yesterday—well, I've never been around much of that before."

"I daresay. Did you have a horse there, or is riding a new experience, too?"

Holly grinned. "You've been spying on me!"

"Not really," her great-uncle said. "I saw you from my window this morning. And yesterday morning."

"Oh. Well, there was this ranch near us in Indio, and when I was in high school. . . ." She trailed off, studying him. "Ichabod, what exactly is it you want to know?"

The old man laughed. He seemed to be completely relaxed in her company now. "Checkmate, again! I saw you riding with young Jessel."

"Yes," she said, feeling the warmth on her cheeks. "Kevin."

"Kevin," he repeated. "An interesting young man—or so Raymond tells me. Yale, summa cum laude. Not bad for the chauffeur's son. With his degrees, I'm surprised he doesn't have some fancy job in New York or somewhere. Oh, well, he's got his life ahead of him. . . ."

Holly thought about that. She'd never wondered. She didn't even know what Kevin's major had been. "You've known him all his life, I should think."

"Not really," he said. He waved a hand, indicating the room. "I rarely leave here. I've seen him around since he was tiny, but I've probably spoken to him a grand total of five times." He seemed to be studying her face. "He's very handsome, though."

"Yes," Holly said.

"Popular with the ladies, according to reports from below stairs."

She shrugged. "I suppose. . . ."

"Do you like him?" he asked abruptly.

Holly smiled again. "Yes, I do. I like him very much."

"Hmm. Well, be careful. You're an heiress now,

don't forget, and a lot of people are going to come crawling out of the woodwork. And more than a few of them will be handsome young bucks like Kevin Jessel."

Now Holly blushed. "Ichabod! You're beginning to sound like my parents!"

He leaned back, smiling. "Forgive me, Holly. I'm a very old man. When you reach my age, you'll have learned to come right out and say exactly what you mean. You never know how much time you have." He took a long breath, regarding her. "And as for sounding like your parents—well, they're gone now."

Holly blinked. "I meant my parents in Indio. Mr. and Mrs. Smith."

He nodded. "Ah. But they're not your real parents."

"No," she agreed, "they're not." Now she leaned forward, studying him as he had studied her. "Do you—do you remember them?"

"Of course," he said.

So, she thought, we've finally come to it. My real reason for this interview. She took a deep breath. "What were they like?"

So, he thought, we've finally come to it. My real reason for this interview. He took a deep breath. "I can show you what they were like. What we were all like. . . ."

He was aware of her watching him as he rose from his chair and went over to the crowded book-shelves near the door. He selected two of his three scrapbooks, pulled them down, and carried them back to the table. Settling into his seat again, he reached for one and opened it. He waved to her, indicating that she should get up and come around to stand beside his chair. She did.

"I have three books full of memories," he began. "This one is the family. The one still on the shelf over there could not possibly interest you: it is about my career in chess."

"I'd like to see it sometime," she said. "And the third?"

He smiled at her and patted the arm of his chair. She settled down onto it. "We'll come to that presently." He smoothed his hand over the first page of the volume. Two wedding pictures, the one on the left extremely old and yellowed. "These are our parents, Emily's and mine, on their wedding day. Over here we have your grandparents, Emily and James Junior." He turned the page. "That's all of us at Emily's wedding reception, right here in the Great Hall. That's your great-grandmother, Ellen, next to the bride. . . ."

She sat on the arm of the old man's chair, staring at the cavalcade of images that arrived before her as the sun outside began to set and the shadows in the room lengthened. His voice continued to narrate the history.

". . . and that's your father when he was, let me see, about three, with the baby, John. Emily had just brought him home from the hospital. . . . A picnic in the woods near the pond, Alicia and Emily and Jimmy, your grandfather, and the two boys.

See how they'd grown! Jim was about fourteen here, and John would have been eleven. . . . Jim's high school graduation. How handsome he was in his cap and gown. I don't know where Emily found that awful hat! I'm not sure who the girl is, the other graduate with Jim. He has his arm around her, so she must have been his steady at the time. Perhaps her name was Cindy, or Candy; something like that. . . . Here's Jim at Yale, in his football uniform. His friend there next to him became a lawyer, I believe. . . ."

"Yes," Holly said, studying the photograph. "His name is Gilbert Henderson. He's my lawyer now. He's the one who arranged for my adoption by the Smiths."

Ichabod glanced up at her, then back at the album. "Fancy that! Well, anyway, he was your father's closest friend. . . . Here they are, Jim and Gilbert, graduating from Yale, just before Jim went to work in the New York office of NaFCorp. . . ."

On it went through the years, through births and weddings and funerals, Christmases and summer outings and various parties and business functions. Alicia cutting a ribbon outside the new Randall Public Library. Holly's grandfather, James, receiving a citation from NaFCorp. Her father and several other young people, including Gil Henderson, at what might have been a debutante ball. Two shots of her grandfather, with two successive presidents of the United States. Her grandparents and Alicia with Elizabeth Taylor and Dina Merrill, taken at the family's house in Palm Beach. The Randalls with the Biddles. The Randalls with the Mellons. The Randalls with the Mountbattens.

At last, he turned to the final page. "And this is everyone, the whole family, at the Waldorf in New York. Jimmy and Emily and Alicia and Jim and John. I'm not in the picture because I'm up on the dais, receiving some silly thing from the International Chess Association. Lifetime Achievement, if you please!" He chuckled a moment, then his humor faded. He stared sadly down at the picture. "This was the last photo of—everyone. All together." He sighed and closed the book.

It was now very dark in the room. Holly stood up from the arm of his chair and walked over to the window. Twilight had fallen, and the light from the downstairs windows stretched out over the lawn and the drive. Soon it would be time for dinner.

His voice continued from the darkness behind her. "I've shown you all this because I wanted you to see how it was, what the Randall family once was. Before they were banished from the garden. And then, as before, it was the work of a serpent. An attractive, seductive reptile named Connie. Constance Hall."

She looked out at the lawn, thinking, Yes.

Then his voice again, the merest whisper. "Come back to the table, Holly."

He waited until the girl had resumed her seat on the arm of his chair. He reached up briefly and patted her arm.

"Please remember that this has nothing to do

180

with you," he told her. "Your father was a decent man, a kind man. But he was young, and young people sometimes make reckless decisions."

"Yes," the girl whispered.

He picked up the other scrapbook and opened it to the beginning. "He met her at a party, the opening night party for the off-Broadway play in which she was appearing. . . ."

She looked and listened. She already knew most of this story, having pieced it together from the extensive newspaper coverage she'd found in the library in Palm Springs. Rich young corporate executive with bachelor pad in Greenwich Village meets beautiful young actress. Dates. Parties. Whirlwind romance. Photographs from various gossip columns, Suzy and Cindy Adams and all the others. Jim and Connie at a restaurant. Jim and Connie on a yacht. Jim and Connie dancing. Two beautiful, blond, blue-eyed young people in love. Published rumors, from the very beginning, that the Randalls of Randall, Connecticut, were Not Amused.

She studied the woman in the pictures. Tall, slender, very pretty. Shoulder-length blond mane in a then-fashionable style made popular by some movie star. Always laughing, flashing even white teeth at the cameras. There were a couple of production shots of her onstage during a performance, in an evening gown with her hair up, holding a martini and smirking at an actor in a dinner jacket. A Playbill of the production, a revival of *Private Lives* by Noël Coward.

"Where did you get this?" she asked her great-uncle, pointing to the Playbill.

"When I went to see the play," he said. "Emily and Jimmy were invited, and so was Alicia, but they all refused. They never met her. They thought she was a 'phase.' But I went: I always liked your father, and he was always kind to me, and I guess I'm just not a Randall. I didn't care that he was dating an actress from Nowhere, Long Island."

Holly nodded. "So, how was she? In the play, I mean."

The old man shrugged. "Well, she was no Gertrude Lawrence—but she was no slouch, either. She was quite good, actually."

Then he turned the page, and Holly felt a small shock. It was a glossy photo of her parents at City Hall, and her mother held a little bouquet in her hands. Beside them, smiling at the camera, stood John Randall and Ichabod. "You went to the wedding?"

"Of course. I was living in New York then, so I saw them a few times. I saw her in the play, and I went to the wedding, and once—no, twice—they had me over for dinner. I had them over for dinner once."

"Did you like her?"

Ichabod looked up at her then. "I don't know: I never really thought about it. I liked *him*, your father, and I was aware that he was hurt by my sister and Jimmy and Alicia, the way they ignored the situation. They never met Constance, not once. He'd really severed all ties with his family by that point. Except his brother, John, oddly enough. And me. So John and I were the relatives, you see?" He paused a moment, thinking. "But did I like *her*? Well, not really. She was very dramatic, very actressy, rather loud. And rather cold. She always smiled at me, but it wasn't a real smile. And she insisted on calling me Icky, even after Jim asked her not to. I don't think she liked me, particularly. She had a habit of—well, staring." His right hand came up to the birthmark on his face.

"I see," Holly said. And she did. Her mother had not been well-bred, that was certain. The steadily increasing public jokes about Ichabod's blemish had driven him, ultimately, to life as a recluse. No, Constance didn't sound like a nice person.

He turned another page.

Holly stared down at the yellowed clipping from the front page of the *New York Post*, dated April 2, twenty-four years ago. At the screaming, one-word headline:

MURDER!

There was more, much more. Headlines and articles and photographs. APRIL FOOL! Her father's body on the floor of the bedroom in Greenwich Village, a big, dark stain on the front of his white shirt. Her mother in sunglasses, head bowed, flanked by police. THE APRIL FOOLS' KILLER: THE JOKE'S ON HER! The funeral at the little cemetery here at Randall House, with the family and a crowd of others in black, including Gil Henderson. Her mother again, handcuffed, being helped out of the back of a van by a grim-faced woman. The lettering on the door of the van identified it as belonging to the East Side Women's Detention Center. Another headline: CONNIE RANDALL PREGNANT WITH DEAD HUSBAND'S BABY—NO (APRIL) FOOLIN'! Editorials in the *New York Times* and various other papers: WOMEN AND THE DEATH PENALTY. And on and on.

Ichabod had been thorough in his collection of information. The trial came next. RANDALL TRIAL BEGINS; CONNIE SAYS, "NOT GUILTY!" . . . STATE ARGUES FIRST DEGREE; JUDGE KEENE UPHOLDS SECOND . . . "DEFENSE HAS NO CASE!" SAYS D.A. . . . WHERE IS CONNIE'S FAMILY? . . . CONNIE SOBS ON WITNESS STAND: "HE ATTACKED ME!"

There were no defense witnesses, but several for the prosecution. Maids and waiters and actors, all painting a portrait of a cold woman with an often violent temper. Slapping Jim once in a restaurant. A marital scuffle backstage at the theater. The cleaning woman who'd overheard several violent arguments in the apartment in the Village, and who'd cleaned up broken glass on more than one occasion. A fellow actress who stated that the defendant had told her more than once that she'd married James Randall III for his money. A doorman who told the court that Mr. Randall would often disappear from home "for weeks at a stretch," during which time he frequently saw Mrs. Randall in the company of "other gentlemen." On cross-examination, he was unable to identify any of the "other gentlemen," but the public defender's motion to strike the door-man's testimony from the record was overruled.

However, the single most damning thing about the whole trial, Ichabod told her, was the absence of any family. Neither the Halls nor the Randalls ever appeared in court, and they declined to make any statements to the press. Constance's mother would finally appear once, years later, on a national news program, denouncing her daughter as a cold-blooded killer, and blaming her for her father's early grave.

The jury was out for less than an hour. Constance Hall Randall was found guilty of second-degree murder. She was later sentenced to life and trans-ported from the detention center to the Kingston Women's Correctional Facility. Two subsequent ap-peals were unsuccessful.

Ichabod went to Randall House to be with his sis-ter after the murder. He had moved into this guest room, and he had never left. Emily died a year after her son.

"There was more to the Constance Randall story," he said now. "She made headlines again, twice, while she was in prison. Fights with other inmates. One of them lost an eye, as I recall. You can imagine how that affected the parole people. She was there for nineteen years."

"Yes," Holly said. "And a year after she got out, she killed herself. On April Fools' Day. I guess she at least had some kind of a sense of humor. . . ."

Ichabod nodded and turned to the final pages of the album. Several more clippings, ranging from the sober *New York Times* (CONSTANCE RANDALL DEAD,

A SUICIDE) to the snide, obviously delighted tabloids (CONNIE FRIES! and JOKE'S OVER FOR THE APRIL FOOLS' KILLER!, and even FOOLED US TWICE—SHAME ON HER!).

There were pictures of the burned seaside cottage and the covered body being loaded into an ambulance. The final picture in the album, accompanying a small notice of her burial in a Long Island cemetery, was an early publicity still. In it, her mother was once more young and blond and beautiful, grinning into the camera, without a care in the world.

Ichabod closed the album. They sat there, he in the chair and she on the arm of it, for several moments. He reached up and took her hand in his. When he looked at her, he saw that she was staring down at the closed scrapbook.

"Why?" she whispered at last. "Why do you suppose she did it? What the hell *happened*?"

He squeezed her hand and shrugged. "Why, indeed? It's a question no one has satisfactorily answered, not even the prosecutors. Not even Constance herself. She obviously had a violent nature: there is too much evidence to deny it. Too many people saw and heard things. Even if you ignore the gossipy doorman, what about the cleaning woman? And the actress, and the waiter? I hardly see it as an elaborate conspiracy. No, she and Jim had a bad relationship, that much seems clear."

He could almost feel her confusion. "They were only married a year and a half. Eighteen months. . . ."

She shifted on the arm of the chair, looking down at him. "Do you have a theory?"

"Yes," he said. "I do." He rose from the chair, pulling her up by the hand as he did so. They walked together over to the window and stood, holding hands, staring out at the dark landscape. "I think your father changed his mind. I think this young woman, this actress, met a handsome, extremely rich young man and, well, latched onto him. He was dazzled, of course, but only for a short time. He wanted to be independent: he'd already moved out of this house and taken an apartment in the city. He wanted a life apart from Randall House. I think he saw something irresistible in the concept of familial disapproval. Raising a ruckus, as we used to say. Shaking things up a bit. Emily was my sister, and I loved her more than anything, but she and Jimmy could be the most awful snobs. Your father told me once, just before the wedding, that he was rather happy about the fuss he was causing. He was—what?—thirty years old, and he'd never misbehaved before. Not once, not *ever*. John was always the bad boy, not Jim. I think he married her because he knew he wasn't *supposed* to marry her. It was a lark, you see?"

His great-niece removed her hand from his and turned to face him. "Yes, I see. And then, afterward, when they were actually married, he . . ."

"He saw what she was really like," he said. "He got a dose of her temper, and her violent behavior, and her—well, her commonness. I believe the doorman, incidentally, at least about Jim's taking off for weeks at a time. I'm sure he did. And then one day he told her. He wanted a divorce."

Holly stared. "Did he ever confide any of this to you?"

"Oh, my dear, no! I was his mother's brother. He wouldn't have dared. If his parents learned that he'd admitted he'd been wrong—no, he kept it all to himself. But that's what I think happened. I think he told Constance that he was leaving her."

"On April Fools' Day," Holly added. "Yes, I see. And she became violent."

"*Again*," he said.

She nodded. "*Again*. Only this time—where was the gun?"

"In the drawer of the bedside table."

"Yes," she said, still nodding. "And he was found on the bedroom floor. . . ."

She turned to look out of the window again. He studied her quietly, noting that she didn't seem to be particularly upset by the story, or by the scrapbooks. Of course not, he reminded himself. Her parents—her parents of record—were Mr. and Mrs. Smith of Indio, California. Until a few weeks ago, she'd never so much as heard of the Randalls.

Now was the time to tell her the rest. About his feeling, his theory. His awful suspicion.

But she was a beautiful young woman. She was gazing out at the grounds—*her* grounds now—assimilating a terrible scandal in which she'd played no part, though it profoundly affected her. She was tough: he could say that for her. Even now she was turning back to him, a smile on her lovely lips.

No, he would not tell her. Not now. Not today.

And yet . . .

Then he had an idea.

"Thank you," she said, reaching up to kiss his cheek. "I'm glad I met you. I'm glad you're here."

Her great-uncle smiled and squeezed her hand. "I'm glad *you're* here! I hope you will come to visit me. We could play again." He gestured toward the chessboard.

"I'd love to," she said, and she meant it. "Would you consider joining us in the dining room for Thanksgiving?"

His bright smile faded, and he shook his head. "Thank you, but no. I—I'd really rather not. I'm sure Raymond will be bringing me some turkey here."

"In that case, may I join you?" she asked. "Catherine said we're having the big meal at about three in the afternoon. I'll eat a little there, and then I could join you here later. Would that be all right?"

She saw the look of pleasure on his face, and she was pleased, too. She preferred this man's company to John and his wife any day of the week.

"That would be delightful," he said, his eyes gleaming.

"It's a date, then," she replied. "I'll tell Mr. Wheatley."

With that, she turned and headed for the door. His voice stopped her.

"One moment, Holly."

She stopped in the doorway, watching as the old man went over to the table and picked up the scrapbook they'd just been perusing. He brought it over and handed it to her.

"Why don't you borrow this for a while?" he said. "I have a feeling you may want to look through it again."

She smiled. "Thank you. You know, it's funny: I was just thinking of asking you for it. I *do* want to read it again. I guess it's—well, it's really all that's left of them. I mean—"

He nodded, holding up a hand. "I understand. Yes, look through it again. Look—carefully."

She stared at him a moment, and she almost opened her mouth to speak. It was the way he'd said it, with that little pause before the final word. But then he was smiling again and holding the door open for her. So she smiled, too, and walked away down the hall, the big scrapbook under her arm. The door clicked shut behind her.

He shut the door and leaned back against it, closing his eyes and breathing deeply. Then he expelled the breath in a long sigh of relief.

She had taken the scrapbook.

What's more, she had promised to look through it again. She even seemed interested in doing so. She was a very intelligent young woman. Very perceptive.

Very observant.

Perhaps, he thought, I won't have to tell her my suspicion. Perhaps *she'll* tell *me*. Perhaps she will see the connection, too. If it *is* there, if I'm not simply imagining it. If I am not going mad.

He continued to lean against the door, weak from the exertion of talking more than he had talked in years. He breathed slowly in and out, waiting for his strength to return and his heartbeat to slow to normal, thinking:

Your move, Holly Randall.

She sat at the little table in the corner of her room later that night, just before she went to bed. She had placed the scrapbook on the table, and now she was gazing down at the paisley print cloth-bound cover. She ran her hand over the smooth material, remembering the tea and the chess game and the long conversation with her great-uncle Ichabod.

Here it is, she thought. Between these covers is a terrible history. The unofficial recording of the incident that shaped my life, that made me who I am. My mother's legacy.

Her life: Indio. The constant, merciless heat of the Coachella Valley. Ben and Mary Smith. Public schools with the children of date pickers. The university in San Diego with a crowd of future yuppies, Gregory Sandford III and all his condescending friends. A cramped, shared apartment in Palm Springs. Explorers Travel Agency, with its attendant daily phone arguments with airlines and hotels and car rental services. Endless dreary paperwork, surrounded on all sides by glorious Ektachrome posters of Hawaii and Australia and the Swiss Alps. And the Greek islands, always the Greek islands, shimmering in the Aegean on the wall beside her desk.

Then she lifted her gaze from the table and looked slowly, appreciatively around the bedroom. This was her room now, for as long as she wanted it. This house, Randall House, would soon belong to her. This was her father's legacy.

"You're Holly Randall now."

She smiled, thinking, Perhaps it all evens out in the long run.

With this, Holly pushed the scrapbook away from her and stood up from the table. She would look at it some other time, later. When she was ready. Now it was time for bed.

Her last thought before she slept that night was of the little black and white chessmen being moved so carefully, so methodically around the exquisite marble board.

CHAPTER SEVEN

The Watchers

The following three weeks were busy ones for Holly. First came Thanksgiving, that pleasant double celebration she gracefully managed to divide between her relatives in the dining room and her kinder, gentler relative upstairs. She and Ichabod played two games of chess that day. He won both, but she was learning a great deal about the game simply by watching him.

The cocktail party at Melissa MacGraw's home a week later was a resounding success, as far as Holly was concerned. Missy introduced Holly and John and his wife to her family and friends, who were all very nice people. They were presumably aware of the scandal that had tainted the Randall family, but they gave no outward sign of their awareness. Missy's twin brother, Matthew, was an artist specializing in portraiture. He asked Holly if he could paint her, and she agreed.

She spent three days sitting for Matthew Mac-Graw, and she became friendly with him and his wife, Laura. They took her to Vermont one weekend and taught her how to ski. She and Missy and Laura went shopping in New York a few times. In the second week of December there was another party at someone's house, and Holly met several more of her wealthy neighbors. Everyone seemed to like her.

She rarely went into the village. The local townspeople had made their feelings for her—or, at least, her family—all too clear, and she avoided them as much as possible. The lone exception to this was the police chief, Pete Helmer, whom she occasionally encountered on Main Street as he made his daily rounds. She always spoke cordially to him, and he always gave her the impression that he was glad to see her.

Mildred Jessel frequently saw Holly with Kevin, riding or walking or going off together in a car. This pleased her, I think, though she was careful to keep her feelings to herself. Besides, she had other things to keep her busy. There was the house to run, and the upcoming Christmas party, and there was her husband. Mr. Jessel was up and about again, but he still had a persistent cough that worried her. He did not go back to work in the garage, and Mrs. Jessel insisted that he stay close to home. Everyone could see that he did not look well.

When she was roaming around the estate, which

she did almost every day, Holly would sometimes be joined by the German shepherd, Tonto, and his master. The three of them became a familiar sight in the distance, exploring the woods and the cove and the wide lawns in companionable silence. She and the boy, Toby, were occasionally seen riding horses together, with Tonto loping along beside them.

John Randall and his wife were always careful to be friendly with Holly, and she usually joined them after dinner for card games in the library, or in the music room, where they would all watch television. But at least twice a week she would spend the later evening hours upstairs with her great-uncle, perfecting her chess game.

Mrs. Randall was very busy all through those first weeks of December, arranging for the party on Christmas Eve. She and the Greenwich caterer planned an elaborate menu for an estimated one hundred fifty people, most of whom had already written or phoned to accept their invitations. A local decorator was contracted to arrive on the day of the event to quite literally deck the halls. An enormous tree was ordered for the Great Hall, and there would be a supplementary staff of twenty to help the permanent staff with the party: waiters, bartenders, kitchen help, and parking attendants.

It occurred to me in that time that we, all of us, were watching Holly for one reason or another. John Randall and his wife, certainly. Kevin Jessel, in hopeful anticipation of romance. Ichabod Morris, who saw everything from his windows. The boy, Toby Carter, who always seemed to be around somewhere. The cop, Pete Helmer, who tended to stare at her whenever she ventured into town. Even Dora Jessel, in her rare appearances, though after the meeting in the cemetery she remained a respectful distance from Holly.

So the time passed. It was a particularly rough winter that year: the weather grew sharply colder as the new year approached, with more snow than had been recorded in the area for a long time. Later that season, in February, after the scandal had begun to die down, New York City and the surrounding area would twice be brought to a standstill by blizzards. But in December, as everything around her slowly froze, Holly seemed to be slowly melting, relaxing into her new lifestyle and her new role as mistress of Randall.

And then, almost before we knew it, December 20 arrived. It began like many other days that season, full of the promise of the impending holiday, but it didn't remain that way. Looking back from this comfortable distance in time, I'd say it was the beginning of the end.

That snowy twentieth of December, the day of the next death.

Holly entered Saks Fifth Avenue that day with a sense of purpose bordering on urgency. She knew the place would be mobbed, which it was, and she was determined to make all her purchases and have them wrapped in a reasonable amount of time. The only way to do this, she knew, was to be organized.

She pulled the gift list she'd made from her purse

and studied it. John, Catherine, Ichabod, Missy, Matthew and Laura MacGraw, and Kevin and his family. The other servants were getting cash bonuses, which she knew they'd appreciate more than a token gift, and she'd already sent packages to Ben and Mary Smith in California. So, ten presents. Twelve, she amended: she had to get something for Toby and Tonto.

Kevin had dropped her off at the entrance on Forty-ninth Street, and he was now finding a nearby garage for the car. She was meeting him at the ground-floor information desk in thirty minutes, so she decided she'd use the half hour to find his gift. She'd already decided what she was getting everyone, so now it was just a matter of finding things.

She'd rarely been anywhere so crowded. Hundreds of people clogged every aisle in the big store. But that was part of the holiday experience, the trees and garlands, the thousands of twinkling lights adorning the store's many displays, and laughing crowds laden with bags and brightly wrapped boxes. It was beautiful, really.

She'd chosen Saks because it was the one place where she knew she would find everything under one roof. The crowds at Macy's, the other logical choice, would be worse than this, far worse, and she wanted to get back to Randall at a reasonable hour: she had a date for a chess game. Smiling at the friendly bedlam around her, she pushed off through the densely packed wall of bodies in search of Men's Accessories.

She found the appropriate counter and selected three pairs of Italian leather driving gloves. Kevin and his father could use them, of course, and Toby would get a pair as well, for riding. Kevin needed an extra gift, however: she looked at the ties on display, but she ended up buying a rather expensive aftershave lotion instead.

Now she would need a silver pipe and cigar lighter for John, a gold cigarette case and lighter for Catherine, silk scarves for Missy and Mrs. Jessel and Dora—she supposed she *had* to get something for Dora—and a household gift for the MacGraws. That left Tonto: if Saks had a Pet Accessories department, and it probably did, he'd get a big rawhide bone. If not . . . well, she'd get the bone somewhere else.

Her gifts would be fairly impersonal, she knew, but she didn't really know any of these people very well. The only gift that would have any personal meaning was the one she was buying for Ichabod. She was getting him a new scrapbook, one she hoped he'd fill with memories of her.

She was so caught up in her planning that she almost forgot to make her way to the information desk. When she remembered, she hurried off in search of it.

Kevin was there, waiting patiently, doing his manly best to ignore the throngs of mostly female customers who milled about him and buffeted him, laughing and pointing. Holly smiled at the sight of him: he'd apparently been there for quite a while. He was a good sport, she realized for the umpteenth time in the five weeks she'd known him. When they were through here, she would take him somewhere quiet for dinner.

Kevin was watching Holly. He was trying to determine whether or not she was pleased with his impulsive surprise. It was difficult to tell, really, because he never seemed to know what she was thinking.

The little basement Italian restaurant he'd brought her to was on Fifty-second Street between Madison and Park, a couple of blocks from Saks. The decor was classic: exposed brick walls, plain wooden chairs, tables covered with red and white checked cloths, and candles in red glass orbs adorned with white plastic netting. The hot, fresh bread and the jug of house white wine had already arrived, and he had insisted on ordering for both of them. They would start with fried calamari, minestrone, and green salads, followed by the specialty of the house, tricolor tortellini carbonara.

He'd been here a few times before, but that had been years ago, shortly after he'd graduated. His love interest at the time was a woman—a rich, older woman—who lived nearby on Park Avenue. He was surprised this evening when the proprietress, Mrs. Amalfi, recognized him and called his name and came over to kiss him on the cheek. Holly had been surprised as well, he supposed, and she had laughed.

Now she smiled over the red candle at him. "This is charming. Thank you."

He smiled back, wondering what to say next. When he'd insisted on taking her to dinner, as opposed to the other way around, she'd been surprised, but she had acceded with grace. He was supposed to entertain her now, he knew, but he didn't feel at all certain of himself. She was sipping her wine, looking at him in polite anticipation.

"I guess I used to be a regular here," he suddenly heard himself say.

She smiled. "Yalie raids on New York?"

"No, after that. After Yale."

Now something apparently occurred to her. "What was your major there?"

He blinked. It wasn't the conversational gambit he'd been expecting, but he found himself going along with it.

"I was a psychology major," he whispered. "I was thinking about becoming a psychiatrist."

He felt a sudden need to elaborate, to explain that extraordinary statement to her. He thought furiously, wondering where to begin. Her next words preempted him.

"I see," she said, looking directly into his eyes. "Your sister." It was a simple statement of fact, and it defied any argument.

He stared, feeling the embarrassment welling up inside him. Then, to his surprise, the embarrassment was replaced by another emotion, one he hadn't been expecting.

Pride.

"Yes," he said. "Dora. I wanted to—to see what I could do about her. She has a lot of problems. She's depressive, certainly, and possibly delusional. She's always been different, ever since we were kids. She was the school weirdo: I learned how to fight at a very early age, defending her from the cruelty of the other kids. But when she was seventeen—well, something happened. She's spent a lot of her adult life in clinics. Hospitals."

"What happened to her?" Holly asked.

Kevin shrugged. "A boy named Leonard Ross. He was an oddball, too, but my parents were delighted when he asked Dora to the senior prom. It was the only date she ever had in her life. She looked so beautiful in her white dress. But a few weeks later—well . . ." He trailed off, embarrassed, unsure how to proceed with the story.

There was apparently no need. Holly nodded her head in understanding. "Oh." Then she appeared to think of something, and she leaned forward. "Was there an abortion? Or did the baby die?"

That surprised him. "No. Why do you ask?"

She shook her head and looked away. "I don't know, I was just thinking—the cemetery. . . ."

"The child was adopted. Miss Alicia and your uncle John helped my mother find an agency in New Haven. But that's when Dora's real problems began. She—she tried to commit suicide. More than once. She ended up in the first of several psychiatric facilities. The Randalls paid for everything. Anyway, I guess that's why I was interested in psychology. I wanted to be able to help her."

Holly was smiling at him again. "That's very nice

of you, but it doesn't explain why you were a regular here, at this restaurant."

He stared at her a moment. Then they both laughed. She had gracefully changed the subject, and he was grateful for that. Too grateful, he later reasoned.

"No," he admitted, "it doesn't. I used to come here because I lived right around the corner. In an apartment I didn't pay for."

He stopped, feeling the heat rising to his face. Why on earth did I say that? he wondered.

If Holly was shocked, she didn't show it. Her expression didn't change. She didn't even blink. "Oh."

Then he told her. Everything. The odd jobs he'd worked at, driving cabs and waiting tables and bartending. And the rest of it, the thing he'd never said to anyone, never admitted to anyone. All about the women—older, rich women—who occasionally sponsored him.

He realized as he spoke that this could well be the last time he would have dinner with Holly Randall. For all he knew, it was the last time she would ever speak to him. Oh, well, he thought, so be it. She'd been friendly with him ever since she arrived. She had never treated him like a servant. And he had repaid her kindness by making his usual plans, the plans he automatically made with rich women. The game, as he always thought of it. Well, no more. Not with this woman.

When he was finished with his litany, with the recitation of temporary jobs and temporary liaisons that had been his life for the last six years, Holly Randall surprised him again. She smiled and nodded.

The main course arrived at that point, so they had to wait several minutes before continuing the conversation. Grated cheese and pepper mills. When the waiter was gone, he forced himself to look at her. Into her eyes.

She was smiling and nodding again.

"I see," she said at last.

Kevin stared at her. "You don't—disapprove?"

Holly shrugged. "It's not for me to approve or disapprove of anyone. I guess I did something similar, in college. That's when I learned about disapproval. There was this group of students there—you know, the glamorous ones, with money and cars and rich parents. I wanted very much to belong to that group, so I started dating one of them. Gregory Sandford the Third, if you please! I wasn't in love with him, not really. But going out with him almost got me accepted."

"Almost?"

She shrugged again. "His family didn't approve of me. His friends didn't approve of me. Hell, *he* didn't approve of me, truth be told. They all made it perfectly clear that I wasn't one of them, that I would *never* be one of them. Greg dumped me for a woman his mother approved of. Janice Holbein, of the Beverly Hills Holbeins. So don't expect me to pass judgment on you, Kevin. I've been on the receiving end of it, and I know how it feels. You've 'knocked around' since college, as Uncle John would say, and you had some rich girlfriends. Big deal."

Before he was aware of it, he'd reached out to cover her hand with his own. "Thank you." Then he quickly withdrew his hand, grinning. "So, have you told Gregory Whoever the Third about your recent change in status?"

She shook her head. "No. I couldn't tell him, even if I wanted to. He's dead. He and Janice Holbein were in a car accident two weeks before they were supposed to be married. He was killed instantly, and she's in a wheelchair for life." She stared down at the table, apparently remembering. "I guess there's a moral in that story, somewhere." She was silent for a moment. Then she looked up at him again and smiled. "So, what happened with the psychiatry idea?"

He wasn't expecting the abrupt change in subject back to him. He looked away from her, at the twinkling Christmas tree in the corner of the restaurant, trying to form an answer.

"It fell by the wayside," he finally whispered.

"Ah," she said, reaching for her wineglass. "And what are your new plans?"

He was still staring at the tree. "I don't have any plans, really. But I think it's time I did. The Big Three-oh is looming before me."

"Yes," she said.

Now it was his turn to ask. "What about you, Holly? Do you have plans?"

She smiled. After a moment she said, "Hell, at this point I'm still getting used to being Holly Randall. But I know what you're asking. I majored in English, but I don't think I'm a writer or anything like that. My other favorite subject was chemistry, if you can believe that. I had no talent for it, though. I didn't exactly blow up the science building, but I'm no Madame Curie, either. After I graduated, I didn't pursue either subject as a possible profession. Until a few weeks ago, I worked in a travel agency. That's the best plan I have, I suppose: to travel. See the world. All of it. Especially the Greek islands."

He nodded. "I understand they're beautiful."

"Yes," she said. "I'm certain they are."

He held up his wineglass. "To Greece."

She laughed as they toasted. "To Greece."

After dinner they had tortoni and cappuccino, and Mrs. Amalfi sent over two tiny glasses of anisette. He paid for the meal, thanked the proprietress, and led Holly out into the snowy evening. They drove back to Randall in a comfortable, almost unbroken silence.

It was, he would later decide, the nicest evening he'd spent in a long time.

Holly came into the Great Hall, followed by Kevin with the shopping bags. She'd told him that she could manage them alone from the car to her room, but he had been insistent. As she approached the stairs, she looked up to see Catherine Randall coming down them.

"Hello, you two," Catherine said, smiling as she descended. "How was New York?"

"Crowded," Holly said as the two women met at the bottom of the staircase. "But we managed to get everything done. We also had dinner, so I won't be joining you this evening. I have a date."

"Oh?" Catherine looked speculatively at Kevin.

Holly laughed. "With Ichabod."

She ran lightly up the stairs and down the hall to her room. Kevin placed the bags just inside the bedroom door and turned to leave.

"Thank you," she said. "For everything."

He stood in the doorway a moment, smiling at her. Then, with a little wave of his hand, he was gone.

She smiled to herself as she got out of her heavy outdoor clothes and quickly slipped into jeans and a blouse. She'd liked Kevin already, before tonight, but his frank confessions over dinner made her like him even more. She glanced at the beaming young woman in the vanity mirror. Remembering her own confession about Greg Sandford, she laughed aloud. We're bonding, she thought. We're beginning to talk about personal things, things that matter. . . .

She rummaged in the shopping bags until she found the big, flat, square package in its bright red paper and velvet bow. She'd ended up getting two gifts for Ichabod, and she'd give him the sweater on Christmas Day. But tonight he would receive an early present. She was suddenly in the mood to give someone a gift. She picked up the brightly wrapped scrapbook and left the bedroom.

When she came back across the gallery toward the guest wing, Holly noticed that her aunt Catherine was still standing in the Great Hall near the bottom of the stairs. She waved to her as she went off toward her great-uncle's room. Catherine smiled and waved, too.

She was watching Holly. She stared silently up at the young woman as she crossed the gallery and disappeared down the hall of the guest wing, thinking, Another date with Ichabod. Another chess game.

She didn't like this. She didn't like it at all.

She stood at the bottom of the stairs for several minutes, gazing upward, deep in thought. Then she went to join her husband in the dining room.

They had finished with the salad and were on the main course before she mentioned it. She wasn't really hungry tonight, she realized, merely pushing the filet mignon around on her plate. John, on the other hand, was shoveling it in like a condemned prisoner. She reached for her wineglass and sipped before she spoke.

"You may have noticed," she drawled, "that we are only two at dinner tonight."

He didn't so much as lower his fork. "Hmmm."

She took the fork from his hand and set it down on his plate. "She's upstairs. With *him*. Playing chess again."

"So?" Clearly annoyed, he retrieved the fork and attacked his mashed potatoes.

"I don't like it," she said. "She's spending entirely too much time up there. I keep wondering if perhaps he might. . . ." She deliberately trailed off, hoping her husband would pick up his cue.

He did. He actually stopped eating. "He might—what?"

She rolled her eyes. "He might *know* something. About us, darling. The plan." God, she thought, sometimes his expulsion from Yale simply announces itself to the world. "What do you suppose they talk about up there?"

He waved his hand in a dismissive gesture before picking up his wineglass and draining it. Then he went immediately back to the steak.

"Chess, I suppose," he said, carving another bite. "What could he possibly know, locked away in that room up there? He's a crazy old man. Don't be paranoid, Cathy."

"Oh, now I'm paranoid!" She winced as she watched him eat. The little migraine she'd been noticing ever since Holly had come home from New York was spreading from her temples to the back of her neck. She stood up abruptly, throwing down her napkin.

"Where are you going?" he mumbled through his food.

"To bed. I'm getting a splitting headache. I can't wait for all of this to be over." She went to the door and opened it. Before she left him there, she turned around for a parting shot. "As you yourself just observed, he's an old man. A *very* old man. And sometimes, very old people have been known to have—accidents."

He was in the act of reaching for the silver bell on the table to ring for more wine. Her words actually arrested him for a moment. He turned in his seat to stare at her. "What are you saying?"

She shrugged, smiling. "Only that it's sometimes

better to be safe than sorry. I can think of a good reason. A hundred and fifty million good reasons, in fact." Then, almost as an afterthought, she threw the last line over her shoulder as she made her exit. "Perhaps you should get in touch with your friend."

He blinked at her. Then he picked up the silver bell and rang it.

Yes, she thought as she left the room and headed for the stairs. Have some more wine, darling. Chew on *that* with your dinner.

When she reached the gallery at the top of the stairs she paused, gazing over at the entrance to the guest wing. Then, with a little sigh of impatience, she went down the hall to her bedroom.

They didn't finish the game.

Holly sat at the table across from her great-uncle, studying him, her light mood slowly dissipating. He'd been very quiet, obviously distracted, ever since she'd presented him with the gift.

He'd torn away the paper, smiling at her in almost childlike anticipation, and she'd wondered when he'd last received a present from anyone. When he'd seen what it was, however, his smile had faded. He'd thanked her gracefully enough, even kissed her cheek, before laying the new scrapbook aside on the table and waving her into her seat.

She was aware within twenty minutes that his mind was not on the game. She was winning, for one thing, which had not happened since that first game in November, when he had deliberately allowed her to win. But tonight he wasn't concentrating at all. He barely glanced at the board: his gaze kept shifting from the new scrapbook to her face and back again.

It was Holly who stopped it. She watched quietly for several moments while the old man leaned forward, his queen dangling aimlessly from his fingers over the board. Then she reached out, gently removed the piece from his hand, and put it down on the table. He blinked, and a long sigh escaped his lips.

"I'm sorry . . ." he began.

"It's all right." Holly rose to her feet. "I guess it's late, and you seem to be tired. We can finish the game tomorrow. Good night."

She was leaning forward to kiss him when he surprised her by fairly jumping up from his chair.

"Don't go," he said quickly. "Please. I—I want to talk to you."

He reached out to grasp her hand, and then he blushed. The dark stain of the birthmark on the right side of his face turned suddenly darker, uglier. As if he were aware of this, he turned abruptly away from her. After a moment, he wandered over to the window. Only then, when he had put distance between them, did he turn around to face her again.

"Well, if you're sure . . ." Holly murmured.

He nodded. "Sit down, Holly."

She felt the first prickle of apprehension as she sank slowly back into her chair.

Ichabod was watching Holly, trying to form phrases in his mind.

Since their first meeting in November, when he had lent her the scrapbook of her parents, they had not discussed the subject again. She apparently had not had a chance to give it further thought, he figured. Her gift tonight, the new scrapbook, was a perfect opportunity to reintroduce the subject that was always foremost in his mind. But now that the opportunity was here, he didn't know what to do with it. He wasn't at all certain how to proceed.

Proceed with caution, he thought, and he actually smiled at her. She smiled back, but he could tell that she was waiting for him to say something.

He was disconcerted by her gaze. He turned around again to stare out the window at the dark lawn and the drive, which were visible in the light from the downstairs windows. The snow was falling again, he noticed, as it had done intermittently for most of the day. He studied the gentle snowfall as he finally began to speak.

"You know, I can see everything from these windows. I've been observing the world from here since—well, since just before you were born. Ever since I retired from chess. From the world. I've seen the seasons come and go, and people as well. I've seen Kevin Jessel and his sister grow from small children to adults. I've seen my sister and her husband and their elder son buried. And Alicia, buried. And, more recently, the return of the prodigal son, with his wife. And now"—he turned from the window—"you. The only happy addition in years."

211

He smiled at her then, and he was glad to see her smile back.

"I loved my sister Emily," he continued, "more than anything in the world. More than chess, certainly. I never married, although I wanted to, once. I came close to asking the woman. But I knew no woman would ever—" He broke off here, raising his hand to his scarred face. "So, Emily was my world. Emily and her family. And then that awful thing happened, and nothing was ever right again. Emily died. And one day I realized that I just didn't want to leave this room anymore."

Holly was still in her chair, watching him. He went over to stand before her.

"My dear, I told you on the day I first met you that when one has reached my age, one has learned not to dissemble. And yet, that is exactly what I have been doing with you. Well, I'm not going to do that anymore."

She stood up. Slowly, with great gentleness, she raised her hand and placed it lightly on the scarred side of his face.

"It's all right, Ichabod," she whispered. "Whatever it is. Tell me."

He looked at her, into her eyes, thinking, Yes. She can take it. She is a remarkably intelligent young woman. More than intelligent: capable. He took a deep breath.

Then he told her.

Holly sat at the little table in her room, staring down. The paisley-covered scrapbook was opened before her, as it had been for the last half hour. She leaned down, studying the grainy images in the photographs. Then, for the fourth or fifth time in that half hour, she turned back to the first page and started again. The headlines, the reportage, the editorials. But, above all, the photographs.

Before she had fairly run from his room thirty minutes ago, Ichabod had picked up a magnifying glass from his desk and handed it to her. It was not a regular, round contrivance with a handle, but a rectangular sheet of clear plastic that served to magnify entire sections of text. She slid the implement over the faded pictures once again.

She couldn't breathe. Her heart was pounding in her chest, and there was a pressure, an odd roaring in her temples. She dropped the magnifier and raised her hands to her forehead, massaging, but the throbbing would not go away. If anything, it seemed to be increasing.

She closed her eyes, breathing deeply. Okay, she thought. I'm okay. She repeated the words silently to herself, over and over, willing herself to believe them. After several moments, the pounding in her head and her heart slowly faded, returned to normal.

Normal, she thought.

Then, alone in her magnificent bedroom, Holly began to laugh. She slammed the scrapbook shut and pushed it away from her, stood up from the table, and went into her bathroom. She swallowed two aspirin tablets with a glass of water, then leaned down and splashed cool water on her face. Straightening up, she regarded her reflection in the

213

bathroom mirror. She examined every detail of her face, trying to find the connection, but the answer eluded her.

Then, with a rueful smile and a shrug of her shoulders, she turned away from the mirror and left her room. She wandered down the hallway and around the gallery to the guest wing. When she arrived before Ichabod's door, she raised her hand and knocked lightly.

There was no reply.

"Ichabod," she whispered through the door.

Still no reply. He's gone to bed, she reasoned, and she went reluctantly back to the gallery and down the stairs to the Great Hall.

The library was empty, as were the living room and music room. She even checked the kitchen and the office, but there was no one, anywhere. The staff were upstairs on the third floor, presumably asleep at this hour, and Mrs. Jessel had gone home to the gatehouse for the night.

As for John and his wife, well, who knew? Upstairs in their rooms, or out somewhere. They occasionally went out for the evening. New York City wasn't far, and there were clubs in Greenwich. There was even that charming little movie theater on Main Street in Randall.

Where *is* everybody? she wondered.

She briefly considered calling the gatehouse, asking for Kevin. But he, too, would probably be asleep. She would only be waking up the entire family. Mrs. Jessel and her husband, who was unwell, and

214

the sister, Dora. No, she couldn't call Kevin, much as she wished she could.

Mary Smith. She thought of this, even going so far as to glance at her watch. It was three hours earlier in Indio. Mary and Ben would be in the living room, watching television. She could call them, hear Mary's voice. The voice of the only woman she would ever accept as her mother.

No. She could not call Indio. Ben and Mary loved her, she knew that. But they were not a part of this. She would not allow herself to involve them in it.

She was alone.

Then, as she had done too often all her life, Holly accepted it. She was alone here, on the ground floor of Randall House, and there was nothing she could do about it. Not tonight, anyway.

Tomorrow . . .

She stood uncertainly at the bottom of the stairs, gazing distractedly up at the huge green tree beside it. The tree would be decorated sometime soon, she knew, in preparation for the party. Her birthday party. Four nights from now, on Christmas Eve, her birthday, this hall would be ablaze with light and filled with people.

But now, tonight, she was alone.

Yet not alone. There was no one here with her, but she was aware of them, all of them. The images from her recurring dream came back to her, the dream she'd been having ever since she'd arrived here five weeks ago. She was naked in the town square, and they were watching her. And here, now, alone in the Great Hall, she could feel the eyes.

Then, as if drawn to it, as if it were inevitable, she went slowly back upstairs to her bedroom, aware with every step of the watchers. That constant, invisible audience with their silent gaze.

When she was safely back in her room, she locked her door. Then she undressed, picked up the scrapbook from the table, and got into bed.

Tomorrow, she thought, opening the scrapbook. Tomorrow I must find a phone number. I must call and make an appointment for as soon as possible.

As soon as possible . . .

She sat up in the bed long into the night, reading slowly through the scrapbook again and again, burning the words and the images into her mind.

Alec Buono, actually Alessandro Buonaventura, sometimes known as Ed, was watching Holly. From his position in the drive at the edge of the trees near the stable, he could just see her head through the partially opened curtains of the extreme right, second-floor bedroom. He'd been watching her for a while, and he could see her better now that the snow had finally stopped falling. He adjusted his powerful binoculars. She was sitting up in bed, reading.

He wondered what she was reading. It was warm in her room, in her bed. Shaking snow from his coat, he thought about being there with her. If I were there with her, he thought, smiling to himself in the darkness, she sure as hell wouldn't need that book, whatever it is. . . .

Oh, well, to work. He lowered the glasses until

they were hanging comfortably from the strap around his neck and crept silently down the drive past the stable, to the garage. With a quick glance over at the dark gatehouse, he slipped into the garage through the little side door. He closed the door carefully behind him before pulling the flashlight from his coat pocket and switching it on.

He made his way slowly down the row of cars to the blue BMW. This was the car John Randall had told him about, the one she drove. He shone the light up and down the length of the back wall of the building until he saw the shelves. Three wooden shelves, about two feet in length, attached to the wall, one above another. Yes, just as Randall had described them. He went over to the wall and felt along the right side of the middle shelf until he found the little latch. The entire shelf unit swung outward, revealing the row of keys hanging on pegs. The third one from the left was labeled BMW.

He unlocked the driver's door of the car, reached in toward the dashboard, and popped the hood. There was a loud click when he did this, and he froze for a moment, holding his breath. When he was certain there was no sound from outside, he went around to the front of the car.

He'd never seen the engine of a BMW before, and he was relieved to see that it was similar to most other engines. He followed the brake line with the beam of the flashlight, nodding to himself. Yes, a slow drainage. She'll lose the brakes somewhere on the highway. He'd used this method twice before, both times successfully. One of them had caused quite a pileup on the Brooklyn-Queens Expressway. The final body count was seven, he recalled, but one of the bodies had been his mark, a croupier from Atlantic City who'd been pocketing profits.

He wondered what the body count would be this time. It didn't make a bit of difference to him, as long as one of them was Holly Randall.

He closed the hood, returned the key to its peg, and shut the concealed cabinet behind the shelves. In seconds he was out the door and moving quietly through the trees to the outer wall of the estate, fifty yards behind the garage and stable. He leaped up and pulled himself over the high stone wall, dropping into the adjacent property, the abandoned farm, just a few yards from the dirt lane where his car was parked.

Mission accomplished. Well, dry run accomplished, he amended as he walked down the snow-covered lane toward his car. This was his last visit before the actual mission. Now that he'd decided on the means, there was no need for any more weekly reconnaissance visits. It was five days to Christmas. A week after the new year, John Randall and his wife were off to Europe. One week after that, he, Alec, would return.

Sometime soon after *that*, he knew, Holly Randall would get into that car, either as driver or passenger. The BMW was only used for her, John had assured him. If the chauffeur—or boyfriend, or whatever he was—was driving, well, so be it. The result would be the same.

But she had definitely looked warm and cozy in

that bed, he thought as he got into the red Infiniti and started the engine. Shrugging off the thought, he turned the car around in the lane and drove toward the main road. He was on the road, headed toward town, before he switched on the headlights.

It was nearly midnight. He passed no one on the road, and the village of Randall was definitely in bed for the night, the only lights coming from street lamps and the Christmas decorations that festooned various houses and the trees in the park in the central square. Even the little police station was bedecked with flashing red and green lights. The only person he saw in the town was a big blond man in a heavy overcoat leaning against one of the sedans in front of the station house, smoking a cigarette. The big man looked up and nodded to him as he drove by. He nodded back. Then the town disappeared behind him and he was turning onto the highway.

The Kismet Motel was about three miles down the highway toward Greenwich. He'd checked in and had dinner there before driving out to Randall House. He'd stay the night and meet John Randall at the appointed time, ten o'clock tomorrow morning, in the lane beside Randall House. He enjoyed staying at the Kismet. It was set far back from the highway in the Connecticut countryside, which was a hell of a lot more quiet than Flatbush Avenue, where he lived in a two-room rental above a very popular Hispanic nightclub. His ex had gotten the house, damn her. . . .

He drove into the motel's lot and parked in front

of his room, which was at the end of the long row farthest from the office and the bar-restaurant in the center of the strip. He paused on the little sidewalk in front of his room, looking toward the restaurant, debating. The lights were still on down there. Did he want a couple of beers before retiring?

He decided against it, remembering the grumpy bartender in the usually empty room where he'd eaten earlier. There were only two other cars parked along the row of rooms, on the other side of the office from him. A real jumping place, he thought. Besides, he was tired. He yawned as he pulled his room key from his coat pocket and went inside.

He was just stepping out of his pants three minutes later when he heard a soft knocking on his door. He froze for a moment, then reached automatically for the gun in the holster he'd placed on the night table.

"Yeah?" he barked.

"Phone message, sir. It came while you were out."

It was a low, muffled voice, Alec noticed. It could be a man or a woman. He pulled the gun from the holster.

"Message from who?" he called.

There was a slight pause. Then he heard, "Uh, J.R. Yeah, that's what it says, J.R."

Alec relaxed and put the gun down on the table. J.R., he thought. John Randall.

A message from John Randall. Perhaps there'd been a change in plans. Something urgent, something that had to be discussed now, tonight, before tomorrow's meeting. Perhaps another job, in addition to Holly Randall . . .

"Okay, just a sec," he said. He pulled up his pants and fastened them. Then he walked over to the door and opened it.

He had only a brief glimpse, an impression of a dark figure standing before him, holding something up above its head. Something that might have been a hammer. Then that something, whatever it was, smashed into his forehead, just above his eyes, sending him staggering backward into the room.

Amazingly, Alec didn't fall. There was a horrible pain where he had been struck, and he could feel the wetness cover his eyes and nose as the blood poured down. But he remained upright. Reflexively, he turned around and fumbled for the night table. His hand was inches from the gun that lay there when the second blow came, at the back of his head. He heard a dull cracking noise and realized that it was his skull smashing into his brain. He saw bright whiteness, and he had the sensation of falling forward across the bed. Then everything went black.

He wasn't alive to feel the third blow.

CHAPTER EIGHT

The Prisoner

Holly had been driving for almost two hours, but as she neared her destination she realized that she was reluctant to arrive. The realization surprised her, because for the preceding thirty-six hours she had thought about nothing else but learning the truth. And the truth was here, ahead of her, in the place where she was going. She was sure of it.

Yesterday morning, after a long, wakeful night of staring at the scrapbook, she had found the telephone number she wanted and placed the call. A friendly switchboard operator had rerouted the call to the appropriate office, where another friendly voice asked her to please hold for a few moments. There was barely a pause before the person she'd asked for—a woman, as it turned out—came on the line.

The woman, a Mrs. Jackson, was brisk and

businesslike, but Holly liked the sound of her voice. It took a few minutes of explaining before Holly could arrange the meeting she wanted. Mrs. Jackson must have been curious, Holly knew, but she politely refrained from asking any questions on the telephone. She had merely agreed to see her at two o'clock the following afternoon.

Holly checked her watch as she drove through the somewhat undistinguished-looking town. One-twenty. Plenty of time. She glanced again at the scribbled instructions the woman had given her. She took the appropriate road away from the town and began looking for the signs that would lead her the rest of the way. There had been no snow today, but the gray landscape around her was still covered with it, as were the naked trees lining the road.

At last she found the sign that led her to the gate, where she rummaged in her purse for identification. A uniformed officer in a kiosk checked a clip-boarded list and made a phone call that took several minutes. Then the gate swung open and she was waved into a large enclosed property, where further signs pointed the way to a fairly empty visitors' parking lot. She parked and got out of the car.

One forty-three. She had seventeen minutes. But, judging from the routine at the gatehouse, it could very well take her that long just to get inside. No time for second thoughts; she was here now, and that was that. Swallowing her feeling of dread, she squared her shoulders and moved.

What stood in the distance before her was a con-glomeration of aggressively nondescript gray buildings, all connected to a slightly larger gray building in the center. The long, three-story wings looked rather like dormitories, which, she supposed, was exactly what they were. She began walking toward the central place, where steps led up to gray double doors and more people in black and gray uniforms.

Inside the entrance, Holly was pleased to learn that Mrs. Jackson had left word that Ms. Randall was her guest, and that she need not be submitted to the usual ritual for visitors. A polite young woman checked something on a clipboard at the desk, made a brief phone call, and led Holly away down a long, industrially lit corridor to the right of the main entrance, through two locked doors, and into a reception area that might have been in any office building in America. Several secretaries at computer terminals glanced up at her with unconcealed curiosity as the woman led her past their desks to another door. This was a big, polished oak affair bearing a brass plaque in the center which read:

New York State Department
of Correctional Services
KINGSTON WOMEN'S
CORRECTIONAL FACILITY

NAOMI JACKSON
Superintendent

The young woman officer knocked on the door, and after a moment Holly heard a soft buzzing sound. The officer stood aside for Holly, who walked into a medium-sized, carpeted, wood-paneled room dominated by a large desk that faced the door. A pretty, rather heavyset, middle-aged African-American woman in a dark blue suit stood beside the desk, smiling at her. As the door behind Holly closed with the distinct click of an automatic lock, the woman came forward, hand extended.

"Ms. Randall," she said.

Holly shook her hand. "Mrs. Jackson. Thank you for seeing me on such short notice."

"Of course. I must admit I was curious to meet you. Please, sit down. We've just had lunch, and I was about to have coffee. Will you join me?"

"Thank you." Holly sat in one of the two padded chairs facing the desk while Mrs. Jackson went around to her chair, picked up her phone, and ordered coffee for two. There was a computer terminal off to the side of the desk, and a thick manila folder on the blotter. A small, artificial Christmas tree twinkled rather forlornly in a far corner, just below the inevitable framed color photographs of the current governor of New York and the president.

Mrs. Jackson leaned forward, resting her elbows on the folder. She seemed to be making a study of Holly, assessing her. Holly sat quite still in her chair, enduring the scrutiny. Finally, the other woman broke the silence.

"So, you're Connie Randall's daughter. I guess everyone knew she had a child, but I never expected to meet you. There's been a bit of a buzz around the place since you called yesterday. Some of the staff have been here a long time; they remember Connie, and they were as curious as I was."

Holly remembered the furtive glances of the secretaries outside, followed by the swift averting of eyes and industrious pecking at keyboards. "Yes, I understand. Mrs. Jackson, I've only recently been informed of my—my true parentage, so this is all rather new to me. May I ask, how long have you been superintendent here?"

"Twelve years next April. Connie was here for the first six years of my tenure. My predecessor probably knew more about her than I, but I'm afraid he's no longer with us, rest his soul. If you're simply interested in finding out general things about her, I think this will help." She picked up the thick folder and held it out.

Holly took the folder and opened it, glancing quickly through the contents. There were photocopies of official-looking documents, several sets of mug shots from the front and side, and what were apparently progress reports signed by various wardens and parole board members, and by Mrs. Jackson and a man named Charles Kendall. The predecessor, apparently. There was also another set of papers: a running medical history signed by a succession of doctors and nurses, including a flat, thin plastic bar to which was attached a complete set of dental X rays. She held these up to the light, studying them.

"It would help," Mrs. Jackson said, "if you told me exactly what it is you want to know."

A secretary knocked and was buzzed in. She

carried two cardboard cups of coffee, sugar and sweetener packets, and several containers of half-and-half, which she placed on the desk. The two women watched her in silence, waiting. She took a good look at Holly before scurrying out. The auto matic click sounded louder this time.

Holly placed the folder on her lap and picked up one of the cups. "I want to know what kind of woman she was, from someone who knew her better than my relatives at Randall House. I've read all the newspaper accounts, and so forth, but I—I don't have a feel for what she was *like*." She shrugged. "Does that make any sense?"

"Yes, it does," Mrs. Jackson said. "But are you sure you really want that information? Perhaps the past is better left—well, in the past. When you called, I assumed you would want her medical history—you know, in case you were thinking of getting married and having children, something like that. . . ."

Holly had never thought of that. "Is there anything medical that I should know?"

"Not at all. She was perfectly healthy. Very few illnesses over the years, no allergies, no disabilities or menstrual problems. She was quite normal—physically."

Holly leaned forward. "And, otherwise? Please, Mrs. Jackson, I want to know."

The superintendent leaned back in her chair, sipping her coffee. She regarded Holly for a long moment in silence. Then, apparently having made some decision, she put down the cup and folded her hands before her.

"She wasn't a nice woman, Ms. Randall. You know why she was here, of course. We don't have many women here who could be described as 'nice,' but she was worse than most. She was arrogant and vain, completely self-centered. She regarded the other women as little more than servants. She got in a lot of trouble. Fights. If you look through that folder, you'll find details. She broke a woman's arm once, and she assaulted another woman with a shiv—I beg your pardon, a homemade weapon she'd fashioned from a soda can, of all things. She stabbed that woman in her right eye, and the doctor was unable to save it. That cost her several more years here, when she might have been paroled or even released much earlier.

"Most of these things happened before I arrived, but I certainly heard about them. I myself once witnessed an incident in the mess—the dining hall. A fight, more like a rumble, that she started when she called one of the other inmates a name. Let's just say it's a name *I've* been called, too. I had to bring in state assistance, and there was a forty-eight-hour general lockdown, so you can imagine what the other women thought of her. She was put in solitary several times, for one reason or another. She was an angry, violent woman, and I was relieved to see the back of her."

Holly stared. "But you *did* see the back of her."

"Oh, yes. Eventually." Mrs. Jackson smiled grimly. "Her last three or four years here were—different.

She seemed to change a bit, for the better. She calmed down, I guess, and she volunteered for extra work. She even made a couple of friends, one in particular. It took her some fifteen years, but she actually began to adjust to the life."

Holly leaned forward again. "Extra work—what does that mean?"

"Oh, well, the women here have certain routines, certain duties. The kitchen and the laundry and the general cleaning are rotated, so everyone does a bit of everything. This is in addition to classes and voluntary counseling and various sports activities. Some of the more ambitious ones—the ones who are looking to get out early—can volunteer for certain duties. A couple of the secretaries you passed on your way in here are actually inmates. Or they can help the counselors or the chaplain or the medical staff. Like that."

Now Holly was watching the woman closely. At last, she felt, we're getting somewhere. "And what—what did my mother volunteer for?"

Mrs. Jackson smiled at her. "During her last couple of years here, Connie worked in the infirmary. She helped Dr. Roth with the medical records."

Holly opened the folder on her lap and picked up the dental X rays. "Medical records like this?"

"Exactly. She was his file clerk."

"I don't understand it," Lena said to the desk clerk as she came into the motel's front office. "That's the second day in a row. What's going on in Fourteen, anyway?"

"Don't bring that thing in here," the desk clerk, Ron, told her. He pointed at her cleaning cart. "Mr. Jaffrey will have a cow if he sees that in the office!"

Lena rolled her eyes as she pushed the cart back outside. "Yeah, right. But what's with Fourteen? The DO NOT DISTURB sign has been hanging on the door for two days now. I couldn't go in yesterday, and I can't go in today, either. And something smells kind of funny down at that end. I want to clean the room."

Ron shrugged. "I guess Mr."—he glanced down at the registry—"Edwards doesn't want to be disturbed. Maybe he's sleeping one off. Maybe he's got a woman in there. Who knows?"

"I just want to do the room!" Lena insisted.

"What room?" asked a voice behind her.

The two turned to see that the owner of the Kismet, Mr. Jaffrey, had joined them.

"Fourteen, sir," Lena said. "The guy in there hasn't come out for two days."

Mr. Jaffrey looked over at Ron. "Did he pay for a second night?"

"Uh, no, sir," Ron mumbled, blushing.

The owner frowned at him and turned back to the maid. "Go knock on the door, Lena."

"But, what if he's asleep or something?"

"Then wake him up. Send him down here to me. And clean the room."

"Yes, sir."

Pushing the cleaning cart before her, she trudged off down the walk. The funny smell became more pronounced as she neared Fourteen. She stopped the cart, planted herself before the door, and rapped on it.

"Housekeeping," she called.

She waited, but there was no response. She knocked and called again, louder this time. Nothing. Finally, in exasperation, she pulled the key ring from her pocket, unlocked the door, and went inside.

The room was pitch dark. All the curtains were drawn, and the smell was now much stronger, overwhelming. Wrinkling her nose in distaste, Lena reached over and switched on the light.

Her scream brought the others running.

The two women in the prison's administrative office sipped their coffee in silence. After a while, Holly looked up at the superintendent.

"Tell me about her friends," she said. "You said my mother made some friends in her final years here, one in particular. Who was that?"

Mrs. Jackson gazed off at the Christmas tree, apparently remembering. "Jane Dee. A sad case if there ever was one—and there have been plenty here. But Jane's history was particularly tragic. She'd been found on a church doorstep in Brooklyn, and some imaginative type called her Jane Doe, which was later altered slightly. She was brought up in a series of orphanages and foster homes. Then came the usual: drugs, shoplifting, juvey halls. More drugs. Arrests for prostitution. Several abortions, I think. A boyfriend for a while, an ex-con who got her to steal for him. A couple of years in prison, during which the boyfriend disappeared. And on and on.

"She came here for armed robbery, shortly after I took over. Very quiet, cried a lot. But later she shared a cell with Connie, who took her under her wing. And Jane changed overnight: I swear, that woman was absolutely devoted to your mother. Connie got her into rehab, even taught her to read—"

"Excuse me," Holly said. "This woman, Jane—what did she look like?"

Mrs. Jackson shrugged. "Tall, blond, blue-eyed. Nordic—I think that's the word. Very pretty."

"In other words," Holly murmured, "she looked a lot like my mother."

"Why, yes, come to think of it, I guess she did. Anyway, she and Connie were inseparable, and I think she had a lot to do with Connie's attitude improvement."

"I'd like to meet her," Holly said. "Is she still here?"

Mrs. Jackson blinked. "Oh, no. She was released a few years ago, and I'm glad to say she hasn't been back. Well, not *here*, at any rate."

Holly was watching the woman again. "When was she released?"

"I don't know, about five years ago. About a year after your mother left, I'd say."

"Do you know if they ever saw each other again?"

Mrs. Jackson shook her head. "I'm sorry, I don't. We don't keep tabs on them once they're—wait a minute! April Fools' Day, that was the day your mother . . ." She trailed off, clearly embarrassed.

"Yes," Holly said. "That's when she committed suicide. Five years ago."

"Yes." Mrs. Jackson leaned forward, nodding. "I remember now. Jane was released just a few days before that. I remember her leaving, and then, just a few days later, I saw the news about Connie. Boy, the irony! Poor Jane Dee, left all alone again." She settled back in her chair, shaking her head. "I wonder where Jane is now. . . ."

Holly wasn't wondering about any such thing. She was thinking of the newspaper photographs in Ichabod's scrapbook. The seaside bungalow, charred and smoking. The body on the stretcher, covered with a sheet, burned beyond recognition. So badly burned that it had to be identified from—

She looked down at the folder in her lap.

—dental records. . . .

It took a few moments, but at last she became aware that Mrs. Jackson was speaking again. The woman's lips were moving, at any rate, but the sound was not registering. Holly blinked. "I beg your pardon, what did you say?"

Mrs. Jackson was smiling again. "I said, I'm glad I was able to tell you something positive about your mother. Teaching Jane how to read. That was Connie's one big passion, you know, reading. She was always buried in a book. She said her passion came from her mother, who was reading in the hospital when she was pregnant. The day she gave birth she was reading *Lady Chatterley's Lover*, so she named the child Constance, after the heroine in the book. Well, Connie took after her mother, all right. She read everything: fiction, nonfiction, new, old, whatever. But she always went back to her favorite books. . . ."

"What were her favorite books?" Holly heard herself ask. She didn't care, but she had to say something. She was trying mightily to focus on the conversation.

Mrs. Jackson chuckled. "Jacqueline Susann, I'm afraid." Then she thought of something else, and her smile faded. "And *Wuthering Heights.* Dear Lord, she must have read *Wuthering Heights* about a hundred times!"

Holly was silent for a while, adding this information to everything else she'd learned in the last few minutes. Then she stood up and placed the folder on the desk.

"Well, thank you, Mrs. Jackson," she said. "I'm grateful to you for being so helpful. And I'm glad to learn that my—my mother had some positive qualities. I'm glad she had at least one friend, considering that her family and the Randalls would have nothing to do with her. . . ."

Mrs. Jackson, who had risen and come around the desk to say good-bye, inadvertently delivered a final surprise. Her eyes widened in obvious confusion, even as she was reaching out to shake Holly's hand.

"Nothing to do with her?" she asked, clearly confused. "What on earth makes you say that?"

* * *

Pete Helmer seemed to fall in love about once every three days, ever since the divorce. Today he was in love with the police station's new receptionist, Debbie Dobson.

She was a thirtyish redhead, tall, pretty, divorced, no kids. She was also an outrageous flirt. In the two weeks she'd been here, since Mrs. Proctor had quit to take care of her ailing sister, Debbie had made the station house a much more exciting place to be. She was not as beautiful as Holly Randall, whom he still saw around the village occasionally, but she was more in his league, that was certain. And she was available: she'd made that very clear to him. She always smiled rather provocatively at him whenever the two of them were alone in the office together, as they were now.

He was therefore surprised when she answered the ringing phone, listened a moment, and turned to him wearing a distinct frown.

"Bad news," she said.

And it was. He grabbed the phone from her and listened to the shrill voice of Mr. Jaffrey, the owner of the Kismet Motel. Then he threw down the receiver, grabbed his coat, and headed for the door.

"Call the Two Stooges and get them over to the Kismet *now*," he shouted back to her as he ran to his car.

"Ten-four," she called after him.

Pete rolled his eyes and chuckled grimly to himself, thinking, *Ten-four*. Oh, well, she's new, he thought as he pulled out of the lot and raced off toward the highway. She'll get over that "ten-four" nonsense real fast.

He was amazed to see that his deputies, Hank and Buddy, were already there when he pulled into the Kismet lot. Mr. Jaffrey and a chubby young man stood near the official cars, tending to a young woman in a pink maid's uniform who sat on the ground between them, sobbing. Buddy was speaking into his handset, probably calling the hospital and the M.E.'s office in Greenwich, and Hank was keeping the other guests out of the way. The Two Stooges were improving.

The first thing Pete noticed as he approached Room Fourteen was the red Infiniti parked in front of it. He strode past it and into the room, thinking, Now, where have I seen that car before . . . ?

When he saw the stiff on the bed, he remembered.

Holly would never be able to remember saying good-bye to Mrs. Jackson, or being led back the way she'd come by the friendly woman officer, or making her way across the vast parking field to her car. She had obviously been able to find all the correct roads leading back to the highway on the other side of town again, but she didn't recall that, either. Her next clear memory was of crossing the state line back into Connecticut, some ninety minutes later.

"She was his file clerk."

She almost missed the turnoff to Randall, so deep was her concentration. The words and phrases from the interview jangled in her head as she drove toward town. As they had done all the way from Kingston.

"In other words, she looked a lot like my mother."

"Why, yes, come to think of it. . . ."

She heard sirens in the distance, from the highway behind her. But the sound didn't really register: she was listening to the voice of Mrs. Jackson.

"April Fools' Day . . . Jane was released just a few days before that."

She passed through Randall, not seeing it. She passed Toby and Tonto, who were walking along the verge toward the estate. The boy waved, the dog barked. She waved distractedly to them as she drove by, not thinking to stop and offer them a lift. She continued toward the point, toward Randall House, remembering the prison superintendent's final disclosure.

At least four times a year, every year she was in prison, Constance had received one visitor. That visitor was John Randall.

John Randall, she thought.

Constance. . . .

When Holly reached the entrance to Randall House, she pulled the blue BMW over to the side of the road and stopped. She sat there with the engine idling, staring through the wrought iron gates at the mansion in the distance.

"The day she gave birth she was reading Lady Chatterley's Lover, *so she named the child Constance, after the heroine in the book."*

Constance, she thought again. Her mother had named her Constance for Constance Chatterley,

the unhappy wife who found fulfillment with another man.

"*And* Wuthering Heights. *Dear Lord, she must have
read* Wuthering Heights *about a hundred times!*"

The sky was gray, overcast. There would be snow
again. She slipped the car in gear and drove through
the gates into the estate. She parked the car in its
space in the garage and got out. She would walk the
rest of the way. She felt like walking. She felt a sudden urge to walk forever, until she couldn't walk
anymore. But she knew she couldn't do that. She
had to go home. And that house on the hill before
her, Randall House, was now her home.

Wuthering Heights, she thought: Catherine Earn-
shaw.

Catherine.

Slowly at first, then with growing resolve, Holly
walked up the curving drive and went into the
house.

CHAPTER NINE

Happy Birthday

Good King Wenceslus looked out
On the Feast of Stephen,
Where the snow lay round about,
Deep and crisp and even.
Brightly shone the moon that night. . . .

The big double doors of the music room stood open, and the lovely singing of the children wafted out into the Great Hall. Mildred Jessel paused a moment, her arms laden with freshly laundered linen napkins, listening. The children were rehearsing for their performance at the party tonight. Yes, she thought as she listened. Beautiful.

She looked around the big room, nodding in satisfaction. A woman and a man were on A-frame ladders beside the twelve-foot blue spruce tree, hanging ornaments from the upper branches. They had already strung it with tiny white lights, and next would come tinsel and candy canes. On the balcony above her, several people were draping garlands of holly around the marble balustrade, being watched over and instructed by a rather excitable man in a blue denim jumpsuit. Other workers were placing holly wreaths with big red bows on doors and in windows. One industrious young woman had the sole job of setting holly-bedecked red candle centerpieces in strategic places throughout the house.

And that was just the decorating team. Madge Alden, the caterer, had arrived early this afternoon with a team of people in a big van. Out of that van had come some three dozen enormous platters for the buffet: a wide variety of hors d'oeuvres, turkey, ham, roast beef, chicken, vegetables, several pasta and potato dishes, three desserts, and what looked to be enough green salad to feed the entire town of Randall.

Ms. Alden's people had been followed by the drinks people in another van, who proceeded to unload case after case of Dom Pérignon champagne, red and white wines, fruit punch and apple cider, mixers, soft drinks, Perrier water, and every upscale brand of liquor on the market. Then the bakery truck had come with the huge, three-tiered birthday cake.

Mrs. Ramirez was in her domain, calmly but firmly issuing orders to the army of caterers, cooks, waiters, and bartenders who had descended on her. Even the usually implacable Ms. Alden seemed to be a bit in awe of her, and that, Mildred thought with satisfaction, was as it should be. Nina Ramirez was, among other things, a cordon bleu chef, and she ran her kitchen as a four-star general commands an army base. Mildred liked to think that Randall House had the best domestic staff in Connecticut, and she knew she wasn't far from wrong.

This made her think of Raymond Wheatley, the only member of the staff who actually remembered the famous Randall Christmas parties of old. Mildred had assisted her mother-in-law on a couple of those parties when she'd first arrived here, but that was near the end of the annual tradition, and the parties she'd witnessed were not nearly as elaborate as the earlier ones she'd heard about.

Mr. Wheatley was outside somewhere with Zeke and Dave, and the three of them were instructing the local boys who had been recruited to help with the parking. Three hours from now there would be a gleaming assortment of expensive cars lining the drive from the gatehouse all the way to the chapel. The field beyond the cemetery would also be full. They were expecting at least seventy cars, probably closer to a hundred, and Mr. Wheatley would be sure that the boys were ready for them, and that they took the utmost care with them.

The orchestra from New York had just arrived, and the seven musicians were currently using two of the guest bedrooms to change into formal clothes. Their instruments and music stands were piled in a corner of the Great Hall, waiting for them. The children in the music room were the glee club from the Randall grammar school, identically clothed in red choir gowns and white pinafores embroidered with holly borders.

Holly, Mildred thought, looking around at the garlands and candle arrangements. Mrs. Randall has been very clever, using that particular Christmas green throughout the decor for the party. The guest of honor, the birthday girl, was its namesake. Even as this thought occurred to her, she heard the children begin to rehearse another carol, the obvious request.

> *The holly and the ivy,*
> *When they are both full grown,*
> *Of all the greenery in the wood*
> *The holly wears the crown.*
> *O, the rising of the sun*
> *And the running of the deer . . .*

She smiled again, gazing approvingly around at the bustle of activity. It really was like the old days, she thought, when Miss Emily and Miss Alicia had presided at such festivities once a year. Mildred's mother-in-law had been there to ensure that everything ran smoothly. And now, more than thirty years later, Mildred would do likewise.

Mrs. Randall might not prove to be the hostess her predecessors were, Mildred realized, but tonight was going to be a memorable event, just the same—she and Mr. Wheatley and Mrs. Ramirez would see to that. The three of them had discussed it: they didn't care for Catherine Randall, not one little bit, but they were all very taken with their new employer. They would do their utmost best to make certain the party was a success, because they were doing it for Holly.

> *O, the rising of the sun*
> *And the running of the deer,*
> *The playing of the merry organ,*
> *Sweet singing in the choir . . .*

The sweet singing of the choir followed her as she crossed the Great Hall and went into the dining room to see to the folding of the napkins.

The first guests had arrived at seven, and by eight-fifteen most of them were milling happily around the ground floor of the house, eating and drinking and chatting. Holly stood at her bedroom window, watching a latecoming couple get out of a white Porsche in the drive below. One of the local men hired for the evening drove the car away, and the couple came into the house. Holly closed the curtains and went back over to her dressing table.

She studied her reflection in the mirror. The royal blue satin Donna Karan evening dress went well with her eyes, and the bare shoulders and upper bosom were appropriately dramatic. No jewels, a light makeup, and the hair was perfect. A simple sweep back into a French twist.

That had been the most difficult part of today. They had driven into Greenwich this morning, just the two of them, to have their hair done for the party. She had spent some two hours with the woman, smiling and talking amiably. And all through the long ordeal, the driving and the hair dryers and the facials, Holly had stolen surreptitious glances at the woman, wondering in retrospect why she hadn't been able to see it immediately, why she hadn't simply *known*.

But she hadn't known. Now, two days into her knowledge, she was still getting over the shock. She had not assessed it completely, examined all the possible repercussions. Not yet. But soon she would have to do that. She would have to go away somewhere—back to Indio, perhaps—and try to figure out what to do. Until then, she would have to survive as she had survived the last two days, on automatic pilot. And she must start with this party.

Ten minutes, she thought. In ten minutes, at eight-thirty, I am to make my entrance.

Kevin would be there, thank God. And Missy and her brother and his wife. And Gilbert Henderson, with any luck. When she'd been told about the party, she'd asked if the lawyer could be invited, and she'd later been told that he had been notified. Friendly faces would help considerably. Ichabod would not be there, of course, especially now. Now, more than ever, he had no intention of leaving his room.

Ichabod. She'd gone to his room that evening, after she'd returned from Kingston, and told him what she'd learned. He'd listened in silence as she recounted her interview with Mrs. Jackson. He'd remained silent for a long while after that, staring down at his chessboard. Then, at last, he'd said what she'd been hoping he'd say, that he was going to leave it all up to her. He would let her decide what they were to do with their knowledge.

She would have to decide soon. Even now, that woman was downstairs with her husband, her longtime associate whom she had *not* met five years ago in Monte Carlo. Heaven only knew what she was planning. Holly shuddered, remembering the fate of the last person who had threatened that woman's access to the Randall millions, not to mention the unfortunate fellow prisoners who had crossed her. And Jane Dee. Poor, lonely Jane Dee, lying in a pauper's grave with another woman's name on it, alone and unlamented.

Perhaps she was planning another murder.

Automatic pilot. With a last, deep breath, Holly forced herself to smile at the woman in the mirror. It was an easy smile, she decided; unaffected, blithe. She knew she might have good reason to worry for her safety, but the others must not know that. A hundred and fifty people were waiting downstairs for her, and none of them, not one of them would see what Holly saw, know what she knew.

Then she stood up and left the bedroom. She walked down the hallway to the gallery and took her assigned position near the top of the stairs, exactly on the stroke of eight-thirty.

It was time for the charade to begin.

There was a sudden flourish of music, and a hush fell over the big crowd of people in the Great Hall. Holly saw only the back of the woman in the sequined red dress who stood on the bottom steps, a little above the others, and made the announcement.

"Ladies and gentlemen, the guest of honor: my niece, Holly Randall."

As Holly came down the grand staircase, the children began to sing. "The Holly and the Ivy." Of course. She grinned around at the applauding throng as she came down to join the woman at the bottom of the stairs. The woman held out her arms. Still smiling, Holly stepped forward into those arms and embraced her mother, Constance Hall Randall.

"Hello, Cathy," she said.

A light snow began as Dora Jessel came out of the gatehouse and made her way across the grounds, keeping close to the border of trees near the front wall of the estate, toward her favorite place.

She had been sitting in her bedroom upstairs, trying to concentrate on her writing. But the constant arrival of cars and the loud activity of the parking attendants at the front gates had finally driven her out into the night to seek a quiet solitude. She had returned her current journal to its hiding place beside the others before going down the stairs, tiptoeing past the living room where her father was asleep in his chair, and leaving the house.

Now, as she crossed the dark lawn, she could hear music in the distance. The main house was brightly lit, and even from here she could see the silhouettes of a hundred happy partygoers at every downstairs window. The music and the movement gave an impression of happiness, of contentment, of safety. But she, alone of all people, knew that this impression was false. It was an evil house, and evil people lived there: that phrase came to her every time she looked at it.

She knew better than to go there. She had made that mistake once recently, a few weeks ago, but she had been confused that day. She occasionally had spells of confusion, she knew, whole days and even weeks when she was not at all certain what she was doing. But that episode had been the worst one in a long time. She'd broken some figurines in the living room, she was later told, and she'd shouted things. Things that, had she been behaving responsibly, she would never have said, no matter how much she wanted to say them. When Kevin had asked her what she'd meant, she had not replied.

She couldn't tell Kevin. She couldn't tell anyone. It would mean the loss of her parents' employment, and the loss of their home. The only home she'd ever known. And she would be blamed. No, she would never tell anyone.

But it was all in the diaries she had filled over the years. The whole, terrible story.

As she moved, tiny flakes of snow drifted down and landed softly on her face, only to melt immediately. It was not an unpleasant sensation, however. The cold snowflakes refreshed and invigorated her. She was aware of every sense: she felt acutely alive tonight.

In the darkness and the light snow, Dora arrived at her destination, the fence above the cliff. She couldn't see the water far below her, but she could hear the waves crashing against the rocks. It was a lovely sound, especially mingled with the new sound from the mansion behind her. Across the lawn she now heard the singing of the children.

> *The holly and the ivy*
> *When they are both full grown . . .*

Holly, she thought. Very clever.

Holly Randall seemed to be nice, and she was certainly beautiful. But Dora frowned when she thought of her: she had been confused the day she found Holly Randall in the cemetery, and she had only succeeded in frightening her, when all she'd wanted to do was warn her.

She must be careful in the future, careful not to disturb people. If her occasional bad days became a burden to her family, they would send her back to the clinic. She did not want to go there again. The clinic was another evil place, just like the house on the hill behind her.

Clutching the fence railing in her gloved hands, Dora closed her eyes and listened to the distant singing.

> *O, the rising of the sun*
> *And the running of the deer . . .*

It is Christmas Eve, she thought. That beautiful young woman's birthday, or so she'd heard her mother say. That was the reason for the party. That was why all those people had come here tonight. There had not been a party like this one at Randall House since Dora was a little girl, before Mr. James's wife had killed him in New York City. Since the murder the Randalls had been—what was that word, the one she'd read somewhere and had to look up in the dictionary? The word she loved because it so perfectly described the Randalls . . . ?

Pariahs. Yes, that was it. The Randalls were pariahs.

Between the singing and the rhythmic sound of the breakers, Dora Jessel never heard anyone approaching. She stood at the railing, staring out into the darkness. She was thinking about her long-lost baby again, unaware that she was no longer alone on the cliff until the gloved hand reached out from behind to grasp her arm. She was whirled around, not brutally but firmly, to confront the figure standing behind her. A wave of numbing shock coursed through her as she stared into the eyes of the Devil.

"You!" she cried.

The children were beautiful. There were some twenty of them in two semicircular rows at the bottom of the stairs, and each child was holding a single white candle. When they were done with "The Holly and the Ivy," they sang "Good King Wenceslas" and "Do You Hear What I Hear?" and "Silent Night," followed by a charming, comical rendition of "Jingle Bell Rock." Then they led the entire party in singing "Happy Birthday" to Holly.

She thanked the children profusely and handed

out gifts to each of them. Amid much loud applause, they were then sent off for cake and ice cream before being driven to their homes. When the birthday cake had been passed out and consumed, the orchestra started playing again in a way that made it clear that dancing was to begin.

Holly searched the Great Hall for her uncle. She even looked in the living room and the music room and the library, but he was nowhere to be found. This was unfortunate: everyone else in the Hall was politely holding back from the dance floor, waiting for John and Holly to start them all.

She didn't see "Aunt Cathy" around, either.

Just as Holly was ready to give up the search, the front door opened and John came hurrying in from outside, shedding his coat and gloves as he rushed toward her. Mumbling something about having helped one of the elderly, early departing couples to get their car from the attendants, he took Holly's arm and led her out onto the floor.

There was a burst of applause as the two of them waltzed around the black and white marble tiles, and soon the guests began to join them. In moments, a hundred people were whirling to the music. Holly would later remember that the waltz seemed to go on forever, but she made the best of it, grinning at her uncle in a perfect semblance of delight, as if this was the one thing in the world she wanted to be doing.

John smiled at the grinning young woman in his arms as they waltzed, thinking, Where the hell is Ed?

The man he'd hired to do the job for him had proved to be remarkably efficient until now. For this reason, John was beginning to worry about him. He'd been here four days ago, checking out the BMW in the garage, just as John had suggested he do. John had told him where the keys to the cars were kept, behind the shelf. The two men had spoken on the phone briefly that day, John having called the motel from a pay phone at a highway rest stop. Ed, or whatever his name really was, had promised to meet him in the lane the next day.

But Ed had never arrived.

Today, John had debated with himself about calling the motel again. But Ed would be back in New York, he reasoned, and the message could not be conveyed to him until he arrived there again. That could be weeks from now, for all John knew. No, he wouldn't chance another message.

But where the hell *was* he?

John smiled again and told Holly that she looked beautiful tonight. She smiled and thanked him and told him that he looked very nice, too.

As they danced, John wondered what to do. He didn't have an address for Ed in New York, and the unlisted phone number in Brooklyn was useless. John had tried it twice, and it just rang and rang. Ed obviously wasn't the sort of man who would have an answering machine.

He didn't want to bother his friend J.T. again. J.T. had done more than enough for him already, and it was never a good idea to overstep the bounds.

He would wait, he decided. He'd wait a few more

days, until after the holidays. If he still hadn't heard from the man by then, he'd bite the bullet. He would call J.T. and ask for an address.

He wouldn't tell his wife about it. Her last words on the subject had been a suggestion to call Ed and include Cousin Icky in the plan, which John had pretty much decided *not* to do. Icky was not a threat to them: he was certain of it. She was just being paranoid. Besides, she'd already made it very clear that she didn't want to know any details. She wanted to be innocent of the whole thing.

This struck John as terribly funny. Innocent, he thought. *Her?!*

He looked around the Great Hall, finally spotting his wife's red sequined dress through the crowd. She was standing just inside the front door, being helped out of her coat by one of the guests. What the hell had she been doing outside? he wondered. She was laughing at some joke the man was telling her, looking for all the world like the lady of the manor.

Good, he thought. If we play our cards right, that's exactly what she will be.

He smiled at Holly again.

He decided that he would be immensely relieved when the waltz was finally over.

Holly decided that she was immensely relieved when the waltz was finally over.

Then, her duty done, she handed Uncle John off to "Aunt Cathy," who'd finally appeared again, and began to leave the dance floor. But she didn't quite make it. The band began to play another number, something slow and romantic, just as Kevin Jessel, looking terrific in a black dinner jacket, materialized in front of her. With a big Irish grin, he stepped forward to take her in his arms, and she was dancing again.

This dance was considerably more pleasant than the first, she decided.

"Good evening," he said. "You're looking beautiful, as ever."

"Thank you. I'm glad you're here."

He smiled. "As a guest, you mean? I understand I have you to thank for that. I'm fairly certain that if it were up to your uncle and Mrs. Randall, I'd be parking cars rather than dancing with you."

Holly shook her head. "Tonight, you are my guest."

He leaned forward then, and kissed her lips. "Happy birthday, Holly."

They glided gracefully around the Great Hall, their bodies pressed lightly together, until the dance came to an end. There was a smattering of applause from the other couples, but they stood quite still on the dance floor, the two of them, regarding each other. Holly realized in that moment, surprised, that she had a sudden, almost overwhelming urge to tell him everything. But not now, she knew. Not here.

"I hope we'll be able to have another dance tonight," she said instead.

Kevin shrugged. "I hope so, too. But now I must leave you for a while. My mother cornered me in

the kitchen and asked me to go down to the gatehouse. She wants me to check on Da and—and my
sister."

Holly nodded, noting his hesitation, his vague
embarrassment. She remembered her meeting with
Dora in the cemetery, but she had never mentioned
it to him. She suspected that Mildred Jessel's current anxiety was not strictly for her husband.

"I understand," she said, smiling at him as he
turned to go. Then she remembered the presents
she wanted to give him. "Wait a minute, Kevin."

She took his hand in hers and led him through the
crowd to the Christmas tree. It was a while before
she could find the gifts she'd placed under the tree
earlier, because the number of brightly wrapped
packages there had grown dramatically. These are
all for me, she realized as she rummaged around for
signs of the Saks wrapping paper. Presents for me
from a lot of people I don't even know . . .

She found her packages near the back, behind
piles of others, and handed him the five presents for
his family. Two pairs of driving gloves, the aftershave lotion, and the two designer scarves. She
smiled, wondering if Mildred Jessel and her daughter would ever wear the boldly patterned silk
scarves. Both women seemed to favor black. Oh,
well . . .

"Put these under your tree," she said, "to be
opened tomorrow morning. And there are two
more here, for Toby Carter and Tonto, but I don't
know where to find them."

"Give them to me," Kevin said. "Whenever they

come around, their first stop is always the stable. I'll leave the gifts there. They'll find them."

"Thank you. And hurry back, please. You're practically the only person I know here tonight, and I could really use the moral support."

He laughed. "And all this time I was hoping you wanted me for my body."

"Well," she replied, "that, too, of course. But please come back as soon as you can."

"Yes, ma'am!" Kevin said. He leaned forward and kissed her lips again. Then, with a final grin, he went off through the crowd toward the front door.

Holly was standing there, smiling as she watched him go, when she felt a tug on her arm.

"What was *that* all about?" Missy MacGraw, looking splendid in emerald green, was standing at her elbow, grinning away. Holly turned around and embraced her.

"Oh, Missy, am I glad to see you! *That* was all about falling in love with a future psychiatrist. And I have a present for you under the tree—"

"Whoa!" Missy cried. "We'll get to all that later. And I want to hear everything about Kevin, simply *everything*! Future psychiatrist—I never imagined him in that line. But first, you have to do the guest-of-honor thing." She pointed toward the dancers. "You can start with my brother, whose work goes on display in the living room at midnight."

"Oh, gosh, the painting!" Holly said. "It's finished? It's *here*?"

"Yes and yes," her friend said. "But you can't see it until the unveiling. Now, dance!"

With a light laugh, Holly went to find Matthew MacGraw. She danced with him, then with Uncle John again, and then the cutting-in began. Holly danced with practically every man at the party: old, young, fat, thin, drunk, sober. They arrived before her in an endless line, and she barely caught half their names. But she smiled and thanked them all.

For the hour or so that it took her to dance with everyone, she had little chance to worry about "Aunt Cathy," who was actually doing an admirable job as hostess. Holly admitted this grudgingly to herself as she saw the woman at various times in various places: dancing, overseeing the wait staff, making sure everybody was included in conversations and had whatever they wanted. Yes, Holly supposed, the party is a success, and "Aunt Cathy" is responsible.

Her lawyer, Gilbert Henderson, never showed up. She thought about him as she danced. He had been her father's best friend. Perhaps he was the one to ask for advice. . . .

No, she would not ask anyone for advice. This was a family matter, a private matter. And it was now her family, for better or worse. It was her responsibility, hers alone, and she would meet the challenge. Looking around the enormous, glittering Great Hall, at the staircase and the marble tiles and the chandeliers, and at the gentle, beautifully attired men and women who even now were swirling around her in a bright profusion of color, she knew that it was worth it. She was Holly Randall now, and she would see to everything.

She wondered, briefly, where Kevin was. But before she could go looking for him, another complete stranger presented himself before her and asked her to dance. With a determined smile, she accepted.

Kevin came out of the gatehouse at a dead run.

He'd arrived home a few minutes ago after first dropping off the wrapped packages for Toby and Tonto at the stable. He'd found his father asleep in the living room, and he'd been careful not to wake him as he placed Holly's gifts under the little tree in the corner. Then he'd gone looking for Dora.

She wasn't in the kitchen, or her bedroom, or anywhere else. She wasn't in the house. She'd wandered off again.

No, he thought. Not tonight, of all nights!

And he'd burst from the house, propelled by terrible visions of Dora in her black cape meeting up with guests who might be wandering around outside, and frightening them. Not that she would mean to, but . . .

Two of the local boys parking the cars were at the front gates near the house, huddled together, smoking something that didn't smell like cigarettes. Kevin rushed over to them and asked if they'd seen his sister, but they groggily shook their heads. He turned away from them in frustration: Patton and all his troops could storm through the gates and attack Randall House, he thought, and those two wouldn't even notice.

He moved swiftly up the drive, peering off across the dark lawns and among the trees. No sign of her.

He ran toward the summer house. All the lights were on, and several partygoers with drinks had braved the cold to come out there and chat. No, they hadn't seen anyone matching Dora's description. He thanked them and continued down the sloping lawn to the cliff. She wasn't there, either.

In the next half hour, he made a complete tour of the grounds. She wasn't among the small crowd near the pool. She wasn't in the pool house, though he did find a young couple there doing something naughty. The chapel and the cemetery were dark, deserted. Even the apple orchard was empty, and the little forest beyond the east lawn.

He stopped beside the pond in the forest, trying to control his panic. He wondered, fleetingly, whether she might have wandered away from the estate, into town, but he immediately dismissed that notion. She had never left the grounds of Randall House alone, not ever.

Which left only one place.

Slowly, with a growing sense of dread, he made his way through the falling snow, back to the fence at the top of the cliff. He followed the fence to the stone stairway that went down the side of the cliff to the beach. He paused at the top of the stairs and peered down over the railing. He could hear the waves crashing against the rocks far below him, but it was too dark to see anything.

Kevin took a slow, deep breath, closed his eyes, and prayed. Then he opened his eyes. Clutching the rough wood rail in his trembling hand, he began the long descent into the darkness.

* * *

The portrait was unveiled at midnight, just at the start of Christmas Day.

It was a big painting, life-sized, and it wasn't at all what Holly was expecting. In the three days she'd posed for Matthew MacGraw, he hadn't let her see what he was doing. But there she was, smiling rather mysteriously out from the canvas, wearing the very dress she now had on. Her pale hair was up, and her hands were folded rather demurely in her lap. She looked serene, and very elegant. Her eyes seemed almost to glow.

She'd known that Matthew did this for a living, but she hadn't seen any examples of his work until now. He was better, infinitely better than she'd guessed. This painting was a true work of art, and it prompted a tremendous round of applause from everyone. Her uncle John immediately announced that it would be hung here in the living room, alongside the portraits of Ellen and Alicia.

Holly stared at the picture for several minutes, trying to define the odd feeling it prompted in her. Immortality: that was it. She had been rendered immortal. When she could no longer decently stare at herself, she embraced the artist and led the way back out into the Great Hall.

She would later remember exactly where she was standing a few moments later, when it happened. She was at the bottom of the stairs, in front of the Christmas tree, and Missy had just brought over a group of friends who were preparing to leave. "Aunt Cathy"—her mother, Constance Randall—

was standing nearby, saying good night to another group. People were dancing in the Hall behind her. The maid, Grace, arrived beside her with little cups of eggnog on a silver tray.

Eggnog, Holly thought. Why not?

In that moment, just before it, Holly was actually feeling happy. She was here, at Randall House, among friends. There was a beautiful portrait of her in the living room. She was very attracted to a handsome man who obviously liked her. As for her uncle and her mother—well, she would do something about them soon. She was Holly Randall now, and she'd had a lovely birthday party, and it was Christmas.

She and Missy were reaching out for the cups when Grace looked past her, toward the front door. The maid uttered a little cry, and the tray slid from her hands and crashed on the floor, sending shards of glass and milky liquid flying. The orchestra stopped in mid-note. All conversation came to an abrupt halt, all movement froze. Holly was still looking blankly down at the mess on the floor when she heard Missy gasp.

Then she turned around.

She stood there with a hundred other people, staring. She heard another gasp behind her, followed by a flurry of muffled noises from somewhere near the dining room, and she knew that Mildred Jessel had seen, and fainted.

Kevin Jessel stood at the entrance to the Great Hall, holding his sister in his arms. He was soaking wet, and the limp figure he held was covered with a light dusting of snowflakes. The hood of her dripping cape had fallen back to reveal the pale white face and jet black hair. Her eyes were closed, and her head lolled at a horrible angle against her brother's shoulder.

There was a long moment of absolute silence. Nobody moved. Nobody breathed. The room, the house, the whole world seemed to have come to a complete stop.

Then Kevin threw his head back and screamed. It began as a guttural moan deep in his throat, increasing in volume as it rose up to engulf Randall House. His anguished cry went on and on, resounding through the farthest rooms.

As Holly watched, a thin, watery trickle of blood descended Dora's pallid cheek and splashed down onto the white marble tile at her brother's feet.

PART THREE

HOLLY RANDALL

CHAPTER TEN

The Funeral

Memory is a funny thing. So many images are swept away with time, while others remain forever. It seems at first almost a random process, what we forget and what we remember. And yet it is not random, not at all. The mind makes choices: there is an elaborate, sophisticated process of selection. I'm not certain that I understand the process, but I'm certain that this is what happens.

The events at Randall House several years ago are a good example of the principle at work. I witnessed some of them firsthand, while others have been related to me after the fact. Sometimes I blur the line between them, even in my own mind. I vividly recall images I could not possibly have seen, and words I never heard spoken. Yet I know that everything I'm telling you is true.

It is true, for instance, that the early morning

hours of Christmas Day were full of activity. Pete Helmer and one of his deputies arrived, as well as the county police, and an ambulance to take away the body. The scene in front of the house was one of constant comings and goings.

The guests at the party still remaining when Kevin Jessel made his extraordinary appearance in the Great Hall probably wished they'd gone home earlier. Their names and addresses were taken down, in case it later became necessary to contact them. It was after two-thirty in the morning when the last of them were finally allowed to go.

And go they did, never to return. They had gone out on a social limb, to their way of thinking, by coming at all. The Randalls were already tainted, and the arrival of a dead body in the middle of the Christmas party did nothing to restore their reputation. Nor did the fact that most of the guests had never so much as met a police officer before that night, to say nothing of having their names and addresses taken down in a public record. They'd all had quite enough of Randall House.

John Randall and his wife were questioned in the library, and Mildred Jessel and her husband met with the police in the gatehouse. Kevin had gone in the ambulance with his sister's body, to fill out all the necessary forms and provide information at the hospital morgue.

Only Holly, the birthday girl, was spared, because she was an outsider. She didn't know Dora Jessel, and she had not left the house all evening, so she could not possibly have seen anything. But she did not go to her room. She remained in the library with her relatives, holding their hands and serving coffee, until the last official visitors were gone. Then she went upstairs with them, embracing both of them at their bedroom doors before going through her own door, and locking it.

Dora Jessel's death was ruled a suicide. Her extensive history of emotional instability and several previous attempts at suicide were soon made known, as were the expert opinions of the psychiatrists who had most recently treated her. Because she had never been declared legally insane, and because the doctors did not believe her to be so, there was no hope of a ruling of accidental death. This proved to be very unfortunate.

An examination of the cliff and the beach by Helmer and his men on Christmas Day proved futile. There was no evidence of a struggle, or even of anyone else having been there with her. Because of the weather that night, there was no evidence at all, really. No one at the party had seen anything of Dora during the evening, and there was no reason to assume that anyone in Randall wished her harm.

The village's resident district court judge had his own holiday celebration interrupted long enough for him to sign the appropriate papers, and Dora's body was released for burial. But there turned out to be a problem with that.

The Jessels were Catholic, but old Father O'Brien, their priest of many years, refused to preside at the funeral. She had committed the ultimate sin, he informed the devastated family. According to him,

Dora could not receive the sacraments of burial, or even be buried in sanctified ground. He was very gruff with Brian Jessel, and when Mildred got on the phone to plead with him, the priest simply repeated to her that his hands were tied.

It was at this point that Holly truly became the mistress of Randall House. She did three things in rapid succession on December 26 that no one in Randall would ever forget. In doing so, she earned the eternal censure of the town—and the eternal gratitude of the Jessel family.

First, she announced that Dora would be buried in the Randall House cemetery beside her grandparents on December 28, at her expense. She ordered a beautiful ebony coffin to be delivered immediately, and she commissioned the construction of a small marble headstone.

Second, she called the archdiocese in New Haven and argued with several people there until a priest was located who would perform the service. This man was a local legend, according to a sympathetic secretary in the monsignor's office, a notorious rebel who worked with homeless people and teenage runaways out of his storefront parish. But he was an ordained Catholic priest, and he was eventually brought to Randall House in a limousine provided by Holly. Exactly how much she paid him for his services is unknown to me.

The third thing Holly did that day is the one that eventually caused all the talk. As soon as she had made all the arrangements for the funeral, she called Father O'Brien at his office in Randall.

Mr. Wheatley—a Catholic—was in the room when she placed the call, and he later told the story with great relish. Holly informed the priest that while she was in charge of Randall House, he was never to set foot in its chapel again. She then called Reverend Ellsworth at the Methodist church across the street and pledged a donation of ten thousand dollars, which the bewildered man gratefully accepted. The fact that Ellsworth would never have consented to preside at the funeral, either, made no difference to her: it was the gesture that counted. She smiled then, according to Mr. Wheatley, as she contemplated what this would probably do to the long-standing rivalry between Randall's two religious leaders.

John Randall announced at dinner that night that he and his wife would be going into New York City immediately after the funeral. They would be staying at the apartment there for a couple of days, but would be back to celebrate New Year's Eve with Holly. She received this news with a profound sense of relief.

Memory is indeed a funny thing: it comes and goes. I don't remember what I had for lunch yesterday, if I had lunch yesterday. But I remember everything about Dora Jessel's funeral.

Holly stood at the graveside with some thirty other people, looking around. The priest from New Haven ("Call me Father Bob") was performing the usual ritual to the satisfaction of everyone, especially Mildred. This was the important thing, as far as Holly was concerned. Mildred Jessel and her

269

family stood together in a tight group closest to the coffin and the gaping hole that had been dug in the frozen ground to receive it. If they were pleased, then she was pleased.

She was uncomfortable in her new black dress, and the wide-brimmed hat was worse. But she decided it was definitely better to have this ponytailed, earringed young man here than Father O'Brien. She grimaced, cursing the dreadful Father O'Brien for what must have been the hundredth time in three days. All of this must be endured, she reminded herself as the maverick priest recited the familiar litany. Ashes and dust, Holly thought as she listened, and all that business about commending Dora Jessel's soul to Heaven. Indeed.

She had met the woman only once, if it could appropriately be called a meeting. She remembered the bizarre scene in this very graveyard, with the swirling fog and those intense eyes burnishing their gaze into her. Most of all, she remembered her own panic, her fear at being alone and vulnerable in this awful place with that distraught creature. She wondered what Dora Jessel had been doing with the doll, and what had prompted her to leap from the cliff on Christmas Eve.

But it was not her place to wonder about such things. It was now her duty to be the hostess of these grim proceedings, and she would perform her duty as best she could. She would take these people back to the house afterward, for the tea and the wine and the baked meats, and all the rest of it.

She gazed around, surveying the assembly. Father Bob, the ostensible star of the group, was garbed in the classic black suit and collar, reminding Holly of an avant-garde actor who had suddenly found himself cast in an extremely conventional production of a Shakespeare play. The Jessels were huddled close together, arms around each other, staring down at the gleaming coffin before them. Brian's sister and her husband had arrived from Chicago to be with them. Uncle John and his wife, her mother, were beside Holly, looking decorously mournful. The staff, led by Mr. Wheatley and Mrs. Ramirez, stood at silent attention. The police chief, Pete Helmer, hat in hand, was near the servants. A dozen other people—friends of the Jessels, apparently—rounded out the group. Well, not quite, Holly realized. Toby Carter and his dog were standing off among the trees, away from the others, watching, and she noticed that Uncle Ichabod was there too, among the trees behind the boy and the dog. He was apparently being careful not to get too close to the crowd, or to let any of them see him. She looked over at Ichabod and nodded. He nodded back.

The service in the chapel had been mercifully brief. Father Bob had recited the usual words, assisted by two boys who were obviously there without Father O'Brien's permission. Holly silently thanked the boys and their parents for their mutiny. Then the coffin had been carried here, to the cemetery, followed by the silent congregation.

She shuddered as the soft snow began to fall around them, thinking, God, I hate this. . . .

As the eulogy came to an end, the six men who

had carried the coffin here—Zeke and Dave, who would ultimately bury her; Chief Helmer's two deputies; George, the stableman; and Mr. Miller, the pharmacist—stepped forward. They were moving the coffin closer to its final resting place when Brian Jessel suddenly uttered a small moan, clutched his chest, and sank slowly to the ground. Mildred reached out desperately with her hands, but she was too late to help him. She clawed at empty air.

Everyone at the graveside reacted in one way or another, but none more swiftly than Chief Helmer. He was immediately kneeling beside the fallen man, doing something Holly could not see because his body blocked her view. Moments later, Brian Jessel sat up on the ground, still moaning. Pete Helmer and Kevin lifted him between them and carried him over to Helmer's car. Mildred followed them and got in with her husband, indicating to Kevin that he should return to the ceremony. He nodded and went back to stand beside Holly. As everyone in the little cemetery watched in silent confusion, the police car sped away toward the main road.

Before she even realized what she was doing, Holly stepped forward. With a wave of her hand, she indicated to the priest and the pallbearers that the ceremony should continue. The final words were spoken, and Kevin placed a single red rose on the coffin. Then, before the coffin was lowered into the cold earth, Holly took Kevin by the hand and led the mourners out of the cemetery and across the back lawn to Randall House.

* * *

John and his wife were in the library alone one hour later, away from the others, when the call came from the hospital. Mr. Wheatley came in and told John that Chief Helmer wanted to speak to him.

Pete Helmer informed him that Brian Jessel had suffered a heart attack, but that he was expected to recover. Mildred was with him, seeing to his needs, and he would be kept in the hospital until further notice. John thanked the police chief for the information and was about to hang up, but the chief's next words stopped him.

"Mr. Randall, I meant to ask you earlier, but there was never a good time for it. Perhaps you can help us with another matter. A week ago, just before Christmas, a man was found dead at the Kismet Motel out on the highway. He'd been beaten to death and robbed. You may have read about it. Well, he was registered under the name Edwards, but his real name was Buono. Alec Buono, of Brooklyn, New York. On the night of his murder, I saw his car—a red Infiniti—driving through Randall from the direction of Randall House. Do you know anything about this?"

John swallowed hard, his mind racing.

"Uh, no," he finally managed to say. "I don't know anyone named Buono." He grimaced, thinking, At least that's true enough. I only knew him as Ed.

"Well," the chief continued, "I was just wondering. We don't know anything about the man, but my colleagues in New York are very interested. It seems he was a member of a mob family in Brooklyn."

"Oh?" John heard himself saying. "How very . . . melodramatic."

"Yes," Pete Helmer concurred. "Well, I'm sorry to have bothered you with this at such a time. But, could you ask around? I mean, your staff and so forth. Maybe someone at Randall House saw something that night It was the twentieth, five days before Christmas."

"Of course," John said, amazed at the steadiness of his voice. "I'll ask them, but I don't hold out much hope for you. That road goes right on up the coast: he could have been coming from anywhere, and I'm certain he wasn't around here. A mobster, you say. . . ."

"Yeah, well, it was worth a shot. I'm not really involved in that investigation. The county police are handling it, but I told them I'd ask you. Please tell Kevin Jessel that his father is going to be all right."

"I will, Chief. Thank you."

When John replaced the receiver, he looked over to see that his wife was watching him intently. Without a word, she stood up and left the room. Reluctantly, he followed her.

When the last of the guests were gone, Kevin went off to the hospital to join his mother and Holly went wearily upstairs. She removed the dress and the hat and kicked off the uncomfortable black shoes, took a long, hot shower, then put on jeans and a sweater. She was tired of wearing black.

She called the kitchen and asked for a glass of white wine. A few minutes later Mr. Wheatley knocked on the door, brought the wine into the room on a silver tray, and left without a word. When she was alone again, Holly went over to the phone and called Missy MacGraw.

She got the message almost immediately. Missy was polite, as her breeding dictated, but evasive. She hemmed and hawed around Holly's invitation to lunch the next day, finally blurting out that she expected to be very busy through New Year's Eve, and for weeks after that.

Holly hung up the receiver, staring down at it. So, she thought, that's that. That's how it's going to be, not just with Missy, but with everyone else in this place as well. I'm Holly Randall now.

With a little shake of her head, she picked up the wine and drank it.

The black dress and hat from the funeral were lying on the chair where she'd dropped them. She could leave them there, she knew: she had servants now. But force of habit, some vestige of Holly Smith, prompted her to pick them up and carry them over to the walk-in closet. She would save the dress, she supposed, if only for funerals. But she would hide it at the very back of the row of dresses, behind everything else, where she wouldn't have to look at it. It was a small decision; unimportant, really.

But it changed everything.

She switched on the closet light and walked past all her other clothes to the back. She was reaching for a padded hanger when she heard the voices from the other side of the wall. She froze, holding her breath, listening.

". . . just *wonderful*!" her mother was saying. "So, what do we do now?"

"I don't know," John replied. "I'll think of something. I'll call J.T. and see if—"

"Oh, please!" Constance snapped. "It was J.T. who sent you *this* guy, this Buono person, and look what happened to *him*! He's dead! *Murdered!*"

"Come on, Cathy. How could anyone have predicted there'd be a robbery at the Kismet, of all things? It was just bad luck, that's all."

Holly strained against the tiny sliver of light shining through one back corner of the closet walls, taking it in. Why did her uncle call Constance "Cathy," she wondered, even in private? Had she made a mistake?

No, she reasoned, there had been no mistake. Calling her Cathy was practice, discipline, so that John would never make a mistake in public. The woman was Constance Randall, all right. The next words Holly heard through the wall served to confirm this.

"Don't tell me about bad luck!" the woman snapped. "I know all about bad luck. I had nineteen years of it, thank you very much, and I will not tolerate any more. If anyone has earned the Randall fortune, it is I!"

"All right, settle down," John murmured. Then he said an odd thing, something Holly didn't understand. "If you think about it, my emotional stake is as high as yours—if you've been telling me the truth, that is."

Her mother's reply was equally cryptic. "I've told

you the truth. *Always.*" There was a sound of foot-steps, and then she said, "Where are you going?"

"To get ready, Cathy," he replied, and Holly could hear the weariness in his voice. "We're leaving for the city in twenty minutes. We have a dinner reservation at the Oak Room, and theater tickets, remember? I—I'll call J.T. from the apartment. I'll get someone else to follow the same plan. You and I will go to Paris on the seventh of January, as scheduled, and they'll fix the brakes on the BMW while we're thousands of miles away."

There was a slight pause then, during which Holly heard her mother's bedroom door open.

"So, *that's* the plan?" Constance said. She apparently hadn't known.

"Don't worry, darling," John said. "She's as good as dead. Now, for heaven's sake, get ready. I'll meet you downstairs in ten minutes."

The door closed. Holly stood at the back of her closet, breathing slowly in and out, her eyes tightly shut, her mind struggling to process all of the information she'd just learned. The next sounds she heard shattered her fugue state, forcing her to move. There was a sudden, loud thump against the hollow wall beside her, followed by the distinct rasp of hangers sliding and dresses brushing against each other. Her mother's closet was obviously on the far side of this wall. Its door had probably been standing open, which explained the clarity of the voices. Swiftly and silently, Holly backed out of her closet into the bedroom.

She sat down on the edge of the bed, her mind

racing. Only minutes ago she hadn't been able to think of anything at all, but now the images were crowding in, flashing through her brain with uncanny speed.

They were going to have her killed sometime in the middle of January, while they were in Europe.

My mother, she thought. The woman who bore me is planning to kill me. First her husband, now her daughter. She's planning to murder her own daughter for one hundred fifty million dollars, or thereabouts.

Holly thought about that, about the money. She imagined simply giving it to them; signing it over, or whatever. Getting rid of them.

No. She knew they would not accept it, not like that. It would be a virtual confession of guilt. And they would never do anything that might serve to expose their plan. If they did, Constance could go back to prison for the rest of her life, and John would be in another one.

She could see to that, simply by picking up the phone. Calling Pete Helmer, who was so enamored of her, and getting him onto it. A dead man named Buono at someplace called the Kismet, whatever that was. Someone named J.T., who was apparently a friend of Uncle John's. She could expose them, the whole plot, right here and now.

No. She had no proof of anything, merely an overheard conversation. She knew nothing of the law, but she doubted whether this was enough to indict anyone, let alone convict them. If her mother and her uncle walked away from the charge—and they probably would—she would only be in danger all over again. No . . .

Jane Dee. The name arrived unbidden in Holly's mind, startling her. Jane Dee must be dead, she reasoned. It can't have happened any other way. She could make an accusation, which would be followed by an order of exhumation, or whatever it was called, on the grounds that her mother, Constance—now Catherine—had murdered her. An examination of the two women's dental charts at the prison in Kingston . . .

No, she wouldn't do that, either. Even if Constance were successfully charged and convicted, it would only leave Uncle John still at large, with more reason than ever to wish her harm. He'd kill her for revenge—not to mention a hundred and fifty million.

So, she thought, what now?

She smiled involuntarily, in spite of her predicament, remembering the words she'd heard through the wall, so similar to her own thought.

"So, what do we do now?"

Then she remembered something else, the cryptic exchange between her uncle and her mother only moments later.

"If you think about it, my emotional stake is as high as yours—if you've been telling me the truth, that is."

And the reply: *"I've told you the truth. Always."*

Holly shook her head absently and frowned, thinking, What the hell does *that* mean?

The sound of a car pulling up in the drive drew her over to the window. John and Constance were standing on the front steps, their bags beside them. As she watched, Zeke got out of the Mercedes and put the bags in the trunk. He then handed the keys to John. The couple got in and drove away, and Zeke came into the house.

Holly waited until the car was out of sight down the drive. Then she went back into her closet and switched on the light. She walked directly to the back wall and felt along the cracked corner with her fingers. It only took a moment for her to find what she'd imagined, what she somehow knew, was there.

It was a little latch, a dead-bolt lock at waist height. She unlatched it, put her fingertips in the crack in the corner, and pushed. The wall slid quietly to the side, forming a little passageway between the two closets—and between the two bedrooms.

Of course, she thought. This house was built a hundred years ago, and old John Randall had designed it. He had the master bedroom, now Holly's room, and his wife, the original Alicia, had been in the bedroom next to it. Her great-great-grandfather had cleverly included a discreet means of passage between the two rooms. She examined the other side of the secret door: nothing. The sole means of operating it were on the master bedroom side. The man's side. How quaint, she thought as she began to slide the wall back into place. And how fortunate: that's how I was able to hear the voices.

She was about to relock the bolt when she stopped, arrested by a sudden feeling of curiosity. She had never seen her mother's room, and she knew that it was always locked. Giving in to the urge, she slid the moving wall aside again and stepped through the opening. She walked through her mother's closet and out into the bedroom. Then she made her way over to the door and switched on the light.

She stood there for a long moment, gazing around. This big room was the complement of Uncle Ichabod's room, architecturally speaking, but there the similarity ended. Where his room was dark and crowded and masculine, this white-carpeted one was light and airy and distinctly female. The walls were a creamy white, and there was a frilly white lace spread on the king-sized bed. A lace-skirted vanity table between the two windows, a small chest of drawers, matching small bedside tables, and a white armchair in the corner with a standing reading lamp beside it. Lots of open space around the huge bed. There were no bookshelves, she noticed, and no artworks of any kind.

But there were mirrors. Everywhere. Holly stared around at several glittering reflections of herself. There was the big round one above the vanity table, ringed with lightblubs in the fashion of a theatrical dressing room. The theater, she thought: of course. There were also full-length mirrors, one on the bathroom door and one on the door to the closet. And on the wall near the bed, where normally one would find shelves or paintings, was a huge, elaborate, framed mirror with etched Art Deco designs along the borders.

Holly took it all in. Then she began to move swiftly and methodically around the place. She inspected the wide array of cosmetics in the vanity drawer, and the impressive collection of sweaters and lingerie in the bureau. She went briefly into the mirror-tiled bathroom and found the things she knew would be there: dark hair dye and all the accoutrements for contact lenses. There were even several extra pairs of dark brown–tinted lenses stored in the medicine cabinet.

Back in the bedroom, she pulled out the drawers of both bedside tables and noted their contents. She smiled when she found the stash of Tootsie Rolls in one of them, and the dog-eared copy of *Valley of the Dolls*. Mrs. Jackson at the prison had mentioned Jacqueline Susann. . . .

Then, with a fleeting pang of guilt at invading someone else's fiercely guarded privacy, she returned to the bedroom door, switched off the light, and moved quickly back the way she'd come, through the closets to her bedroom, locking the sliding wall once again behind her.

If she'd been unsure of the woman's identity before, she was certain of it now. That bedroom was a dead giveaway, and not merely because of the dye and the contact lenses and *Valley of the Dolls*.

The dead giveaway was the mirrors.

She thought about the facility in Kingston, the gray walls and barred windows. She imagined the tiny, cramped, double-occupancy cubicles behind those windows, with narrow bunks and virtually no floor space. Then she thought of the room next door, with its creamy walls and thick white carpet and that huge, lacy bed. And the mirrors: the one thing missing from every prison, even the bathrooms, because mirrors could be shattered and fashioned into weapons.

For nineteen years, Constance Randall had been unable to see her own reflection. Now, she had surrounded herself with glass.

In that moment, Holly knew that her mother was insane.

So, she thought again, what now?

What she finally decided on was another hot shower. Then she got dressed again and went downstairs. The maids were still bustling between the dining room and the kitchen, putting away the food from the postfuneral reception. Holly went into the kitchen to tell Mrs. Ramirez not to bother making dinner for her, that she wasn't hungry. But when she arrived there, she saw that the woman had already prepared a tray of cold ham and salad. Mrs. Ramirez reminded her that she hadn't eaten anything after the funeral, while the guests were around. She handed Holly the tray, insisting that she eat now.

Holly ate in the music room, in front of the television. Far from not being hungry, she found that she was ravenous. She smiled as she ate, remembering that first night at the apartment in New York City, when she'd made a similar discovery. That first night on Central Park South—God, had it been only five weeks ago? Closer to six, she reasoned, but even so. . . .

That first night, before she'd met these people,

John and Constance Randall. Now, in retrospect, she wished she'd never met them at all.

Someone came and took away the tray. With a sigh, she stood up, switched off the television, and left the music room. She wandered into the library, briefly scanning the walls of books before shaking her head absently and wandering out again. She didn't want to read. She opened the front door and stood gazing out at the drive as the snow fell softly down. No, she didn't want to go outside, either.

She went back to the kitchen, but it was now empty. Mrs. Ramirez and the maids had finished cleaning up and had retired for the night, turning off the lights before climbing the back stairs to the third floor. Mr. Wheatley and the others would be there, too, either in bed or getting ready for it. She was alone here.

With a sigh, she went upstairs. She walked down the guest hall and knocked softly on Ichabod's door, but there was no reply. She hadn't expected one, really. She always made appointments with him before going there, and she had the feeling that he slept most of the time when he wasn't entertaining her.

There was nothing for it but to go back to her room. She took another hot shower, her third that day. She put on her silk robe and sat on her bed, staring down at the telephone. After a while, she realized that she was weeping, the tears moving slowly down her face.

She was still sitting there, wondering whether

she should call Mary Smith in Indio, when she heard the soft knock on her door.

He was standing at the fence on the cliff, gazing up at Randall House in the distance, when he saw the light come on in her bedroom.

He'd sat with his mother by his father's hospital bed until visiting hours were over. Mildred had asked if she could stay the night, and her request had been granted. But she had sent Kevin home.

He'd stopped in town and gone into the local bar, planning to have several drinks while he watched his old high school chums shoot pool, but he didn't even finish his first beer. He didn't want to get drunk, and he didn't want to be sober. He felt restless, too antsy to sit in a crowded, smoky room listening to meaninglessly light chatter and oppressively loud music. So he'd come home, to the gatehouse.

The empty house was worse than the noisy bar, especially with the floral arrangements. Mildred had sent most of the flowers to the chapel for the service, but several tributes still remained behind, covering every downstairs table in the little house. The cloying perfume of a hundred lilies, the scent of death, drove him out again, out into the snowy darkness.

He'd wandered aimlessly around the estate for a long time before he found himself at the cliff edge, staring down into the dark abyss. He listened to the churning of the water against the rocks; a restless sound, as restless as he was feeling. He stood there, repeating the same thought over and over in his mind:

Why, Dora? Why?

Dora was gone, and he had not done anything to help her. He had not studied for, or even seriously looked into, the profession he had vaguely considered. He had not taken care of his sister, as he had promised himself he would do. He had done nothing useful, nothing meaningful with his life.

He wept now, as he had wept when he'd found her here four days ago, as he had not wept since he was a child. He cried for Dora, and for his parents, and most of all for himself. For the vital, purposeful human being he might once have become.

Suddenly, for no reason he knew, as if obeying some secret urge or primitive instinct, he turned around and looked across the lawn at the house in the distance. Gradually his blurred vision narrowed, became fixated on one specific detail of the facade: the dark windows of the farthest second-floor bedroom on the right.

And then her light came on.

He stared, fascinated, at that light shining through the darkness, through the snow. Before he was aware of what he was doing he was walking toward it, across the snowy lawn to the snowy drive and up the steps to the front door. He pulled the key chain from his pocket and fumbled for the right key, and he was inside. Across the foyer and the Great Hall and up the wide staircase. Around the gallery and down the carpeted hallway to her bedroom door.

Still half asleep, still in his trancelike state, still weeping, he raised his hand and knocked.

CHAPTER ELEVEN

The Island

On December 30, at three o'clock in the after-noon, Holly was on the Long Island Express-way in Kevin's Land Rover, heading east. She was on her way to Suffolk County, and she was making good time in the preholiday traffic. She was still in Nassau County now, but there was no snow today and the road was relatively empty. She was an hour ahead of schedule, so when she saw the exit sign before her she gave in to a sudden, overwhelming impulse. She steered the car over to the right lane and left the highway.

She'd seen the name of the town on the highway sign, and she'd remembered the address from the newspaper accounts and the documents in Mrs. Jackson's office, but she had no idea how to get there. She pulled over into the first gas station she saw. While the attendant filled the Land Rover's tank, she asked him for directions.

It took her a few minutes to find the Hempstead Turnpike, and ten more minutes on the turnpike before she arrived in the little town she was seeking. She found the street the man at the gas station had told her about and turned into it.

She was getting better at handling the big car, she noticed. When she'd asked Kevin if she could borrow the Land Rover, he'd handed her the keys without asking questions, for which she was grateful. Despite their new, intimate relationship, she had no intention of telling him why she didn't want to get into the blue BMW. After what she'd overheard two days ago, she would never go near the BMW again. But she'd decided not to tell Kevin that, or anything else. Not yet, at any rate. Between his sister's suicide and his father's illness, he had enough to worry about at the moment.

Kevin . . .

No. She couldn't think about all that. Not now. Now, she was looking for a street.

As she drove farther into the neighborhood, she began to form an impression of it, and it was not a good one. She knew something about the place. Years ago, this prefabricated town was one of many built around the United States to fill a growing need for reasonably priced housing for lower-middle-class families. Holly gazed around at the rows of drab little cement boxes set close together in the flat Long Island landscape. If this place had ever possessed a quaint charm, that time was long gone. Now it was a

cramped mélange of bare lawns and crowded clothes-
lines and inexpensive, badly maintained cars. She
imagined ill-clad children playing in these streets in
summer, and cheap plastic lawn furniture on the
sparse grass near the cracked, uneven sidewalks.

Indio, for all its intense heat and lack of beauty,
had never been as bad as this.

She found the street and turned into it. She slowed
now, checking the numbers on the battered mail-
boxes before each unit, counting them off in her
mind. 72, 70, 68 . . . here it was: 66. Number 66, Sixth
Street. She pulled over on the other side of the street
and stopped the car, staring.

66 Sixth Street, she thought, remembering Sunday school in Indio. The number of the Beast. The
sign of the Devil.

The reference, she saw, was apt. The house across
the street was even shabbier than its neighbors, if
that was possible. A dreary, aluminum-sided, screen-
doored nightmare, one that its occupants had not
even bothered to maintain. The clothesline here
was empty, and the rusting hulk in the carport had
no tires, but rested on cinder blocks. It was definitely the right address, however. The tilted mailbox beside the driveway had HALL inexpertly slashed
across its side in black paint.

She revved the engine, preparing to drive away,
but it was not to be. There was more. At that moment, the front door opened. An enormous old
woman in a gray housedress, brown sweater, and
incongruously pink fuzzy slippers banged through
the screen door and came down the single step to

the front walk. Her frizzy white hair was in a loose bun, and she carried a can of beer in her right hand. She came forward in Holly's direction, and for one horrible moment Holly thought she had been caught spying. But no: when she reached the sidewalk, the woman turned and waddled over to the mailbox. She stopped to drain the beer can, crumple it, and toss it into the gutter before opening the box. She pulled out several large items that Holly could plainly see were brochures and mail-order catalogs. The woman riffled furiously through these, obviously looking for something that wasn't there. Holly rolled down her window just in time to hear the woman shout a single word.

"Shit!"

With that, the old woman barged up the walk and back inside the house, slamming the screen door and the aluminum front door behind her.

Holly sat there, staring, thinking, Social Security. Late again, no doubt.

She couldn't breathe.

She rolled up her window and slowly raised a hand to her chest. She sat there for several minutes, waiting for her heartbeat and respiration to return to normal. Then she slammed the car in gear and roared away. She circled back to the street she'd originally been on and made her way back to the turnpike. In a matter of minutes, she was once again on the Long Island Expressway, speeding east.

The woman she had just seen was Beulah Jean Hall, Constance's widowed mother.

Her grandmother.

* * *

Kevin was alone in the gatehouse. His father was being kept in the hospital for several more days, at least until after the new year, and his mother had virtually moved into the room with her husband. He'd been to visit them earlier this afternoon, but now he was back home, wondering what to do next. Holly was away for the day on Long Island, so he couldn't spend the afternoon with her, as much as he would have liked that.

Holly . . .

He smiled at the memory of two nights ago, when he'd been drawn, weeping, to her bedroom door. She'd opened the door in a silk robe, and he'd been surprised to see that she was weeping, too. He didn't ask her why. In fact, neither of them had said a word. One moment they stood there staring, and in the next they were in each other's arms. The rest of it was a blur of feverishly flung coat and boots and clothing, and that lovely silk robe fluttering to the floor. . . .

No. He wouldn't think about that now. Later, when he'd decided what to do about himself. About his parents. About Dora.

Dora . . .

He managed to eat half of a sandwich he made with some leftover ham, and he was washing up in the sink when he heard a car arriving at the front gates. He looked out through the kitchen window to see Mr. and Mrs. Randall drive by in their silver Mercedes, on their way to the main house. Back from

New York, he thought idly, staring after the beautiful car. He'd give anything to own a Mercedes. . . .

With a pang of remorse, he subdued that thought. The truth was, he'd give anything to have Dora back. But that would never happen, he knew. Dora was dead. A suicide. And for the thousandth time, he asked the air again.

Why, Dora? Why?

He dried his hands on the dish towel above the sink and wandered out of the kitchen and up the stairs. Perhaps he could sleep for a while. He hadn't been able to sleep since Christmas Eve, since he'd found his sister at the bottom of the cliff. Even the other night with Holly, in her bed. He had lain awake watching Holly sleep beside him, stroking her lovely hair, but sleep would not come to him.

Now, upstairs in the gatehouse, he paused at the door of Dora's bedroom. He opened the door and looked around the small, tidy room. The bed with the quilt comforter his mother had made for her. The big collection of dolls that covered nearly every surface. The sampler above the headboard that Dora herself had embroidered: HOME IS WHEREVER LOVE IS. He stared at the sampler, reaching up absently to touch the sweater he was wearing, the sweater she had made him for his birthday five years ago.

His vision blurred by tears, he went over to the little closet in the corner. He opened the door and gazed slowly around at her simple, well-kept wardrobe. He smiled sadly when he noticed the white dress in the corner, the dress she'd worn to her senior prom. She'd looked so pretty in that dress as she went out the door of the gatehouse, fawned over by her beaming parents, escorted by Leonard Ross.

Kevin blinked, his gaze dropping to the neat row of shoes at the bottom of the closet. Leonard Ross, he thought, her date for the prom. The only date she'd ever had . . .

The baby.

Still staring down at Dora's shoes, he thought, Was that it? Was that the reason she'd jumped from the cliff? Mildred had been as discreet as possible about it, but even fourteen-year-old Kevin had figured it out. The whispered conversations, the trips to the doctor in Greenwich, the six months of banishment to New Haven. Dora had been pregnant, and she'd gone away to have the baby. She'd come home without it. Mildred had warned Kevin not to mention it to anyone, and he hadn't. Later, when he'd asked his mother about the child, she'd told him that it had been given up for adoption. He'd repeated this family secret only once, to Holly, in the restaurant in New York.

Had the baby driven Dora to this? Kevin wondered now. Had years of guilt and remorse for giving up the child led to all the rest of her problems? It was possible, certainly, even probable. And yet, in all these years, Dora had never once mentioned the child. Not to him, at any rate.

He sighed, shaking his head sadly at the memory. He was about to close the closet door when he noticed the box.

It was a big, rectangular wooden thing in one corner beside the row of shoes. There was—or, rather, had been—an intricate design on the lid in gilded paint, now faded to a ghostly series of diamond patterns. Kevin stared at it, wondering what it was. He picked it up, surprised at its heaviness. He went over to the bed and put it down, but when he tried to open it he found that it was locked. There was a tiny keyhole on the front.

He looked around the room for the most likely place to keep a key, and he immediately settled on the top dresser drawer. He pulled it open and rooted briefly among pencils, pens, and a pitifully small selection of cosmetics before he found it. He took the minuscule key over to the box and opened it.

He stood there for several moments, staring down at the box's contents. On the top lay two medium-sized, leather-bound volumes. When he picked these up, he found identical ones under them, and yet another layer after that. Six books in all. Kevin sank down onto the bed and began to examine them.

They were diaries, journals covering some fourteen years. All the adult years of her life, beginning when she was seventeen, when she'd had the baby.

Starting with the earliest one, he began to read.

Holly drove the Land Rover off the ferry that had brought her over from Long Island, and onto the landing dock. She turned right on the main road before her, as instructed, and drove around the coast of the little island. Another turn, and she was headed up toward higher ground.

It was very pretty here, with many trees that would be beautifully green in summer and big, attractive houses spaced far apart. Of course, many of this tiny island's residents were elsewhere for the winter, but the resident she sought was here, and he was expecting her.

After giving the matter much thought, Holly had finally decided to call the lawyer, Gilbert Henderson. Ms. Choi at his office had told her that he was away until after the holiday. When Holly convinced the woman of her urgent need to speak with him, Ms. Choi had promised to call him at his home and convey the message.

He'd called Holly at Randall House five minutes later. She'd explained that she wanted to talk to him about private family matters, but that she didn't want to do it on the phone. It was then that Gil had invited her here, to this island, and she had been happy to accept. So, here she was.

The house was on a hill above the bay, fronted and framed by trees, at the end of a steep driveway. It was a very modern-looking structure, all stone and wood and plate glass. She parked in the drive near the two cars already there, a sleek Nissan and a battered Jeep.

Gil Henderson was waiting for her at the front door, flanked by two beautiful greyhounds. He was grinning, and the dogs were barking and wagging their tails. She smiled as she approached, realizing that she almost hadn't recognized the imposingly handsome lawyer in his cable-knit fisherman's sweater and faded jeans.

"Hello," he said. "Welcome to the island. I hope you didn't have any trouble finding us."

"No," she replied. "Your instructions were perfect."

"Good. Come in, come in. These are my children: the boy is Tristan and the girl is Isolde."

Holly knelt briefly to greet the dogs before following Gil into a living room that could only be described as dramatic. It was two stories high, rising to a central peak, and the entire cliffside wall was glass, affording a magnificent view of water and sky. On the other side of the glass was a big redwood sundeck with a railing. There was a wooden staircase leading up to a second-floor balcony on the inland side, with a row of doors upstairs that were presumably bedrooms. Through an archway under the balcony she could see a gleaming, tiled kitchen.

The living room was a symphony of low-slung leather couches and chairs, with a big coffee table between them. A home entertainment center with a huge television screen filled one entire wall, and a stone fireplace blazed on the other. Several large, ultramodern paintings hung on the walls, and on the coffee table was a small statue, a male nude carved of ebony. A big, round, glass-topped wrought iron table in front of the large window was adorned with linen and candles and place settings for three. Holly stared at this.

"I hope you're staying for dinner," Gil said, following her gaze. "Of course, that means you'll have to stay the night: the last ferry is at seven. I've made up the guest room for you, and I hope you'll say yes."

Holly thought for only a moment. A whole night here, far away from Randall House. She could drive back tomorrow afternoon, getting home in plenty of time for a New Year's Eve celebration with John and "Cathy."

"I'd love to," she said.

"Then it's settled. Sam!"

This last was called through the archway toward the kitchen. Holly turned to see a tall, handsome, dark-haired young man in a flannel shirt and overalls arrive in the living room. The son, she thought. She recognized him from the photograph on Gil's desk in New York.

"Hello," the young man said, extending his hand. "You must be Holly."

"She is, indeed," Gil told him. "Break out some more chops, kiddo. We have company for dinner."

"Cool!" Sam said. "How about some white wine while you wait?"

"That would be lovely," Holly said.

"Comin' right up!" With that, Sam headed immediately back to the kitchen.

Holly smiled over at the lawyer. "Your—son?"

Gil blinked. "Uh, no, he's not my son, Holly."

Oh, she thought, feeling the blood suffuse her cheeks as she looked around at the paintings and the nude statue and the greyhounds named after operatic lovers, both now stretched out by the fireplace. Of course Sam is not his son, you idiot! You can take the girl out of the Coachella Valley, et cetera. Perhaps that explains the rift between this man and my father all those years ago. She thought all of this, but all she managed to say was "Oh." Then, to cover her awkwardness at her naïveté, she asked if she could use the telephone.

Gil smiled and led her over to the couches closest to the fire as Sam came back in bearing a tray with a bottle in an ice bucket and three stemmed glasses. He poured and served while she called Randall from the phone on the coffee table. She told Mr. Wheatley that she would be away for the night and would return sometime tomorrow afternoon. Then she hung up and smiled at her hosts. They smiled, too, and toasted her.

"Hope you don't mind if I have mine in the kitchen," Sam said. "I'm in charge of dinner."

"Do you need any help?" Holly asked.

"Nope. You're the guest. You stay right where you are and keep him out of my hair." And he was gone again.

Holly laughed. "He's charming. Is he a lawyer, too?"

"No," Gil said. "You're obviously not a fan of soap operas. He's an actor, currently breaking hearts on a popular daytime drama. Sam Collins."

Holly stared at the archway through which the young man had disappeared. "Wow! How long have you two—I mean, uh—"

He laughed again. "Seven years next June. But I don't think you came all the way out here to discuss my private life. I rather thought you wanted to discuss yours."

Holly nodded and took a sip of the cool, sweet wine. Then she leaned back on the couch and began.

"Yes," she said. "I wanted to ask you about my father."

John was waiting for her in the Great Hall, at the bottom of the stairs. She had just come from her room to the gallery, preparing to go down and join him for cocktails. Her progress toward the stairs was arrested by a sudden, loud bang as the front door of the house was flung open and a large figure rushed forward across the black and white tiles toward her husband. As she watched from above, her husband turned, alerted by the noise.

She did not hear the blow from where she was, but in the next instant John was sprawled backward across the bottom steps of the staircase, his arms and legs splayed at bizarre angles, a completely blank expression on his face. His assailant towered over him.

It was Kevin Jessel. She recognized him now that he had temporarily stopped moving. Until now the figure had been a huge, presumably male blur of motion. Kevin Jessel had just punched her husband, John Randall, in the face, knocking him down.

She stood quite still at the balustrade, staring, unable either to move or make a sound. There was something surrealistic, absurd, Felliniesque about the scene below, not merely its content but the sight of it from this distance, this angle. There was a sound, an awful, bellowing rasp coming from somewhere, but she couldn't identify its source, so stunned, so awed was she by the sight. By the very idea that this person, this servant, this *nonentity* was assaulting her husband. And yet it was familiar, too, from nineteen years of experience, of repeated exposure to just this sort of behavior. A daily occurrence, really. She'd seen it all—and done it all—before.

Even as she stared, fascinated, the hulking young man reached down and grasped John's throat. He lifted him up from the stairs and held him with one hand while the other reared back in a fist. Two mighty blows followed in quick succession, one to her husband's stomach and the next to his chin. This time she heard a muffled cracking sound as John flew down again to land on the checkered tiles beside the Christmas tree.

It was that sound, and the sudden knowledge that the awful bellowing emanated from Kevin Jessel, that brought her back to reality. This was real; this was happening, now, before her, and she at last reacted. Without a conscious thought, without using any intellectual processes, she turned around, ran back to her bedroom, and unlocked the door. Then she was across the room, flinging open the drawer of the bedside table. She was already back outside in the hall when she heard the next sounds from downstairs, the words being shouted.

"You! *You!* You killed my sister! You *raped* her, you *animal*! That was *your* baby, not Leonard's! I'll kill you I'll kill you I'll kill you I'll *kill* you!"

By this time she was halfway down the stairs. Her husband lay on his side now, moaning, while the crazed young man loomed above him, ranting.

But now the scene had changed. Now *she* was in charge of it. This was familiar; this had happened before. The naked bodies of women, broken and still, on the tiles of the communal shower room, their blood being rinsed away down the drains. Jane Dee, that stupid loser, staring in shock at the gun aimed at her as she was doused with accelerant in the beach house. Her other husband, James William Randall III, charging toward her in the bedroom in Greenwich Village, fists raised, his face contorted by rage, just before his chest exploded into a huge, red flower. This she could handle.

As she had done once before, twenty-four years ago, she calmly raised both arms out straight in front of her, aiming the Smith & Wesson .38 revolver at Kevin Jessel's chest.

"*Stop!*" she commanded. "Stop it!"

The young man looked up at her, at the weapon now pointed at him, and froze. She kept her gaze locked on him: she was afraid that if she looked down at John, she would give in to the impulse to rush to him and take him in her arms. God, she loved him so much, but he was so weak and helpless. He was ruining everything. A useless, rich idiot . . .

Kevin Jessel glared, now speechless. John continued to moan at his feet. She did not move, did not even blink. The three of them remained in that strange tableau for what seemed an eternity, until

Mr. Wheatley came down the stairs to stand beside her. Still aiming the gun sure and true, she calmly instructed the butler to call Chief Helmer and get him here immediately. Without a word, the old man nodded and went past her down the stairs, toward the office.

John slowly, painfully got up from the floor.

"No," he gasped. "No—police."

"Oh, shut up," she said, and then she began to laugh.

"Your father?" Gil Henderson said. "I—I don't understand. What do you want to know about him?"

Holly studied his face as she sipped her wine. Then she put the glass down on the coffee table and said, "Well, for one thing, who *was* he? I mean, I know his name was James Randall, but I don't really know anything else—except that my mother killed him."

The fact that her mother, Constance Hall Randall, was still alive—was even now returning to Randall House from New York, no doubt—was not something she would share with this man. Not now, and probably not ever. That was her burden, her cross to bear.

Gil Henderson's next words drove all of this from her mind, as they drove the breath from her body.

"No, Holly," he said. "His name was not James Randall. Jim—James Randall—was not your father. His brother, John, is your father."

She stared, breathless. She was still seeing Gilbert

Henderson in his well-appointed living room, and she was aware that his lips were moving. But all she could hear in her mind was the cryptic exchange she'd heard through the closet wall two days ago:

"If you think about it, my emotional stake is as high as yours—if you've been telling me the truth, that is."

"I've told you the truth. Always."

Only very gradually did Holly's senses return, including her sense of hearing.

". . . from the moment we first saw each other at Yale," Gil was saying. "Jim and I were together from that moment until that awful day twelve years later. The day he told me about the actress, this woman he'd met, and about his plan to marry her. I—I won't even attempt to explain to you how I felt. That is not part of your story. So he married her, this Constance Hall. They'd talked it over, I gathered, and she was willing to go along with his idea. He wanted to be 'normal'—no, let me get this exactly right: he wanted to *appear* to be 'normal,' whatever his definition of that word was. But that definition obviously did not include me, so I went away. I left him to it, to—whatever it was he was trying to do.

"Well, he hadn't been married more than three months before he learned the truth, and it must have struck him as very sad. He was gay, through and through, and trying to be anything else was a lie. And when we live a lie, we do not live at all. I forget who said that, but truer words were never spoken. His marriage was a joke: he hadn't so much as consummated it. Not that *she* cared, mind you. Constance had her own agenda."

Somehow, Holly found her voice. "Agenda?"

He shrugged. "She wanted his money, and his name. That was all. She never loved him, any more than he loved her. She was supposed to be a beard, you know, for Daddy Randall and the board of directors at NaFCorp. Well, she was an actress, so it wasn't difficult, I daresay. She went along with it because she wanted to be Mrs. Randall. I understand she was from a poor family. I can't imagine how poor it must have been to prompt her to do that."

"I can," Holly said, thinking of 66 Sixth Street, the hag with the beer can. It was one thing about Constance Randall she understood perfectly.

"Well," Gil went on, "they went through all the motions of being a happily married couple, while secretly leading their own lives. Constance fell in love with Jim's brother, John, and he with her. They met at the wedding—are you *loving* this? They were carrying on long before the murder. Oh, they were discreet about it, I guess. Only that doorman who testified at her trial was aware of their secret, and even *he* got it wrong. The 'other gentlemen' he kept mouthing off about were actually only one gentleman: John." He shrugged again.

"And what about my—uh, James?" Holly asked. She'd almost said, "my father." But *John* Randall was her father.

Gilbert Henderson stood up. He went over to the glass wall that Holly now saw was actually a series of sliding doors. He stared out at the cold, gray seascape, the choppy bay and ragged sky. When at

304

last he spoke, his voice seemed to be coming from far away.

"He tried to come back to me. Can you *believe* that? This man I thought I knew, I thought I'd loved. He came to *me*. I sent him away, of course. But there were others, I gather. Other men, quite a few of them. I guess he went a little crazy. There he was, married to Lady Macbeth, or whatever role she was playing. And I told him to drop dead—words I would later regret, in the circumstances. He didn't have a marriage, and he no longer had—perhaps I flatter myself, but I don't think so—he no longer had the one he loved most. So he went crazy. Drinking. Running around. Drugs, too, I wouldn't doubt. Sometimes he'd disappear for weeks at a time. And in his private desperation, he began to—to lash out. At *her*, I mean. I didn't know her, never even met her until the day you were born, but I heard things from mutual friends. I know that he abused her. He beat her up a couple of times, and once he beat John up. Well, I guess you can see where all this is going. I think he attacked her that morning, just like she said. So she shot him. But I think she was already planning to murder him."

Now he turned from the view to look at her. Slowly, as in a dream, Holly nodded.

"Was John involved in the murder plan?" she whispered.

He came over and sat down beside her again. "I have no idea, and I assure you I don't care."

She stared at him. "You've known all this for twenty-four years. You knew I was John's child, and you knew that my grandfather and Alicia would *never* have left me the inheritance if they'd known. And yet you never said a word, to them or anyone. You even helped to get me back here. Why?"

Gil surprised her then. He reached over and gently took both her hands in his own. He leaned forward, staring deep into her eyes.

"My dear," he whispered, "if I have to explain that to you, I can only assume you haven't been listening."

They regarded each other for a long moment, a moment in which she began to understand him, and to like him even more than before. Love, she thought. The great leveler. This man had loved James Randall all his life, even after what James had done to him. He'd loved him enough to send him away. Enough to take the baby away from Constance, his murderer, after he was dead, and to swear that the baby was James's. Enough to lie, if necessary, to keep Constance's lover—and possible accomplice—from getting a fortune. Gil Henderson had always loved James Randall. He still loved him, even now.

Holly knew in that moment that she could not tell him that Constance was alive and well and living in Randall House. She had no idea what he might do. She didn't even want to think about what he might do.

They were still staring at each other when Sam Collins arrived from the kitchen to break the spell.

"Dinner!" he announced.

* * *

Pete Helmer smiled up at Debbie as she handed him a fresh cup of coffee. She smiled back and ruffled his hair. They'd been an item for almost a week now, since Christmas, so he supposed it was okay for her to be so familiar here at the station. Not that it mattered, really: aside from the prisoner, they were the only two people in the building. The Two Stooges, Hank and Buddy, were out on their nightly rounds.

"Did our guest eat his dinner?" he asked her.

"Nope. Didn't even touch it, last I looked."

Pete sighed, took a quick sip of the coffee, and got up from his desk. Moving to the back of the office, he went through the connecting doors to the back room.

There were two small, bar-fronted cells here, side by side, separated by a cement wall. Each cell had a cot, a table, a folding chair, and a sink. They were holding cells, essentially, so there were no toilets. The prisoners simply called for someone and were taken to the station's rest rooms. Well, the men's room: in Pete's nine years as chief here, there had never been a woman in the cells. There were rarely any men, either, unless a fight broke out somewhere, or old Tod Farley got loaded and passed out in his tankard down at the pub. Randall was a very peaceful place, for which Pete was grateful. Of course, there *was* that robbery-murder over at the Kismet, but that wasn't really Randall. That was the highway.

Now, however, they had a guest. Kevin Jessel sat

on the cot in the cell on the right, slumped forward, staring down at the floor. The food Debbie had brought him from the diner—Ilona's special meat loaf, with mashed potatoes and gravy and string beans and Ilona's famous peach cobbler—sat untouched on the table before him. It would be cold now, Pete thought.

"Hey, Kevin," he said to the prisoner. "I sure am sorry about this, but I didn't really have a choice. Mrs. Randall is thinking about pressing charges, but she'll have to wait till after the holiday to find a judge, let alone a lawyer. Now, I can hold you here for twenty-four hours, even without a warrant, but I'm not gonna do that. I'll let you go at nine tomorrow morning, but only on one condition."

He paused, waiting for the young man on the other side of the bars to look up, or to in any way acknowledge that he was listening. Kevin did not move. With a sigh, Pete pressed on.

"The condition is, don't go anywhere near that house or those people, at least until we can get this thing sorted out, okay? Kevin?"

Now, finally, Kevin Jessel turned his head, looked up at him, and nodded once. Pete was surprised to see tears in his eyes. Embarrassed, he quickly looked away at an empty corner of the cell.

"Okay, then," he said. He almost turned to go, but curiosity got the best of him. That, and pity: Kevin had just buried his sister, and his dad wasn't doing too well, either. He looked back at the young man. "What the hell happened, Kevin? Do you want to talk about it? We're talkin' assault and battery here. That can be a very serious charge. You may go to jail—I mean, a *real* jail." He smiled at his paltry joke, but the other man did not. "The good news is, Mr. Randall's okay. You just winded him, and he'll have a bruise on his chin, I should think. But, goddammit, I sure wish you'd talk to me."

At last, the man on the cot spoke. "Thanks, Pete, but I really don't want to talk about it. I—I appreciate your concern, and I'll do what you say. I'll stay away from that sonofabitch, for one reason: if I ever, *ever* see him again, I'm going to kill him. This isn't idle talk, and I guess I shouldn't say it to a cop, but it is God's honest truth. I'll kill him, Pete. I swear to God I will!"

Pete opened his mouth, about to make the obvious response to such a threat. The cop's response, the rulebook's response. Then he looked at Kevin Jessel, into his eyes, and stopped. He licked his lips and said, "I didn't hear that."

"Fair enough," Kevin replied.

Pete sighed again. Then, with a sense of frustration, with a hundred questions that wouldn't be answered in any case, he went back into the front office.

Debbie was no longer the only other person there. Toby Carter stood in the center of the room, his German shepherd at his side. Pete stopped when he saw them. They'd never entered the station house before.

"That dog isn't supposed to be here, Toby," he said.

Toby shrugged, watching him. The dog was watching him, too.

"I guess you want to see Kevin Jessel," Pete said. The boy nodded.

Pete nodded, too. "Have you brought him a file or a stick of dynamite?" He chuckled.

Toby did not chuckle. Neither did the dog. They both watched him silently, gravely, and he was acutely aware that Debbie was watching the scene with great interest, a little smile on her face. She looked as if she'd placed her own private bet on the outcome, and he knew very well whom her money was on.

"So, what are you thinkin'," Pete asked the boy.

Toby reached into a pocket of his down-filled jacket and produced a pack of Bicycle playing cards. He held them up in front of him.

Pete stifled a laugh. With that deadpan look and his constant silence, the kid was somehow disarming. If he ever went into stand-up comedy, he'd be the biggest thing since Buster Keaton. But he'd have to have the dog with him, or it wouldn't work.

"Okay, c'mon." He turned around and went back into the cells. Kevin looked up from the cot. "You have a couple of visitors." He unlocked the cell and swung the door open. Boy and dog silently trooped past him. Pete shut the door and locked them in. "You have two hours."

He stood outside the cell, watching the pantomime inside. Kevin sat up and nodded to Toby, who nodded back. Then the kid pointed down at the tray of food and raised his eyebrows. Kevin shook his head. Toby picked up the tray and placed it on the floor, pulled up the folding chair, sat down, and began shuffling the deck. The dog silently went to work on Ilona's special meat loaf.

With a final sigh, Pete went back outside. Debbie came up to him, put her arms around his neck, crushed her ample breasts against him, and kissed him on the lips.

"Okay," he mumbled, "so I'm a softie."

Debbie laughed lasciviously. "You'd never prove it by me, big boy." And she kissed him again.

Pete stood there kissing Debbie Dobson, thinking, What the hell is going on over at Randall House . . . ?

They sat up very late together, just the two of them. Sam Collins had provided an excellent dinner: broiled baby lamb chops and roasted potatoes and asparagus, with salad before and hot apple pie for dessert. The pie, he'd jokingly confessed, was store-bought. Then Holly got him to hold forth on his career, and he'd kept the table entertained right through dessert and coffee. She'd insisted on helping him put things away in the kitchen, and Gil loaded the dishwasher. Then—she wasn't sure if this was the result of some secret signal—Sam had bid her good night and gone up to bed, leaving her alone once more with Gil.

The fire had burned low, and they were on their second brandies. They had been quiet for some time, she with her new information and he with the memories she'd stirred in him. But her coming here today had not been a mistake, she was certain of it. She had done the right thing.

It was better for her to know the truth. All of it.

How else was she to decide what course was now best to take? If she'd had any sort of choice in it, she would not have chosen her true parents, either of them. But there it was, and wishing wouldn't change it. Beggars would ride, she reminded herself. So, now she had to make a decision.

As if reading her thoughts, Gil said, "So, what's next for Holly Randall?"

She actually laughed, and he joined her. Then they sipped their brandy again, but she knew he was waiting for an answer.

"Indio," she said at last. "I'm going back to Indio. To Ben and Mary Smith. May I use your phone again?"

"Of course."

She picked up the receiver and called Directory Assistance. She got the number she requested and dialed it, aware that Gil was watching and listening. The airline representative struggled nobly to find a flight from New York to southern California, explaining that the holidays were the worst time for reservations. After much searching, she offered Holly a first-class seat on a flight from Newark to San Diego on the fourth of January, if she didn't mind a two-hour stopover in Oklahoma. Holly made the reservation, requesting—after a glance over at Gil—that it be a round-trip ticket with the return open.

Gil watched her hang up and waited a moment before asking, "Are you sure this is what you want to do?"

"Yes," Holly said. "I'm sure. I—I'll be back soon,

but now I just want to get away from there for a while. I don't like John, and what you've told me makes me dislike him even more. And his wife— well, his wife is insane. I want to go home."

"You didn't have to call a commercial airline, Holly. You can use a NaFCorp jet anytime you want, free of charge."

She shook her head. "I don't want a NaFCorp jet. I want—I just want to be Holly Smith again. For a little while, anyway."

He nodded and reached for the brandy, and she was grateful that he asked no more questions. She would not have been able to answer them truthfully, and this lovely man deserved only the truth from her. He had jeopardized his career to enable Holly to inherit the Randall fortune. If his withheld knowledge ever came to light, he would be disbarred. But he'd been willing to do it for her. Well, for her and for the memory of James Randall. Impulsively, she leaned over and kissed him on the cheek.

Gil laughed. "If you're trying to compete with a gorgeous soap opera hunk, you're just about the only woman I've ever met who might win."

Holly laughed, too. "Oh, you just want me for my money."

This, of course, set the two of them off on paroxysms of laughter.

"My dear," he gasped, "you have no idea how close you are to the truth!"

They laughed some more. Then Gil stood up, and now it was his turn to lean over and kiss her cheek.

"I'm so glad you came, and I hope you'll become a regular here. Please forgive me if I don't become a regular at Randall House, but—well. . . ."

She nodded, remembering something. "I guess that's why you refused Mrs. Randall's invitation to my birthday party."

He stared, and his smile disappeared.

"What invitation?" he asked.

"Oh, nothing," she said quickly, realizing in an instant what had happened. Constance. Of course. She wouldn't want this man, of all people, anywhere near her. Her dead husband's lover, the man who'd taken her child away from her. A man who might very well see through the hair dye and the contact lenses and the cosmetic surgery. No, she had not invited him.

"You may stay up as late as you want," Gil said now, "but I'm for bed. Finish the brandy, if you like. Your room is the one on the left at the top of the stairs, next to ours. Good night, Holly."

"Good night," she said.

She watched him go upstairs. Then she poured herself one more brandy and settled back on the couch, gazing out at the darkness beyond the glass doors. She sat there for a long time, reviewing the last six weeks of her life, beginning with the moment she'd stepped off the plane to find Kevin Jessel waiting for her. Smiling at her. Holding up the placard that read, HOLLY RANDALL.

Holly Randall, she thought for the thousandth time. I'm Holly Randall now. I'm Holly Randall, and I'm ready for anything. Whatever fate offers. Whatever it takes to survive.

Then, with a long sigh, Holly Randall, heiress of the Randall millions, drained her glass and went up to bed. She slept well that night because she was not in Randall House, because she felt safe for the first time in days.

Less than twenty-four hours later, she would be very close to death.

CHAPTER TWELVE

Auld Lang Syne

The next day was New Year's Eve, the famous New Year's Eve you've all heard so much about. On that day, Holly Randall's fate moved her swiftly, inexorably toward tragedy. The countdown began at four o'clock that afternoon, when she drove Kevin's Land Rover through the iron gates and up the curving drive to the front of the house. Everything else was destined to follow. There is no escaping destiny.

She arrived in the house to be told by Mr. Wheatley that dinner would be served at eight, and that after dinner the entire staff would be attending the New Year's Eve party at the Randall Town Hall. Holly smiled and nodded. They had cleared this with her two weeks before, but she said she'd forgotten all about it. Mr. Wheatley informed her that dinner would be roast chicken and stuffing, with crème caramel for dessert. There were also two bottles of Dom Pérignon in the bar refrigerator in the library, for later. When she asked for Mr. and Mrs. Randall, he told her that they were not at home at present, that they were in the village for the afternoon. She smiled again and thanked him.

The servants were not in the house at the time of the incident. Mr. Wheatley would later testify that none of them told Holly of the previous day's business with Kevin Jessel and the police, at the request of Mr. and Mrs. Randall. He was thanked by the coroner and dismissed.

The snow had begun at about one o'clock that day, before Holly had left Gilbert Henderson's house and driven back to Connecticut. Now it continued outside, a steady swirl of flakes buffeted by the constant, sharp wind. The snow covered everything—ground, trees, buildings—in an ever-mounting coat of white frosting. From a distance Randall House looked perfectly innocent.

Holly didn't get farther than the Great Hall. She didn't even remove her white wool parka. After Mr. Wheatley left her there, she turned around and went back outside, into the snow.

She wandered around the grounds for about half an hour, circling the main house twice. She went into the summer house and took a good look around. She went to the chapel, where she found a single candle burning before the altar as she'd found one the first time she was there. She went into the pool house, and into the storage room beside it. She wandered the fields, the orchard, and the little forest with the frozen pond. At last, her private inventory completed, she wandered back into Randall House.

At the big desk in the office she wrote letters, including a brief thank-you note to Gil Henderson for his hospitality and a thank-you-but-good-bye letter to the MacGraws. Matthew MacGraw's painting was lovely, but enough was enough.

In the living room, she stood before the painting for several long minutes, gazing up at it. That beautiful woman in the blue satin gown was Holly Alicia Randall. She needed to remember that. She needed to always remember, no matter what happened to her, that she was now the woman in the portrait.

Upstairs, she went into her big closet and began to get ready. Among other things, she found the new, medium-sized Louis Vuitton suitcase she would pack for California.

She paused a moment with the suitcase, thinking, I won't tell them. I'm not going to tell these people— my *parents*, for God's sake!—that I'm leaving. I will simply leave on the morning of the fourth. Clean and easy.

But nothing was ever easy. Everything had a price. She, Holly Alicia Randall, was aware of that.

Constance Hall Randall had had enough of the Randall Police Department. She'd certainly had enough of Chief Helmer. And she'd had enough of her weak, stupid husband.

She'd had enough of everything.

She was perched rather primly on the uncomfortable metal chair beside John, her feet pressed together, her purse clasped on her knees. They'd been sitting here for nearly twenty minutes, but their perfectly simple message apparently hadn't sunk in. Now she silenced her babbling husband with a stern look and leaned forward.

"Look," she said to the chief. "All my husband is trying to say is that we don't want to press charges against Kevin Jessel. Let's just—I don't know—pretend the whole thing never happened."

Mr. Helmer leaned back in his chair, glancing briefly over at the rather ridiculously well-endowed redhead who sat smirking in the corner. "Mrs. Randall, I asked Kevin to explain why he attacked your husband, but he wouldn't say a word. If *you* could explain it to me, I might be able to decide what's best to do about it."

John leaned forward again, ready to shoot off his mouth, but her hand on his knee stopped him.

"We have no idea why he assaulted John," she lied. "We know he's very upset, which is understandable. Poor Dora—it was just awful, what happened. And his father, of course, that dear man. I don't think Kevin is quite himself. And we don't want to bring him any more trouble than he already has, if you see what I mean, Mr. Helmer."

At last the man nodded as if perhaps the message was getting through.

"Very well," he said. "I guess I can lose this report." With a single motion of his arm, he swept the papers on his desk over the edge into the trash can. "This never happened."

Constance smiled. "Good. Come on, dear. We've taken up enough of Chief Helmer's time." With that, she stood up and strode to the door, John hurrying along behind her.

In the car on the way back to Randall House, she finally relaxed. The interview in the police station had unnerved her. Any office of authority had bad connotations for her. Hard-ass Kendall and that bitch, Naomi Jackson. But Chief Helmer's penetrating gaze had been particularly unsettling. He wanted to know the truth. More dirty laundry, she thought. This family definitely has more than its share of that.

She leaned back in the passenger seat and closed her eyes. God, she was tired! Tired and defeated: a dreadful combination. Her husband was a pig, the pig she'd always known he was, despite her lifelong love for him. But raping Dora Jessel! She hadn't expected that particular bit of news. He'd had his way with the village idiot, for heaven's sake, when the poor thing was all of seventeen years old!

He'd told her about it last night, when she had confronted him. As she'd held the ice pack to his swollen jaw, he'd told her the whole ridiculous story. About the provocative, trusting young girl he saw around the estate whenever he came home to visit, and his growing desire for her. How he had followed her down to the beach under the cliff one afternoon in summer, shortly after her senior prom. He'd played with her and flattered her and tried to kiss her. When she'd become frightened, he'd held her down and forced her to submit to him. Afterward, he'd warned the weeping girl that she must never tell anyone what they'd done, or her parents would be fired and her family would be out on the street. She'd never said anything, but she'd meticulously recorded the story in her diary—the diary her brother had apparently found yesterday.

The poor halfwit had spent her entire adult life in mortal fear of John. It was disgusting. *He* was disgusting.

This revelation had been the final straw on an already overburdened camel. Holly had spent yesterday with Gilbert Henderson, her nemesis, that awful creature who had been Jim's great love. God knew what *he'd* been telling her! And Ichabod—the appropriately named "Cousin Icky"—knew more than she or John suspected. She was certain of it.

Oh, God, she thought, what if Icky has seen me? Recognized me? What if Gilbert Henderson has somehow figured it out? What if Holly knows who I am, and what we're planning?

It was all closing in on her. She didn't want to go back to Kingston. She *wouldn't* go back there. *Ever.*

She glanced over at her husband, thinking, Idiot! Then she leaned back and closed her eyes again, bracing herself for the night ahead.

She knew what she must do now.

Holly stood at her bedroom window, watching her father and mother get out of the Mercedes. John waved vaguely toward Zeke, who waited nearby.

The couple came into the house, and Zeke got in the car and drove away.

It was six twenty-three.

That man is my father, she thought. She remembered her foray into the Randall cemetery that day several weeks ago, in the fog. She remembered kneeling over James Randall's grave, wondering why she couldn't feel anything. Now she knew: she hadn't felt anything because the man in the grave was not her father. John Randall was her father.

She shook her head, sighing.

It was now six twenty-seven.

At six-thirty, Ichabod turned off his computer. He was tired of playing chess with an inanimate opponent. But there was something else wrong, as well.

He was afraid.

He couldn't remember now when the feeling had begun. It seemed to have been going on all day, ever since the snow had started falling. The fear had begun as a tingling at the back of his neck, emanating outward from there until it gradually involved his entire body. His withered, useless body. His scarred body.

With a long sigh, he went over to the shelf where he kept the scrapbooks. He pulled down the oldest one, the one that recorded the history of the Morris and Randall families, and took it over to the table. He stared down at the familiar photographs of his sister and his in-laws, and immediately the tears began to flow. Emily. Jimmy. Alicia. Those wonderful people, those victims of Constance Randall.

Oh, God, it is a sin to hate, he thought, but I hate her. I hate her I hate her I—

The fear stabbed into his abdomen. It encompassed him now, a throbbing pain all the way out to his extremities. Something was wrong. Somewhere in this house, in the world, there was evil afoot.

Evil.

He knew all about that. He was eighty-seven years old, and he knew all about everything. The one advantage—or curse—of living this long was the knowledge of every emotional state on earth, good or bad. And this one was bad. Very bad.

Evil . . .

Wiping away the useless, impotent tears, he closed the scrapbook and shuddered. Something evil was in this house. Now. Tonight. And he was powerless against it.

Then the knock came at his door. It was Holly, and he'd never seen her looking so drawn, so tense. He wondered if she felt the evil, too.

"Hi," she said.

He forced a smile. "Hello. How was Long Island?"

Holly smiled, too, but it was not a pretty sight.

"Most informative," she said. "I'll tell you all about it one day when you have two weeks."

They laughed together then, but it was not a natural laugh. Nothing today was real, he noticed, ever since the snow had begun. He thought, Perhaps nothing will ever seem real again. . . .

"I'm having dinner with them soon," Holly said. She didn't have to tell him who "they" were.

"Yes," he said, watching her.

"Then we're going to toast the new year in the library."

"Yes," he said again.

"Will you be up later?" she asked. "I could come up and have champagne with you, if you'd like."

He smiled. More artifice. "Oh, my dear, I'm planning on retiring early tonight. I have a sleeping pill for later. Raymond will bring me some dinner in about an hour, before he goes into town for the party. I shall toast the new year then, with him. Then I'm for bed."

Holly nodded. "That sounds like a good idea. I wish I could go to bed early, too, but duty calls. After I have champagne with—with them, I'm supposed to put in an appearance at the Town Hall. That's where I'll probably be at midnight, when the new year actually arrives."

Good, he thought. She'll be out of this house. This evil house. What he said was "Well, that doesn't sound so bad. And you *should* go to the party. You're the head of Randall House now, and there are certain obligations."

"Yes," she replied. "And I intend to fulfill those obligations." She kissed him lightly on his discolored cheek. "Happy New Year, darling."

"Happy New Year, Holly," he said.

With a last strained, artificial smile, she was gone.

And he was afraid again.

At seven fifty-four, Holly sat at her vanity table, tending to her hair with her grandmother's silver-plated brush. She had applied a light makeup, and she was wearing her blue, gray, and green diamond-patterned sweater, her pleated gray dress slacks with the big pockets, and boots. When she threw a coat over it, she mused, she'd be ready for Town Hall.

She glanced in the mirror at the bed behind her. The Louis Vuitton suitcase was lying open on the bed, and now it was half full. She would not take much from here with her to Indio. All her light clothing was already there, at her apartment.

Indio. She thought about that, about Ben and Mary Smith and Rhonda Metz, her roommate, and how pleased they would all be to see her. Well, she *hoped* they would be pleased. She'd left them six weeks ago a middle-class young woman, but she was returning in an entirely new role. It had never occurred to her until this moment, gazing at her reflection in the mirror, that the people in her old life might not be delighted with her new identity.

Suppose they resent me? she thought. Suppose they want the old model back, the woman they knew as Holly Smith? Suppose they don't like Holly Randall?

Then she shrugged at her image, thinking, No matter. She had changed a great deal in the last six weeks, and in her opinion those changes were all for the better. Not that Holly Randall didn't like Holly Smith: on the contrary, she loved her. She admired her courage and her perspicacity, her cleverness when faced with obstacles, her absolute refusal to remain always as she was. As she had been. Her exuberance to embrace her new persona, her new fate.

However, she thought as she smiled at the

beautiful woman in the mirror, I'm Holly Randall now. Amen.

With that, she cast aside the silver brush, stood up from the table, and left the bedroom. She ran lightly down the hallway, around the gallery, and down the white marble, red-carpeted stairway that always made her feel like a princess. Like Her Imperial Highness, the Grand Duchess Anastasia Nicolaievna Romanov, smiling sleepily as she followed her parents and her siblings down the stairs to the cellar. To the firing squad.

She arrived in the dining room at seven fifty-nine.

John Randall was uncomfortable, as uncomfortable as he had ever been. He sat at the head of the dining room table, flanked by the two women, being very careful not to touch his chin with his hands. Not that he'd ever been in the habit of doing that, but now that he was forbidden to do it, he felt a sudden, neurotic urge. That's crazy, he thought, but there it is.

His chin was covered with something by Max Factor that matched his skin tone, courtesy of his wife. It was concealing the black-and-blue mark Kevin Jessel had given him yesterday. God damn Kevin Jessel, he thought again. If it weren't for him, I wouldn't be aching all over.

That was the least of his problems, he reminded himself. He'd been warned, on pain of death, not to mention yesterday's incident at all. Holly was not to know about Kevin's accusation, or his assault. Helmer had assured them that Kevin would not be around for a while, so they could at least temporarily stave off his telling Holly himself. Perhaps I should pay him, John thought. A few grand would probably buy his silence about the attack, and about Dora.

Dora, he thought. That stupid girl had written it all in her diary. That feebleminded lunatic. John was glad that she was dead.

But now this meal had to be endured. He smiled at the women, who were chatting amiably about some clothing designer he'd never heard of, their light conversation as artificial as their smiles. Well, Holly's conversation, at any rate. His wife was strangely silent tonight, as if she was thinking about something else, something important. Oh, well . . .

He would fire the Jessels. He'd already told his wife of his decision, and she was surprisingly amenable. She usually put up an argument against anything he decided to do, but this time she concurred. Good. He would fire the Jessels, get them out of the gatehouse once and for all, and he would call J.T. Tomorrow, New Year's Day, J.T. would certainly be home. He'd call him and ask for another assassin to get rid of Holly.

With this resolve, he smiled again at the two women and drained his wineglass.

It was eight fifty-two.

Holly felt that she couldn't keep smiling much longer. She was tired of being polite to these people, when all she wanted to do was scream at them. Scream, and throw something.

She wished Kevin were around, but the gate-house had been empty when she'd checked it on her way home today. He would be at the hospital with his parents, she assumed, waiting for midnight. He would celebrate the new year with them, of course, but she wanted him here. She wanted to lean against him, bury her face in his chest. Maybe even tell him everything.

These people are my real parents, she imagined herself telling him, and now I have to leave. I'm going back to Indio for a while. She imagined herself telling him this, and she imagined his strong arms around her, stroking her, and his voice assuring her that everything would be all right. She thought about his Irish grin, his powerful legs, his naked magnificence. She had never seen a more beautiful man—with the possible exception of her father.

She glanced over at her father, at John Randall. Yes, she could understand a little more about the woman across the table now. Men who looked like this—particularly rich ones—were worth a great deal of trouble in a woman's life. Odd, she thought: trouble is exactly what they always seem to bring. It was one of a thousand reasons she sometimes wished she'd been born male. But she was a woman, and a beautiful one, and now she was rich. She was going to be fine, just fine.

The three of them were going to meet again in the library at ten o'clock, for an early toast with the Dom Pérignon Mr. Wheatley had placed in the refrigerator there. She wondered if she could talk them into Town Hall. It was worth a try, she supposed. But her mother was acting very strangely tonight, very quiet and distracted. She wondered what the woman was thinking. . . .

She smiled again at her handsome father and her silent mother. Nine o'clock.

The countdown continued.

Kevin Jessel was sitting in his father's hospital room, watching his parents sleep. Da was in bed, an intravenous hookup attached to his arm with white tape, and Mother was dozing in a chair. The steady, wheezing blipping from the various life-sustaining machines beside the bed were the only sounds in the room.

His father was out of danger, but Dr. Bell had taken Kevin and his mother aside in the waiting room and told them the whole truth. His heart had been severely taxed, and there was some mild brain damage as well. The next attack, when it came, would most likely be fatal.

Kevin sighed. It was all rushing in, one thing after another. His only solace was that John Randall and his formidable spouse were probably not authorized to do the hiring and firing at Randall House; otherwise, he and his family might very well be looking for a new place to live. But Holly would not fire them, not after Kevin explained what John Randall had done.

John Randall. Well, Kevin would wait. He would bide his time, at least until after he had spoken to

Holly. After that, John Randall was in serious trouble. He and his simpering wife would rue the day they met Kevin Jessel.

Holly. He wanted to see her, now, tonight. There was something he wanted to tell her, to make clear to her. After long, careful consideration, he had decided that now was not a good time for him to embark on a love affair. He had thought about it a great deal while he sat in the cell. His fascination with her had been doused by the subsequent events in his family, not to mention hers. There was an irony here, certainly: after years of chasing rich women, he was now turning one away. He was not sure how he could explain this to her, but he had to try, and soon.

He sighed again. No. He would stay away from there, as Pete Helmer had instructed. For now, anyway. He would stay here and toast the new year with his mother. The friendly nurses, who giggled together whenever they saw him, were keeping a bottle of Taylor on ice for him. He wished his father could join them, but it was not a chance they dared take. Besides, Da would probably sleep right through midnight.

Kevin settled back in his chair, glancing at his watch. Nine forty-seven. He would be here, in this chair, for a long time. Oh, well . . .

He was still there less than an hour later, when the paramedics arrived at the hospital with Holly Randall.

* * *

Holly came out of her bedroom at nine fifty-eight. She'd finished packing for Indio, even though it was still four days away. She hated putting things off to the last minute. She was ready now.

She knocked on her mother's bedroom door. After a moment the door was unlocked and opened, and her mother stood before her in the beaded red dress she'd worn at the birthday party.

"Aunt Cathy," Holly said, "I'm going into town in about an hour, to the party at Town Hall, and I was wondering if you and Uncle John would like to come with me."

Her mother, Constance Hall Randall, blinked, assessing this.

"Why, yes," she said at last. "That might be fun. I tell you what: you go down to the library and tell John. I'll join you in about fifteen minutes. If I'm going out in this weather, I'd better change into something warmer."

"Okay," Holly said. "I'll tell him."

Her mother closed the door, and a second later she heard the little click of the lock. Then Holly proceeded on her way to the stairs.

Constance sat at her vanity table, staring at her reflection in the mirror. She had quickly changed into her long-sleeved, navy blue velvet dress. Not that it mattered, she thought. Oh, well . . .

She thought about her daughter, Holly, and John, and all of the events of the last six weeks, culminating in Kevin Jessel's shocking accusation. It was all closing in on her. It was all coming to an inglorious end.

She had made her extraordinary decision hours ago, in the car on the way back from town. Now she had to act on it. She'd gotten through dinner, and she'd spent the last hour here, in her room, writing. Now, she would join her husband and Holly in the library. After that, she would come back up here and finish it. . . .

She reached for a Kleenex and wiped the useless tears from her unnaturally darkened eyes. Her false brown eyes that concealed the blue, as the dye in her hair concealed its true shade. The props, the small details that had kept her from spending the rest of her life as Constance Randall, prisoner.

As she stared in the mirror, Jane Dee came quietly into the room behind her, followed by Jim Randall. They stood behind her, one on each side of her, grinning. With a little cry, she swiveled on the vanity stool to confront them, only to find the room behind her empty. Yet she fancied she could hear their laughter hanging in the air. With a little shrug, she turned around again.

It's time, she told the desperate woman in the mirror. It's time for all of this to end.

But she would put it off a few more minutes. With a sigh, she reached for a lipstick and began repainting her already perfect lips.

Holly paused at the bottom of the stairs, gazing around. The servants had all left in the van half an hour ago, and Uncle Ichabod would be asleep by now. The big house on the headland was silent. The snow was falling outside, cutting them off further from the real world, the world a few hundred yards down the road. She and her parents were alone in Randall House. They might as well be the only people in the universe, she thought.

Oh, well, she told herself. It's time for a toast.

With that, Holly moved forward across the checkered tiles toward the library door. She arrived there at precisely six minutes after ten o'clock.

Her father was waiting for her.

Exactly seventeen minutes later, Ichabod came suddenly awake and sat up in bed. He was groggy from the sleeping pill he'd taken an hour ago, groggy and disoriented. But he was certain that something had awakened him. A loud, sharp noise of some kind, a noise that had reverberated through the house. A noise like—

A gunshot, he thought, and then he nodded in sudden understanding. He'd been dreaming of his sister, of his family years ago, when he'd served in the army in Italy. He'd been dreaming of a confrontation between the Allies and the occupying Germans in the little village where he'd been stationed. He'd shot a man that day, killed him. The sound he thought he'd heard had probably been in his dream. . . .

He rolled over and drifted back to sleep. He was awakened for a second time, some ten minutes later, when he heard the sirens outside the house. He sat up in bed again.

This was not a dream. This was real, very real. The wail of several approaching sirens filled the room, and he could now see the flashes of red and blue and white lights against the drawn curtains at his windows.

He stood up from the bed and made his unsteady, drugged way over to the door. He moved slowly down the hall to the top of the grand staircase, where he stopped abruptly, suddenly awake, arrested by the shock of the sight that met him.

Holly was lying on her side on the black and white tiles at the base of the stairs, and she was vomiting. That local kid, Toby Carter, knelt behind her, his arms around her waist. He was apparently forcing her to be sick. The German shepherd, Tonto, stood near them in the Great Hall, watching. As Ichabod stared, several people, led by Pete Helmer, ran through the open front door and dashed across the tiles to kneel beside Holly and the boy.

When he could think, when he could move again, Ichabod rushed forward down the stairs.

Holly lay back on the tiles, vaguely aware of the hands reaching out to her, touching her. She'd been sick, she knew: she tasted vomit in her mouth. But she could not open her eyes.

There were sharp voices all around her in the Great Hall. She thought she was in the Great Hall, at any rate. She'd staggered out of the library a few minutes ago, after she'd dropped the phone receiver on the floor.

The phone receiver, she thought. I called the police. I spoke to Pete Helmer. . . .

A wave of pain burst in her stomach, and she was

sick again. She'd been poisoned, she remembered that much. The Dom Pérignon . . .

Then she was floating through the air. Several pairs of strong arms were lifting her up from the cold marble floor and moving her across the foyer toward the front door.

The last thing Holly Randall felt was the freezing cold as the snowflakes fell down on her upturned face. Then, in a final burst of pain, she slipped into unconsciousness.

The call had arrived at the station at ten thirty-two, and a startled Debbie had immediately handed him the phone. Pete Helmer had heard a sound like ragged gasping, followed by a whisper. It was Holly Randall.

"Please . . ." she breathed. "Please come to Randall House . . . poison, I think, in . . . champagne . . . my uncle . . . dead . . . she . . . she left and went upstairs . . . gunshot . . . hurry, please hurry. Oh, God, I think I'm dying. . . ."

Those words had been followed by a sharp crack and a clattering sound, which Pete would later identify as the receiver landing on the wood floor of the library.

He'd moved immediately, shouting instructions to Debbie as he ran. She'd acted quickly and efficiently. By the time his squad car roared past the crowded Town Hall, he heard the distant sirens from the ambulances as they rushed to join him at Randall House.

The front door had been standing wide open, and the first thing he saw as he entered the house was the macabre scene at the bottom of the stairs. Holly Randall lay there vomiting, and Toby Carter, of all people, was holding her. The dog stood nearby, watching, and an old man in a bathrobe with a huge birthmark on his face was at the top of the stairs, staring.

Within seconds, Pete and the paramedics had relieved Toby of his post. Holly was whisked away on a stretcher, and Toby and the old man with the disfigured face had jumped in the back of the ambulance with her. The dog had tried to go, too, but a sharp whistle from the boy had stopped him. The shepherd stood in the drive at the base of the front steps, watching the ambulance scream away.

Then Pete had gone into the library. Two more paramedics were there, working on John Randall, who lay on his back on the floor. He was not responding to their ministrations, and after a few moments they stopped. John Randall was obviously dead, a shattered champagne glass on the floor beside him. He, too, had been sick.

Pete glanced around the room. Another glass lay on its side on the coffee table, a stream of champagne emanating from it. The receiver was on the floor by the table. There was a big, mostly full bottle of Dom Pérignon on a tray next to the base of the phone. A single, full, untouched champagne glass was on the tray beside it.

Pete shook his head, grimacing, putting the awful scenario together in his mind. Then, remembering Holly Randall's gasped words on the telephone, he left the library and went quickly up the stairs.

He tried two other doors in the wing to the right of the stairs before he found the locked one. He went back to the top of the stairs and called down, relieved to see that Hank and Buddy had finally dragged themselves from the party at the Town Hall. The Two Stooges came up to join him, and it took the combined shoulders of both of them to force the bedroom door.

A gunshot, Holly had whispered on the phone, and she had been right.

Mrs. Randall was lying on the carpet beside her vanity table, a Smith & Wesson .38 revolver in her outflung right hand; he recognized the gun from yesterday's incident with Kevin Jessel. There was an enormous splash of red on the wall to her left, dripping down, darkening as it dried. Mrs. Randall would not be needing the paramedics: most of her head was no longer attached to her body. It lay in several pieces on the floor beside her.

On the vanity table was an envelope of creamy white linen. Across the envelope in an elegant, sloping hand were written the words, *To whom it may concern.* Pete picked up the envelope, opened it, and read the letter.

My name is Constance Hall Randall. For the last five years, I have been posing as Catherine Shaw, later Catherine Randall. . . .

It was a very detailed story. The woman had gotten out of prison six years ago, and one year later she'd murdered someone, a woman named Jane Dee. She'd left the other woman's burned body in her house in Long Beach, Long Island, and gone to Europe for a prearranged meeting with her lifelong love, John Randall. A plastic surgeon in Zurich had operated on her three times, changing her nose and her cheekbones and her jawline. Two years ago she'd married John Randall.

Ten months ago, the letter stated, she and her new husband had come here, to Randall House, to wait for Alicia Wainwright to die so they could claim the inheritance. That's when they'd learned that the Randall fortune had been left not to them, but to Holly Smith.

Holly Smith, it turns out, was their daughter.

It was there in every horrible detail, the whole, sad story. Pete read it with a growing sense of disgust. This woman and her husband had hired Mr. Buono, the stiff from the motel, to rid them of Holly. But Constance had been having second thoughts, a delayed sense of guilt—*very* delayed, Pete thought grimly. And now, after learning of her husband's perfidy with the tragic Dora Jessel, Constance had decided on her final course of action. Better this, she'd concluded, than prison.

The final paragraphs of the letter were a detailed description of Constance Randall's actions tonight. She'd written the letter first, apparently. She would poison her husband and daughter in the library shortly after ten o'clock, she wrote. Then she would come up here, to this room, and take her own life with her husband's revolver, the revolver she kept in the drawer in her bedside table.

Pete read the three pages twice. Then he slipped the letter back in the envelope and put it down on the table. He went out of the room and down the stairs to the Great Hall. Glancing around, he saw that the county police were there now, and the people from the Greenwich medical examiner's office. There was nothing more he could do here. Circling the pool of milky vomit at the base of the stairs, he went out the front door to his car.

As he drove through town on his way to the hospital, he heard the bells of Randall ringing in the new year.

CHAPTER THIRTEEN

Breaking the Silence

Holly awoke to the sensation that she couldn't breathe. She was lying on something soft, and she was vaguely aware of a large shape hovering over her, reaching down to her. It is an angel, she thought. I am dead, and this angel is reaching down for me, to take me to Heaven. Then her vision came into focus, and she saw that the angel was a nurse.

She could breathe after all, but only with difficulty. Something cold made of clear plastic was fitted over her nose and mouth, and there was an awful hissing sound all around her. She tried to sit up, but the angel restrained her, pushing her gently back down against the pillows.

"Don't move," the angel said.

She didn't move, but she did come fully awake. She was in a white bed in a white room with white uniformed people around her. An emergency room or an ICU, she reasoned. But she wasn't there for long.

"How do you feel?" An elderly man in white had arrived beside the angel-nurse.

"Who are you?" Holly asked, half expecting him to answer, "I'm God."

"I'm Dr. Bell, Ms. Randall," God said. "You're at Randall Hospital. You've just had your stomach pumped, I'm afraid, which will explain any pain you're feeling in your abdominal region."

Groggily, she shook her head. "No. No pain." Then she sat abruptly up on the bed. She remembered, even in her confusion, to use the appropriate relationships. "My aunt and uncle. Where—where . . . ?"

Dr. Bell shook his head sadly as he took her hand in his. "I'm sorry, Ms. Randall. They're dead, both of them. The police are here, and they want to talk to you as soon as you're in your room. You've been poisoned. Arsenic, as well as I can tell. Your uncle was poisoned, too, and Mrs. Randall—well, Mrs. Randall shot herself."

Holly was fully cogent now. "She—she poured the champagne, but she didn't drink any. I—I was wondering about that. . . ."

"Yes. Well, the chief will ask you to tell him the whole story. I think we can move you out of here now. You're going to be fine. That young man saved your life."

Holly stared at Dr. Bell. "Young man? What young man?"

"Shh," the doctor said.

Then she was moving, floating out of the white

341

room and down a long white corridor. The angel-nurse was still beside her, and there were two large men, one at each end of the floating bed. Holly settled back against the pillows and allowed herself to be led.

Then she was in a small, beige room, being lifted from the floating bed into a solid one. A gurney, she thought: I was on a gurney, and now I'm in a private room in Randall Hospital.

"I'll send the police away," the angel—a pretty young African-American woman, Holly now saw—was saying.

"No," Holly replied. "Please help me to sit up. I—I'm all right. I want to do this now."

"Very well, Ms. Randall," the nurse said.

"What's your name?" Holly asked her.

"I'm Nurse Reed, Ms. Randall."

"No," Holly said, "I mean your first name."

The girl blinked. "Selma."

"I'm Holly, Selma. Please don't call me Ms. Randall. I'm just—Holly." Then she smiled at the startled nurse. "Please send the police in now."

The girl nodded and disappeared. Moments later, the beige door opened and Pete Helmer came in, followed by Ichabod and Toby Carter. Holly smiled, half expecting Tonto. But the dog was not here. Of course not, she thought. You're in a hospital, Holly, and there are rules. . . .

Suddenly the door opened again, and Kevin was in the room with them.

"Hi," Pete Helmer said to her. Then he turned

around, apparently surprised that the others were here with him. "Hey!"

"Please let them stay here," Holly said. "They're my friends." She studied the trio behind him a moment before adding, "They are my only friends."

Pete Helmer shrugged and pulled a beige armchair over to the side of the bed. He sat, but the others remained standing near the door.

"Okay," he said, pulling out a notepad. "I guess we'll begin with your name." He laughed halfheartedly at his rather weak joke.

She smiled at him, and at the three men who stood behind him. She smiled at everyone, at the whole, wide world.

"My name," she said. "My name is Holly. Holly—Alicia—Randall."

With that, the questioning began.

Ichabod was relieved when the police chief finally left the room. They'd all listened to Holly's story—as much as she seemed to know of it—with a growing sense of wonder. Ichabod, of course, knew more than the others, so he wasn't particularly shocked by Mrs. Randall's actions tonight. But the others were, especially by the revelation in the suicide letter that "Catherine" was actually Constance Randall, the notorious murderess.

Holly was perfect. She looked appropriately surprised when Chief Helmer told her that the woman who'd tried to kill her tonight was her mother, Constance Hall Randall. She stared around at them all, seemingly unable to take it all in, and Ichabod suppressed a smile.

Then his amusement faded. He remembered his foreboding from earlier tonight, the terrible, constricting sense of evil all around him. Now, of course, that feeling was explained for him. Connie Randall had shown her hand at last. More scandal for the family, he thought grimly, realizing that even as they were here in the hospital room, the journalists and camera crews would be gathering, some of them here but most of them outside the gates of Randall House. He must call Town Hall, he thought, and get the servants away from the party. Raymond Wheatley, at least, should be at Randall House with the various police forces and the reporters. . . .

Then Chief Helmer told Holly something that put his mind at ease. The servants were already home, he said. His deputies had been at the party when someone named Debbie had contacted them, and they had told Mr. Wheatley. Randall House would be safe.

Ichabod looked slowly around the room, and it occurred to him that something here was odd. There was a presence that needed explaining. . . .

The boy.

Toby Carter stood near the door behind him, staring at the woman in the bed. Ichabod studied his face a moment, and in that moment he realized that here was someone who might just know more than all the rest of them. Randall House's own Greek chorus, omnipresent and possibly omniscient. Yes, and silent, too. But now, perhaps . . .

Then he realized what was bothering him. It wasn't the boy—or, rather, it wasn't *merely* the boy. It was something he'd seen earlier, at Randall House. Something about the tiles, the sea of black and white marble slabs that paved the floor of the Great Hall. He'd been standing at the top of the stairs, gazing down, noting yet again the floor's resemblance to a chessboard. He'd spent his entire life hovering above them, studying them, analyzing strategies. And there was something—one specific thing—that had been out of place on that particular chessboard.

Yes, he thought. Oh, dear me, *yes*!

At last the police chief finished with his questions and left, and Kevin Jessel went over to the bed. Ichabod and the boy waited quietly by the door as Kevin asked Holly if she needed anything. Then, after she'd promised him that she was all right, Kevin left the room.

Ichabod went to the bed and looked down at her. She was pale, which was to be expected, but otherwise she looked to be in good spirits. He shook his head, thinking, She came close; this is as close as anyone should ever come to death.

"You're going to be fine, Holly," he assured her. "You just need some rest. But first, I want you to talk to Toby. I saw him outside my window earlier tonight. He's always around Randall House. He may be able to shed some light on all this, on what happened to you tonight."

Holly smiled weakly up at him.

"Toby's not going to shed any light on anything, Ichabod," she said. "Toby doesn't speak."

Ichabod reached out to stroke her hair. "Perhaps that's because nobody ever listens."

With that, he turned to go. He regarded the boy in the corner for a moment, aware that he was watching him. Then Toby nodded once. Ichabod returned the nod, and left the room.

Holly reached behind her and adjusted the pillows. Then she leaned back against them and faced the boy across the room.

"Are you the young man Dr. Bell was talking about?" she asked. "The young man who saved my life?"

Toby nodded.

She regarded him, this tall, handsome boy with the glistening blond hair and the pale blue eyes. He was watching her, silent as ever. Silent and unblinking.

"Why did you do that?" she asked him.

He continued to watch her, his grave face revealing no emotion. Then he stepped forward, out of the shadows by the door into the pool of light around the bed. He came right up to her, and after a moment he reached out for her hand. Startled, she placed her hand in his, studying his face as he slowly licked his lips. For the very first time, she heard him speak.

"I think . . ." he whispered, pausing to lick his lips again before he continued. When he did, his voice was clear and strong. "I think I'm your brother."

* * *

I stood beside the bed looking down at Holly Randall, holding her hand in mine. Her face registered the shock that was the appropriate response to my words, the appropriate response to my finally—and so dramatically—breaking my long silence. I regarded the beautiful face staring at me. She was the most beautiful woman I had ever seen, and I had fallen in love with her instantly.

"Who are you?" she said at last.

I waited a moment before I replied, savoring her confusion. For once, for perhaps the only time in her life, it was she who was surprised.

"I am the son of Dora Jessel and John Randall," I said at last. "I was adopted by the Carters, who brought me up as their own. They're not very nice, and I don't like it there. But two years ago I got them to tell me about my real mother, and I've been hanging around Randall House ever since. If I'm not mistaken, you are John Randall's daughter."

"Yes," she whispered.

"Yes," I repeated. "John and Constance. The man you poisoned tonight, and the woman you shot."

Now there was absolute silence in the room; you could have driven a truck through it. I squeezed her hand, savoring every moment of my triumph. She was still staring at me, and her eyes were beginning to glaze over.

"That makes me your half brother," I went on before she could say anything. "I just found that out a few days ago, on Christmas Eve. But no matter. Nothing matters now, except the fact that you're alive." I leaned forward, smiling at her. "What's that phrase, 'Hoist with your own petard'? I think you drank too much champagne."

Her shock delighted me. I'd waited a long time to see the stupefied expression on her face. She was speechless.

But not for long. After a moment, she burst into laughter. She laughed for a long time, doubling over in the bed and letting go of my hand to cover her mouth lest the policeman outside hear her. But she continued to giggle, shaking with the mirth that had been pent up during all her weeks at Randall House. Then she began to gasp for breath, and to cough. I reached out again and grasped her by the shoulders.

"Holly!" I cried. "You're ill!"

She continued to gulp air as she shook her head vigorously.

"No," she gasped. "Not anymore. You've cured me, Toby, once and for all!"

I leaned forward, and we embraced. I held her tightly against my chest until her shaking subsided. Then she leaned back again.

"So," she said presently, "you saw everything tonight. I guess you've been watching me since I arrived, in November."

I nodded.

"Talk to me," she said.

So I did. I told her all about Alec Buono, the man I'd watched while he watched her. The man I'd heard talking with John Randall in the little lane near the estate, plotting and planning everything.

The man I'd followed one night, back to that squalid Kismet Motel.

I told her all about it. Then I told her all about my mother, Dora Jessel. How I had approached her that Christmas Eve on the cliff. How she had looked into my pale blue eyes and seen the eyes of the Devil— my father, John Randall. How I'd introduced myself, told my confused mother who I was, what I was. She'd slapped my face then, and called me the Devil. She told me who my father was—not her high school sweetheart, which was what the Carters had told me, but John Randall. Then she—she told me to get away from her, and never to come near her again. She said she wished I was dead, and that she was sorry she'd had me instead of getting rid of me before I was born.

It only took a little push to send her over the railing.

Holly listened to all of this in silence, the whole story I'd been longing to tell her. When I was finished, she nodded, more to herself than to me. She didn't seem to be too terribly surprised by what I told her, and I was grateful for that. I didn't want to go on and on about it.

Then, from the depths of her soul, she smiled.

So I told her the rest, everything I had seen at Randall House tonight.

Holly stared up at Toby Carter as he spoke, remembering. She remembered everything now, from the moment she'd arrived back at Randall House from Long Island this afternoon. It had been four o'clock:

she'd checked her watch as Zeke drove the Land Rover away toward the garage.

At Gil Henderson's house the night before, she had decided to get rid of John and Constance Randall. And she'd figured out exactly how to do it.

At four o'clock she'd come into the Great Hall to find Mr. Wheatley waiting for her. He'd told her several things, notably that Mr. and Mrs. Randall were not at home. So she'd used that precious hour to get ready.

She'd wandered around the estate, and her travels included the storeroom, where she poured a small but lethal amount of BEE-GONE into a tiny paint jar, which she slipped into her coat pocket.

She'd wandered into the office on the ground floor of the house, where she'd written letters to Gil Henderson and the MacGraws. And the letter in her mother's remarkably similar hand, confessing everything.

Then she'd gone upstairs to her room, and into her walk-in closet. Among other things, she'd taken down the Louis Vuitton suitcase. The "other things" had included a trip through the sliding wall into her mother's bedroom, and over to the bedside table. For the revolver she'd seen there three days before, when she'd searched the room.

She'd left the revolver and the confession and the arsenic in her bedroom when she went down to join them for dinner at seven fifty-nine.

Later, at approximately ten-fifteen, she was in the library with John, ostensibly waiting for "Catherine" to come down and join them. She'd turned her back to him, slipped arsenic into the bottle, and poured three glasses, murmuring something about a quick one before "Aunt Catherine" arrived. John was amenable to that, of course; she'd known he would be. He'd downed his first glass in one quick gulp, as she had observed him do so many times before. Then he'd held the glass out for another. She'd smiled and poured.

It was remarkably swift. The moment he'd hit the floor, Holly left the library and ran up the stairs and down the hall to her bedroom. She'd taken the revolver and the forged confession out of the drawer where she'd hidden them and gone into the walk-in closet.

Her mother had changed from the beaded red dress into a dark blue velvet dress. That was the first thing Holly noticed as she came quietly into the bedroom behind her. Constance was sitting at the vanity table, painting her lips. She did not look up from her reflection until Holly arrived beside her.

"Hello, Mother," Holly said.

She watched in satisfaction as the woman dropped the lipstick on the table, her temporarily-brown-but-actually-blue eyes widening in disbelief.

"What?" Constance gasped. "What did you call me?"

"I called you mother—Constance." Holly was still watching her face in the mirror.

To her credit, Constance Randall did not so much as pause for breath. She lunged sideways off the vanity stool, toward her bedside table.

"Looking for this?" Holly asked, slowly raising the gun.

The woman sank back onto the stool. Her face was white now, Holly noticed, completely drained of all color. She took several deep breaths before she spoke.

"Holly," she said. "Holly—darling—you must listen to me. I—I'll do anything you say, only please—"

Now Holly pressed the .38 against her mother's right temple. "Anything?"

"Yes!" Constance cried. "I'll do anything you say!"

Holly pressed the gun harder and smiled.

"In that case," she whispered, "go to hell!"

And she squeezed the trigger.

When Holly pulled the letter from her pocket, she got a surprise. There was an identical envelope already on the vanity table, but this one was addressed to John. She picked it up and tore it open. She read it through quickly, then turned around and looked at the bed.

Standing over her dead mother, Holly Randall started to laugh.

There was a medium-sized suitcase on the bed, half full. In the note, Constance had told her husband that she was leaving Randall House tonight. She would take the first available Concorde flight to Paris, and she would meet him there, at the George V, on the seventh of January. John was to tell Holly that a dear friend had become ill and that "Catherine" had rushed to her side. In Paris, she concluded, the two of them would decide on a new course of action.

Still chuckling, Holly swiftly unpacked the bag and put the clothes away in drawers and the closet. Then she tore up the good-bye letter, replacing it with her beautiful forgery, and dropped the paint jar with the remaining insecticide in the wastebasket, where it would later be found. Leaving her mother's bedroom door locked from the inside, she went back through the two closets to her room, bolting the sliding wall behind her.

Then she ran back downstairs.

I noticed Holly flinch as I spoke of her trip upstairs to her mother's bedroom, after she'd left her father to die in the library. I figured—correctly, it turned out—that she was remembering the moment when she shot the woman. But she didn't tell me about it that night in the hospital. She told me later, when we were alone and at our leisure, after the scandal had finally disappeared from the front pages.

Now, I simply filled her in on everything I'd seen. I'd watched her with John through the library window on the ground floor, and then she had left the room, to go upstairs. I kept my eye on him through the window, making sure he didn't get up again and ruin her plan—whatever her plan *was*. He didn't: he vomited once, then lay still. Satisfied, I left my vantage place and went over to the front door.

It was unlocked. Tonto wanted to come in with me, of course, but I made him stay outside. I slipped into the foyer and concealed myself under the grand staircase. A few minutes later I heard the gunshot, so I knew Holly was on schedule—whatever her schedule *was*. But it was good enough for me.

When she ran downstairs again, I thought she'd go back in the library, but she didn't. She went around the stairs—I shrank back into the shadows—and through the dining room into the kitchen. She was there about three minutes. Then she came back past me across the Great Hall, wiping her mouth as she went. Milk, she later told me: two tall glasses of it, to dilute the poison. I waited until she was back in the library before coming out of my hiding place and venturing closer. I heard her phone call to Chief Helmer, with all the affected gasping and mumbling. Then she dropped the receiver to the floor. I peeked through the open library door to see that she was laughing, holding her hand over her mouth as the small, tinny voice of the chief continued to shout through the phone.

"Holly! Holly!"

I had a sudden, incredible desire to join her then, to make my presence known and share her hour of triumph. I had actually begun to step forward into the open doorway when she did an extraordinary thing, stopping me in my tracks.

She cocked her head, listening for something, and I heard her speaking softly under her breath.

"One. Two. Three. Four . . ."

She counted nearly to thirty before the first siren became audible at the end of the front drive. Then she smiled again, picked up one of the two full glasses on the tray, and drank from it.

I nearly cried out. I nearly ran into the room and knocked the glass from her hand. But then I figured it out, what she was doing. I smiled and watched her.

Suddenly she came toward me. I ducked down under the hall table as she came out into the foyer. She went over to the front door and threw it open. Then she walked back toward the Great Hall, passing within two feet of me. She went over to the bottom of the stairs near the Christmas tree and slowly, carefully lay down on her back, waiting for Chief Helmer to arrive.

I nearly left then. I didn't want to be found here in the next few moments, when Helmer burst through the door. I had slipped out from under the table and begun to edge toward the door when Holly stopped me.

She hadn't seen me or anything: that isn't why I stopped. I stopped because she screamed. She clutched her stomach and rolled over onto her side. Then she tried to vomit, but the pain was apparently too great.

"Oh, God!" she moaned. "Oh, God, I don't want to die—"

And I was at her side.

Weeks later, she would admit with a rueful smile that she'd drunk too much of it. She'd known the expected effects, having minored in chemistry at college, but she'd underestimated the potency of the insecticide. All she'd wanted was a trace amount, enough to hold together her scenario. Enough to prove that Constance Randall had poisoned her and her father before going upstairs and shooting herself in her locked bedroom.

Well, it turned out fine, after all. That was precisely what everyone believed, from Helmer and the county and state police to the coroner at the inquest two days later, on the third of January.

And every journalist in America believed it. The next morning, in her hospital room, Holly held the first of several press conferences she would give in the next days and weeks. The press ate it with a spoon: they shouted it from newspapers and television sets for months. So, of course, you all believed it, too.

Yes, you all believed her, and for the most simple of reasons. She had an eyewitness who backed up every single last detail of her story.

Me.

We Randalls have to stick together, you know.

CHAPTER FOURTEEN

Departing

Holly was sitting at her vanity table, gazing at her reflection, when the knock came at her door.

"Come in," she called.

It was Mr. Wheatley. "I'll take your suitcase down, Miss Holly. The car is ready."

She smiled. "Thank you, Mr. Wheatley."

He picked up the Louis Vuitton from the bed. She rose, put on her white wool coat, and looked around the room for a long moment before following him out.

"I want you and Zeke and Dave to supervise the renovations," she told him as she followed him down the stairs. "I want that woman's bedroom completely redone. Mrs. Jessel and I have discussed the new decor, so she'll be in charge of that. Make sure she gets rid of those damned mirrors! I want the room to be perfect for him."

"Don't worry, Miss Holly. We shall see to it in your absence." He paused at the bottom of the stairs and turned to face her. Lowering his voice to a murmur, he added, "Shall I have the men wall up the connecting door between the closets?"

Holly thought about that for a moment.

"No," she whispered at last. "Leave it."

Mr. Wheatley nodded, and the tiniest trace of a smile appeared at the corners of his lips.

"Very good, Miss Holly," he said.

Then he went across the foyer and out the front door. Holly followed, wondering again just how much the inscrutable majordomo knew, or thought he knew. Well, no matter. He was retiring next year to an apartment in New York City, near his grandchildren and great-grandchildren, and when the time came he would be buried beside his wife in the Randall cemetery. Holly was paying for the apartment. She'd pay for the funeral, too.

She came out into the gray daylight, smiling in grim amusement at the inevitable snow. Indio was going to be a veritable treat after this constant freezing cold, she decided. And, after that, Greece . . .

The staff was waiting for her, lined up at the bottom of the front steps as they had been on that day in November, when she'd arrived. It had been snowing then, too. She moved down the line of now-familiar faces, shaking hands. Mrs. Ramirez, Martha, Frieda, Grace, Zeke, Dave. Mrs. Jessel was last.

"Please be sure that Mr. Jessel has everything he needs," she told the housekeeper. "And send all the bills to Mr. Henderson in New York."

"Bless you, Holly," Mrs. Jessel said. Then she stepped forward and embraced her new employer. "God bless you, for everything!"

Holly blinked, wondering—as she had with Mr. Wheatley moments ago—just how much Mrs. Jessel knew. No, she decided; I'm being paranoid. With that, she turned to her relatives.

"Good-bye, Ichabod," she said, kissing his discolored cheek as she would steadfastly do in the future, every time she saw him. "I'll be back to play chess with you again soon. In the meantime, I think you should teach *him* how to play." She jerked a thumb at the young man who stood silently beside him.

"I don't think I'll have to teach him anything, Holly," her great-uncle said. "I think he knows all the moves already."

She laughed. "Checkmate!" Then she turned to her half brother and took him in her arms.

"Your new bedroom will be ready in a few days, Toby," she told him. "You can move in whenever you like."

He nodded.

"Mr. Henderson will be calling you," she continued. "You're going to be signing a lot of papers— the same papers I signed a few weeks ago."

He nodded again.

"You're one of us now, Toby, and I couldn't be more pleased. You and I will share the Randall name—and everything that goes with it. Fifty-fifty." She kissed him and reached down to pat Tonto on the head.

"I love you," Toby said, and then he and the German shepherd went up the steps and into the house.

Holly watched them go. Then she went over to the limousine, where Kevin stood in his father's gray uniform. He was not smiling today. He held the door gravely as she got into the car, then he went around to the driver's side, got in, and started the engine.

Holly leaned back against the soft leather and closed her eyes as the car began to move. Then, on an impulse, she leaned forward and opened the little bar above the facing seat. She took a small bottle of white wine from the cooler and poured into a crystal glass. Then she leaned back again and took a long, appreciative sip.

She studied the back of Kevin's head as he drove. He would not be at Randall House when she returned. He was going back to New Haven to work for a former professor of his at Yale. In the fall, he was going to graduate school. Holly would be paying for it, but he had not smiled when she told him that. She wondered if she would ever see that wonderful Irish grin again. Probably not, she decided. He'd waited until she was out of the hospital to tell her, politely but firmly, that he wanted nothing more to do with the Randalls. Well, he hadn't said it so callously; he was actually rather charming about it. But the message was clear. His delayed guilt over his sister's "suicide" had ended their relationship before it really began. Oh, well . . .

It doesn't matter, she decided. Nothing matters,

except the fact that I'm on my way. A quick visit with the Smiths in Indio, then London, Paris, Rome, Tokyo, Sydney. But first, Greece . . .

And then, when she had seen the world, she would come back to Randall House. *Her* house.

She spared a fleeting thought for John and Constance Randall, buried in a public cemetery at the expense of the state. She thought of Kevin Jessel, and Dora, and Missy MacGraw, and the dead man who had met his kismet in the Kismet Motel. She thought all of this, but all she managed to say was:

"Fuck them. Fuck them all."

She whispered it softly, so Kevin in the front seat would not hear. Then she took another sip of the wine. As the car moved down the curving drive and out through the iron gates, Holly Randall smiled.

She really had no use for these people.

EPILOGUE

Holly Randall Now

It has been seven years since the events I've described here, and a great deal has happened to me. To all of us. First, let me tell you about the others.

Mr. Jessel died of a second heart attack that February, and Mrs. Jessel, my grandmother, followed him a few months later. Not surprising, or so I'm told—people who have been married that long often die within a year of each other.

Kevin got through graduate school and went to work in a psychiatric clinic in New Haven—a clinic in which his sister, my mother, had once been a patient. He's there now. He arrived here for a brief visit last Christmas with his new wife, who is also a clinical psychologist. Holly didn't like her much, but I wasn't really expecting she would. The wife is pregnant, and I thought she was perfectly pleasant, but what do I know?

Mr. Wheatley and Uncle Ichabod both passed away two years ago. They're buried in the Randall cemetery. There was a lot of press attention when Ichabod died, because he was such a famous chess player. Holly handled the press conferences as graciously and gracefully as she'd handled her own press conferences, years before. She told me in private that she was glad to have played chess with him so often in his final years. I used to watch them sometimes, and they would talk quietly together as they played. Ichabod had figured everything out in the hospital, he told her, when he'd remembered the milky white vomit on the chessboard tiles of the Great Hall. She'd had chicken and créme caramel with white wine and coffee for dinner—he'd known that because he was always served the same meals in his room—and champagne in the library. So why, he'd wondered, had she been drinking milk? That tiny detail had nagged at him until the moment in the hospital room, when her strategy had at last become clear to him. The two of them always laughed together when they spoke of this. Then they would call for champagne, and I would join them in a toast. We never told him about my mother.

They played a final game the night before he died, and Holly won. I wasn't surprised to learn that he had left his considerable fortune to her.

Mr. and Mrs. Smith, Holly's foster parents, are still alive. They're in California, and they occasionally come to visit. Once, three years ago, Holly took me to Indio to visit them. I couldn't believe how hot it was there! As for *my* foster parents, the Carters, the less said the better. They were always rather horrible to me and to each other, and age has not improved them. They're divorced now, married to other people. But they have no part in this story, so who cares? Not I, certainly.

Pete Helmer married that redhead, Debbie, the secretary at the police station, and they have two children now, a boy and a girl. He still has those two deputies, and he still hates them.

Tonto is very old now, but he still gets around a little. He sleeps at the foot of my bed, in the bedroom that briefly belonged to Constance Randall. The bedroom in which she died.

Holly is home now, for the time being. She turned thirty-one last Christmas Eve, and the two of us celebrated the landmark alone together. She'd just returned from London, where she seems to have a large group of new friends. She has friends all over the world, rich and tinged with notoriety as she is. Men friends, mostly, but I don't like to think about that. She travels almost all the time, but she always comes home to me.

On that birthday, last Christmas Eve, we at last became lovers. She came through the secret door into my room and got in bed with me. It was the loveliest night of my life. Three days later we drew up wills together, with Mr. Henderson. She says she's leaving her half of the fortune to me, so I told her I was leaving my half to her. She seemed touched by that, but it's not exactly the truth. I don't have to tell her everything, do I?

I'm twenty-three now. I was graduated from Yale

last year with a degree in English literature. I wrote my first attempt at a novel there, but I haven't shown it to anyone. It isn't very good.

But this is, I think. I began this a year ago, right after my graduation, when I came home to Randall House again. It is the fulfillment of the promise I made to myself, to write down the story that plays over and over in my mind, like a song. My only regret is that no one will ever read it. At least, I don't expect anyone to read it. As soon as I print it out, I'll mail it to a lawyer I've retained in New Haven. It is to be published only in the event of my death.

Not that I'm expecting to die anytime soon. I'm perfectly healthy, but—well, you can never be too careful.

You see, I know everything about Holly, but I've promised to keep it all a secret. I know, for example, about the college sweetheart in San Diego and his fiancée. That's why Holly was so amused when she learned what Mr. Buono had been planning with the brakes of the BMW. She'd done the exact same thing to Gregory Sandford III's Porsche years before. He died, and the fiancée is in a wheelchair for life, courtesy of Holly.

But my biggest secret is the one I've kept from everyone, even Holly. It is this:

I said she was the most beautiful woman I'd ever seen, and I fell in love with her instantly. That's true; I did. But it wasn't on that snowy November day when she arrived at Randall House. It was three months earlier, in August, when I first saw Holly on the grounds of Randall House, watching it. She was there for three days, following Miss Alicia whenever she went outside the house. Getting to know her habits and routines. She followed Miss Alicia to the pond that morning, and got in the pond with her. I saw the whole thing, and I remember Miss Alicia's final shouted word.

"Holly!"

It was a startled cry of recognition.

Holly didn't realize that Miss Alicia was going to die soon in any case, and she was impatient to get out of Indio. Now that I've seen her hometown, I can hardly blame her. I would have done the same thing. I wouldn't let one old lady stand between me and freedom, not for a moment. And neither, obviously, would Holly: that's why she went to the pond.

Holly doesn't know I know about it. And she won't ever know, unless this journal sees the light of day. I'm not expecting that to happen anytime soon.

There's one more thing I wish to include in this document. I've told you a secret about Holly, and now, perhaps, it's only fair that I share a little secret about myself.

In a remote corner of the little, well-tended cemetery near the chapel, there is a small marble headstone. For most of the hours of the day it is shaded by a nearby oak, and at night the marble is cold to the touch. I find myself drawn there at odd times, when I want to get away from things, or merely when I want to sit quietly on the ground before it and rethink my life. I imagine how my life might have been—how I might have "turned out," as they say—

if the woman who lies there had been more fortunate. I stare at the stone for hours, and eventually my gaze travels over to the crude little wooden cross that juts up from the earth beside it, where Dave and Zeke found the baby doll buried.

The doll is there now, next to her in the ground, because I decided that this was what she would have wanted. I watched her bury it many times, only to return the next morning and dig it up again.

The doll's grave is my grave, in a way, and sometimes I get up from the ground where I am sitting and walk across it, crushing the soil beneath my shoes, because it amuses me to do so. But the woman who lies beside it is another matter: I have made my peace with her. When I utter her name aloud, she comes up quietly behind me and joins me in my vigil. She reaches out a pale hand from the folds of her black cloak and rests it, ever so lightly, on my shoulder. I expect that, at the moment of my death, I will feel her soft caress. I will look up into those dark eyes in that pale face, and perhaps then she will, finally, smile at me.

That is a long way off, I trust. I'm here with Holly now, inside our iron gates, and I intend to stay here with her forever. I intend to help her keep the secrets of Randall House. If Holly and I have our way, Randall House will always look perfectly innocent—from a distance.

But you should never be deceived by appearances.

Well, that's all, I guess. It's time to print out this manuscript and feed Tonto, and to finish packing. I've been told to pack my lightest clothes for this trip. In the morning, before we leave for the airport, I must remember to go to the chapel and light another candle for Holly.

Tomorrow, she's taking me to the Greek islands.

BARTLETT, SANTIAGO & KLEIN

ATTORNEYS AT LAW

To: Danielle Perez
From: Vincent A. Bartlett
Re: <u>THE INHERITANCE</u> by Toby Carter Randall

Dear Ms. Perez,

Enclosed please find the manuscript, <u>THE INHERITANCE</u> by Toby Carter Randall, as per our telephone conversation of last week.

I am pleased that you have decided to publish this. It is more than a "novel," as you are no doubt aware. It is an important document. I am certain the Randall police will be as interested in it as the general public.

As for the events in Crete one year ago, I'm sure you know as much as I. It was a fortunate chance that the local fisherman witnessed the incident on the beach, and that he testified. Otherwise, Toby Carter Randall's drowning would probably have been ruled an accident. Holly Randall finally confessed to the Greek authorities that she did it for Toby's half of the inheritance, which he had not willed to her in any case. It's ironic, if you think about it: Holly always wanted to see Greece, and now she'll be spending the rest of her natural life there.

Please forward the advance payments and any royalties to me at this address. I will send them on to Toby Carter Randall's sole heir, the new owner of Randall House: his uncle, Kevin Jessel.

I wish you all success in this endeavor.

Sincerely,

Vincent A. Bartlett

Vincent A. Bartlett

PENGUIN PUTNAM INC.
Online

Your Internet gateway to a virtual environment with
hundreds of entertaining and enlightening books from
Penguin Putnam Inc.

*While you're there, get the latest buzz on
the best authors and books around—*

Tom Clancy, Patricia Cornwell, W.E.B. Griffin,
Nora Roberts, William Gibson, Robin Cook,
Brian Jacques, Catherine Coulter, Stephen King,
Jacquelyn Mitchard, and many more!

**Penguin Putnam Online is located at
http://www.penguinputnam.com**

PENGUIN PUTNAM NEWS

Every month you'll get an inside look at our upcoming
books and new features on our site. This is an ongoing
effort to provide you with the most up-to-date
information about our books and authors.

Subscribe to Penguin Putnam News at
http://www.penguinputnam.com/ClubPPI